THE BLINDING BEAUTY

When Alexandra Farrish had to shepherd her younger sister Didi through a London Season, there was one worry she did not have. There was no problem finding suitors for her charge. Every man who met Didi became a slave to her sensationally stunning beauty.

Didi's list of instantly captivated conquests included even the magnificent Marquess of Malvern, the most irresistible lord in London. Alexandra should have been dutifully delighted for her sister. But the call of duty was no match for the siren song of love, urging Alexandra to open the eyes of a man who had to learn that the most bewitching beauty was more than skin deep. .. .

Be sure to read these other Signet Regency Romances by Dorothy Mack:

The Reluctant Heart
A Prior Attachment
The General's Granddaughter

SIGNET REGENCY ROMANCE
COMING IN MARCH 1991

Anita Mills
Miss Gordon's Mistake

Michele Kasey
The Somerville Farce

Margaret Westhaven
The Duke's Design

THE
UNLIKELY
CHAPERONE

~·~·~

by
Dorothy Mack

A SIGNET BOOK

SIGNET
Published by the Penguin Group
Penguin Books USA Inc., 375 Hudson Street
New York, New York 10014, U.S.A.
Penguin Books Ltd, 27 Wrights Lane,
London W8 5TZ, England
Penguin Books Australia Ltd, Ringwood,
Victoria, Australia
Penguin Books Canada Ltd, 2801 John Street,
Markham, Ontario, Canada L3R 1B4
Penguin Books (N.Z.) Ltd, 182–190 Wairau Road,
Auckland 10, New Zealand

Penguin Books Ltd, Registered Offices:
Harmondsworth, Middlesex, England

First published by Signet, an imprint of New American Library, a division of
Penguin Books USA Inc.

First Printing, February, 1991
10 9 8 7 6 5 4 3 2 1

Copyright © Dorothy McKittrick, 1991
All rights reserved

 REGISTERED TRADEMARK—MARCA REGISTRADA

Printed in the United States of America

BOOKS ARE AVAILABLE AT QUANTITY DISCOUNTS WHEN USED TO PROMOTE PRODUCTS
OR SERVICES. FOR INFORMATION PLEASE WRITE TO PREMIUM MARKETING DIVISION,
PENGUIN BOOKS USA INC., 375 HUDSON STREET, NEW YORK, NEW YORK 10014.

Prologue

~~~~~

AN AURA OF GRIM URGENCY enveloped the solitary horse-
man galloping southward along the turnpike. At the post
house where he'd stopped for a light meal he'd had to
wait for the three-quarter moon to rise or risk a broken
leg for the hired horse who could not be expected to
know every inch of Sussex soil as he did. Impatience had
gnawed at him while he made a pretense of eating, and
he'd questioned the decision taken earlier in London to
ride the rest of the way, leaving his carriage to follow
when his exhausted coachman had caught up on the sleep
he'd missed the previous night.

The message had been waiting yesterday when he'd returned from a long day of hunting. His host had tried to
dissuade him from traveling at night and in the rain, but
he'd departed from Leicestershire within two hours, leaving his groom behind to arrange for transporting his
hunters home. He'd taken the reins himself for a couple
of stages to give his coachman a chance to rest and dry
off a bit, but both were the worse for wear and weather
when they finally reached London around midday. The
skies had cleared miraculously by the time he'd roused
from a restorative sleep of nearly four hours. It was then
he'd decided to ride and leave his aging coachman to his
well-earned rest. Despite the necessary delay, he still figured to make better time this way. After the next tollgate
he'd be going cross-country where no carriage could
travel.

He found his way mostly by instinct over the next hour,
guiding the powerful horse around the forest and across
hills and valleys, sensing more than seeing obstacles in

5

their path, driven always by the fear eating away at him. He fought a losing battle to keep his mind clear for navigational problems, for his fears kept pace with the rhythm of the hoofbeats. The welcome sight of the old post windmill gleaming silver in the moonlight rescued him from his thoughts momentarily.

Ten minutes later he pulled his sweating horse to a stop in front of the main entrance to Fairlawns, leaving the animal standing there as he ran up the steps and banged the knocker.

"How is she, Stokes?" he demanded of the white-haired individual who opened the door to him a few seconds later.

"Not good, I fear, my lord. Dr. Maxwell is worried that she might slip away. That is why he sent for you. We were not expecting you until tomorrow, but I am glad you have come so soon. Perhaps seeing you will make all the difference."

Though he had been ridding himself of hat, gloves, and overcoat while the butler spoke, his concentration on the chilling words was intense. "How did all this come about?"

"It is my opinion that Lady Marielle was unhappy, sir, when she came back from Yorkshire. You were away, and she made no calls in the neighbourhood. She took to walking over the hills all alone in all weather for hours on end. She'd come home too tired to eat. It was no wonder she caught a chill, but it descended on the lungs, and the doctor says it is pneumonia, sir."

"Yes, that was in his message. I'll go right up to her. Have someone see to the horse."

Two minutes later he stood over his sister's bed trying to conceal his shock at the wasted look of her as she lay there utterly still, her skin so drained of color it provided no contrast to the pale blond hair.

The nurse who was sitting at the bedside had risen and bobbed a curtsy at his entrance. "She never sleeps more than an hour or so, my lord; it's hard for her to breathe, you see, and her mind wanders sometimes," she warned the silent shocked man, her eyes full of unspoken sympathy.

He nodded. "I'll stay with her while you go get some tea."

For the next half-hour he prowled about the warm, dimly lighted bedchamber, too agitated mentally and physically to sit and look steadily at the corpselike figure that was his nineteen-year-old sister, though his disbelieving gaze was pulled back to the bed time after time as if by a magnet. It was the fatigue and strain of the last twenty-four hours that eventually brought him to a chair a moment or two before Marielle's eyelids fluttered open.

"Ohhhh," she breathed on seeing the masculine outline by her bed, and he thought he detected a spark of joy, quickly quenched, in her blue eyes as he leaned forward and took her hand in his.

"I am here now, my dear. Everything will be all right now," he said firmly, determined to convince both of them.

The pale lips attempted a smile but her voice was little more than a thread as she said, "Robert. I . . . I thought at first that it was Leander." A tear glistened on her lashes.

"Who is Leander?" The question came out more sharply than he intended, and he gentled his voice immediately as he repeated, "Who is Leander, my dear? I'll bring him to you," he added on an inspiration.

There was a tiny negative motion of her head. "No. I thought he loved me . . . but I was wrong."

"Mayhap you were not wrong. What is his whole name, dear?"

She seemed to have drifted off again. The thin hand was inert in his. He gave her fingers a little squeeze.

"Leander who, dearest?"

"Leander . . . Farrish."

She did not speak again. He sat there throughout the night, occasionally talking softly to his unresponsive sister, willing his strength into her quiescent spirit, promising that he would bring Leander to her when she was better.

When the doctor arrived shortly after dawn, he glanced at the hollow-eyed man in the chair as he approached the bed. A moment later he said heavily, ''I am so sorry, my lord.''

1

A SMALL FROWN MARRED the smooth perfection of Miss Alexandra Farrish's brow as she concentrated on deciphering the dainty but nearly illegible script covering the paper in her hand. The crease between her eyes deepened as she thrust the sheet closer to the window, angling her bright head and squinting ferociously in the pursuit of comprehension, then suddenly disappeared, to be replaced by a smirk of triumph.

"Ah, not one blue *bottle* but *bonnet*! And a shockingly dear bonnet too!" she finished on a little gasp of dismay as the price of the item in question steadied and became clear—too clear—to her seeking gaze. She scanned the rest of the bill, hoping there was some error, that someone else's account had been sent by mistake, but the other items listed tallied with her recollection of their recent purchases at Miss Crimpleton's elegant little shop off Oxford Street.

Alexandra sighed, dropping her chin in her hand and replacing the bill on the stack on the table at which she sat. The frown was back and she nibbled her bottom lip while gazing out the window. Nothing in the quiet street below impinged on her consciousness, however, as she methodically went over the events of that morning more than a sennight ago in her mind. At the conclusion of this exercise her eyes were no longer vacant, but troubled.

It was Didi, of course. Her sister had taken one of her passionate fancies to a pale blue velvet bonnet on sight and had been importunate nearly to the point of bad manners on being told they could not afford so extravagant a hat when there were so many essential purchases still to

9

be made before they could consider themselves even min-
imally equipped for a London Season. Alexandra had
steeled herself for the inevitable tantrum with its con-
comitant embarrassments, when Didi's rebellious expression had cleared magically. She had apologized with
pretty penitence and made no further reference to the hat
while they remained in the shop. Her elder sister had
been much encouraged by this evidence that the headstrong girl was at last coming to some rational appreciation of the realities of their situation—the more fool she!
As if it were a tableau in her mind, Alexandra recalled
Didi's annoyed exclamation, after the four girls had gone
a few steps down the street, that she must have left one
of her gloves in the shop. Bidding the others to walk on
slowly, she had dashed back to retrieve the glove before
anyone could suggest that the shop assistant would bundle it up with the order.

And that, of course, was how she had been able to add
the blue bonnet to their list of purchases without having
to account for a package on her return to her waiting
sisters. Didi must have been on the watch for the order
when it was delivered. Obviously the expensive bonnet
was now secreted somewhere in her bedchamber, to be
brought out when she considered it too late for her annoyed sister to return it to the shop.

The worry on Alexandra's face deepened as she passed
her sister's character under mental review. Didi had never
been known to consider the possible consequences of her
actions when in the grip of one of her passions. This
singleminded determination to have her own way at any
cost to herself or others was a trait guaranteed to alarm
a mature guardian, let alone a mere sister, especially a
half-sister whose authority was nebulous at best and hotly
resented at all times by one who, at nineteen, considered
herself quite capable of managing her own affairs.

Alexandra sighed again. If only Didi were not the em-
bodiment of a beauty so extraordinary and riveting that
men stopped in their tracks at sight of it and fell all over
each other in racing to pay tribute to its possessor. If
only she had not been already so thoroughly spoiled by

her doting mama before that lady's death ten years previously that she accepted such tributes as her due. The child had been taught by her proud and foolish parent that beauty deserved homage and entitled its fortunate possessor to first choice of all life's rewards. Not all the moral precepts drummed into her head by a succession of plain governesses had served to dislodge the lessons learned from her beautiful mother. Over the years she had, it was true, heard enough in praise of modesty, a desire to please, and generosity in a female's makeup to consciously counterfeit these virtues whenever they served her purpose, and she had acquired very pretty manners that did her no disservice in the eyes of ladies of an advanced generation. It was perhaps not to be expected that even superhuman efforts would be sufficient to annul the very natural suspicions cherished by other young ladies of one whose mere presence cast them all into the shade, but in any case Didi wasted no pains on trying to ingratiate herself with her contemporaries. Alexandra was under no illusions that guiding her beautiful sister safely through the social pitfalls of a London Season would be anything other than a very tricky maneuver, like walking blindfolded through a forest.

Her eyes fell on the account lying on the table and her soft lips firmed. It was never any good wishing for the impossible or refusing to face up to problems as they arose. She must deal with the present situation in a manner that should leave Didi in no doubt that family policy could not be flouted without payment being extracted. Her musings on this head were interrupted a moment later by a knock on the door, followed by the entrance of a soberly clad individual whose expressionless demeanor proclaimed him an upper servant of impeccable training.

"I am sorry to interrupt, Miss Alexandra," he said, permitting himself this familiarity since there was no one else present, "but someone has called to see you."

"Who is it, Edson?" Alexandra put down her pen and reached for the visiting card on the silver tray being extended to her.

"I am afraid the gentleman is unknown to me, Miss Alexandra."

A slight hesitation before the word "gentleman" and something in Edson's voice alerted his mistress to the butler's disapproval of the visitor. "Mr. Montgomery Dane," she read aloud. "To the best of my recollection, the gentleman is unknown to me also."

"Shall I deny you?"

"No, I think not, Edson. I may as well find out why he is calling. Perhaps it is one of the local tradesmen wishing to sell me something."

"I should doubt that, Miss Alexandra. Mr. Dane is quite young, and his attire would indicate that he aspires to the fashionable."

"Oh. Well, show him in, Edson."

"Very good, ma'am."

The caller who was presently ushered into the small front drawing room fully justified Edson's implied censure, Alexandra decided after a swift assessing glance had assimilated the full glory of his skintight yellow pantaloons, bright blue jacket, wadded at the shoulders and nipped in at the waist, a brocaded waistcoat, and a stiffly starched cravat of monstrous width and complexity. Mr. Dane might aspire to the height of dandyism, but true fashion would elude him as long as he continued to select such eye-catching garments. Unconsciously Alexandra drew herself up to her full height, but her voice was perfectly polite as she inquired, "You wished to see me, Mr. Dane?"

"Well, not exactly, ma'am." The young man looked discomfited all of a sudden as the lady's eyebrows escalated. "That is, are you Miss Farrish? I could have sworn she said her name was Farrish."

"I am one of the four Misses Farrish, five if you count my youngest sister," Alexandra said. "Which one do you wish to see?"

"I didn't quite catch her first name when we met at the theater the other night, but she is extremely beautiful," the young man replied in reverent tones. A hint of amusement in the lady's eyes caused his cheeks above the starched points of his collar to redden. "Not that you are not quite beautiful too," he added with more haste than tact, "but the Miss Farrish I mean is much taller and has black hair and the most enormous brown eyes." His voice trailed off under the cool stare being directed at him from a pair of enormous blue eyes.

"My sisters are all lovely and they are all dark, and we were all at the theater together the other evening," Alexandra said unhelpfully. "I wonder you did not ask the mutual friend who presented you to repeat the name so there would be no possibility of error, Mr. Dane."

"I . . . well, it wasn't exactly like that, you see, ma'am," replied Mr. Dane, wilting visibly under that blue-eyed stare.

"No, I fear I must be rather dim, because I don't see. How was it exactly, Mr. Dane?"

The lady's soft tones were still pleasant, but somehow the gentleman experienced a tightening of his collar. He slipped a finger beneath it and arched his neck before saying somewhat defensively, "The circumstances were such that we simply introduced ourselves."

"I see. And are you saying that my sister gave you her direction, Mr. Dane?"

"Yes, of course. I couldn't have found it otherwise." His tones were bolder now and his slightly protuberant blue eyes had regained their earlier confidence.

"I see," Alexandra said again, and now her voice became crisp, "but I am persuaded you must also see that I could not regard the—shall we say—*informal* circumstances of your meeting with my sister as a sufficient basis for continued acquaintance, so I shall bid you good day, Mr. Dane."

As his hostess had walked over to the bellpull during this damping speech, and the butler had appeared in the doorway with a celerity that suggested he had never departed the immediate vicinity, Mr. Dane was left with nothing to do save remove himself with what dignity he could muster. Red-faced, he bowed formally and did just that.

Having sent their unexpected visitor to the rightabout,

Alexandra resumed her seat, bitterly conscious of yet another drawback to chaperoning her beautiful sister. Didi's
insatiable appetite for masculine admiration had on more
than one occasion led her to disregard the ordinary rules
of decorum obtaining in public. Her rather free manner
had not mattered so much at the Harrogate assemblies,
where the family had a wide acquaintance in the neighborhood, but in London the task of keeping unsuitable
young men like Mr. Dane away from her was suddenly
assuming the proportions of a Herculean task unless Alexandra could manage to convince her willful sister that
it would not add to her consequence to be thought to be
too coming with strange gentlemen.

Alexandra was considering ways to accomplish this
laudable objective without alienating her sister, when she
was interrupted a second time by the entrance of a gentleman into the front drawing room.

"Who was that court card in the yellow trousers I saw
coming out of the house just now?" asked the young
man, who tossed hat and gloves onto the sofa before
flinging his lean form after them.

There could not be a greater contrast between the
weedy youth who had just left in his cheap finery and
her brother, whose handsome lineaments and well-
proportioned form needed no sartorial embellishments,
Alexandra thought, smiling at him with affection. "Just
an optimistic opportunist who struck up an acquaintance
with Didi at the theater and came to try his luck."

The young man draped carelessly over the sofa smiled
slowly with unconscious charm. "I'd wager my new tele-
scope you sent him away with a flea in his ear."

"Naturally. He was quite impossible."

"Didi wouldn't care so long as he was sufficiently wor-
shipful of her glorious self."

"Perhaps you could speak to her, Lee, and explain
that, though men will generally encourage a girl to go
beyond the bounds of what is proper, they don't really
respect the girls who do."

"Lord, Sandy, you know very well Didi wouldn't listen to anything I had to say. She considers me a total washout.''

''That's not true; she is merely disappointed that your friends are not from the Corinthean set she so admires,'' Alexandra said in swift denial, though her brother had certainly not appeared hurt by the unflattering opinion allegedly held by the sister closest to him in age.

''Yes, well, I have better things to do with my time than shoot wafers at Manton's or get up to silly curricle races or spar with a lot of sapskulls at Jackson's.''

''Yes, my dear,'' murmured Alexandra, eyeing him with a mixture of exasperation and amusement, ''and I am exceedingly grateful that you interrupted your studies to lend us your protection this spring while I try to get the girls established, but if you had escorted us to the theater the other night, perhaps that encroaching young man would have contented himself with making sheep's eyes at Didi and not boldly approached her, as seems to have been the case.''

''Oh, but Sir Humphry Davy was lecturing at the Royal Institution that evening. You would not have had me miss that for a stupid play!''

''Not that particular evening perhaps, but I wish you would come with us occasionally, Lee, just until we are settled into a social circle and have acquired some presentable escorts, which shouldn't take long once Didi and the twins have been seen in the right places. At the very least, the girls shall not be perceived to be totally without protection.''

''They'll never be that while you are around,'' Lee said with a boyish grin that transformed his normally serious countenance. ''All right, Sandy, for what it's worth, I'll tag along on a few jaunts until you acquire a larger acquaintance, but not Almack's, please. I couldn't bear to spend hours dancing with a lot of brainless females, and you know I hate cards.''

''I seem to recall one young lady whom you found appealing enough to solicit for a dancing partner last year at Harrogate,'' Alexandra said slyly, enjoying the slight embarrassment on her brother's face.

"Yes," he admitted softly. "Lady Marielle Trent. There was something special about her, though I haven't the wit to put it into words."

"I agree she is a sweet girl and very lovely to look at. I know she was only visiting in Yorkshire, but I wondered at the time why you did not pursue the acquaintance. Did you never see her again after the two assemblies she attended with Lady Standish and her daughter in September?"

"No," he said abruptly. "To what purpose? She is the sister of a marquess. Can you see her family welcoming an alliance with ours?"

"Ours is an old and respected name in Yorkshire."

"Once perhaps, but with Papa rapidly dissipating what is left of the family fortune, we'll soon have nothing but the name left. Her brother would have dispatched me quicker than you got rid of that puppy today."

It had gone more deeply with Lee than she had believed last autumn, Alexandra realized, swallowing an impulse to offer sympathy that would be rejected out of hand. "It isn't quite so bad as that," she countered lamely. "Papa cannot quite ruin us even if his luck should never change for the better. The terms of the entail will preserve the estate for you."

"The estate needs a lot of money spent on the farms and even more on the house if it is not to fall down about our ears one day soon. Oh, no, I am not quite so blind and unworldly as my devotion to my studies would indicate," he said, interpreting her look of surprise. "Since Papa is beyond the reach of reason and prudence, my hands are tied, so I might as well pursue my own interests in the meantime. If ever I am appointed Astronomer Royal, at least I'll have a roof over my head," he added, half in earnest.

There was no point in raising feeble arguments against her brother's ruthless honesty, Alexandra knew, but she said with a hope of extending comfort, "One never knows what is around the next corner. Very likely we shall be often meeting Lady Marielle in London this Season."

"She is probably married by now, and a good thing

too,'' Lee said, dismissing that subject with a finality his sister was compelled to accept.

Lee had gone about his own business and Alexandra had finished dealing with her bills when a slight commotion in the hall below advertised the return of all her sisters, for the good-natured twins had persuaded a reluctant Didi to countenance the addition of thirteen-year-old Penny on their morning excursion. Even with the door to the hall left open, their entrance seemed attended by much less bustle than was usually the case. The reason for this became clear as Alexandra reached the doorway in time to see Didi sprinting soft-footed up the second flight of stairs, her arms full of packages and her glorious dark hair becomingly set off by a high-crowned creation of pale blue velvet.

"I would like to speak with you, please, Didi,'' Alexandra said.

"In a moment, after I get rid of these bundles,'' came the reply as her sister continued her swift ascent.

"Aphrodite Farrish, if you know what is good for you, you will turn smartly around and get yourself in here at once.''

This was not the most diplomatic speech in the world, but the events of the morning had taken their toll on Alexandra's temper. She remained planted in the doorway, aware that the progress of the others up the first flight had ceased while the three younger girls tried to melt into the woodwork. "The rest of you had better get ready for lunch,'' she advised in even tones, raising her voice to repeat, *"Now, Didi!"* as the footsteps on the second flight had ceased while her younger sister weighed her options.

"Oh, very well, but I do not know what is so important that it could not wait a minute or two,'' muttered the beautiful dark-eyed creature who flounced down the stairs and stalked past her waiting sister into the drawing room, where she turned abruptly and faced the much smaller girl, who was closing the door with tight-lipped precision. "Well, what is it?''

Alexandra did not immediately unburden herself to the girl staring at her with mingled defiance and bravado.

"Drop your packages on the sofa," she recommended, nodding toward that piece of furniture as she headed over to the table where she had been seated earlier.

Didi hesitated, then deliberately walked over and dumped her bundles onto a gold brocade bergère chair near the fireplace. This small gesture of rebellion was not lost upon her sister, who sighed inwardly and braced for battle. She reined in her exasperation and tried a conciliatory beginning.

"The hat is lovely, Didi, and very becoming to you, but I am persuaded you know you did wrong in buying it behind my back."

"No, I don't know any such thing. You agreed I must have another bonnet, and this is the one I wanted. You were just being mean and unreasonable not to buy it for me."

It might be thought that familiarity would have reduced the impact that the dark girl's beauty would have on her family, but looking at her sister now with a determinedly impartial eye, Alexandra had to concede that not even the angry pout she was being treated to could detract from Didi's astonishing good looks. A tall graceful figure allied with beautifully sculptured features, and strikingly dark hair and eyes combined with a flawless pink-and-white complexion all added up to a breathtaking total, not a single aspect of which anyone with any discrimination could possibly wish to change. It could not be said of her that she was a shade too tall or might have been improved by more defined cheekbones or prettier teeth. Everything about her was beautiful; to suggest the possibility of improvement was to court derisive laughter. Perhaps it was this visual perfection that made it so difficult to accept that there might be something missing in her character—at least when one was under the hypnotic influence of her physical presence.

Patiently Alexandra tried again. "Didi, meanness does not come into it, as I hope you realize. I would dearly love to be able to dress you and the twins in the height of fashion and elegance without regard for cost, but you know that is not possible. It has taken years of scrimping and saving toward the expenses of a come-out to make this Season a reality, and it is essential that we adhere to a strict budget if we are not to find ourselves run off our legs before the Season is half over. I am sorry you dislike my notions of economy; I don't much care for them either, but believe me, they are necessary. Do you understand?''

Didi pressed her lips together and twitched her shoulders impatiently, rejecting the argument. "You talk as if one little bonnet would make the difference in our ending up in debtors' prison. It is too nonsensical.''

"It would not be if Cassie and Arie had both sneaked back and bought extravagant items as you did. We would soon find out what it is like to be lodged in the Fleet," Alexandra snapped, her patience exhausted.

"Well, they didn't!''

"No, and you are not going to do it either.''

"Wh-what do you mean?'' Didi's magnificent brown eyes grew apprehensive, and her hand went in an unconscious gesture to the satin bow beneath one ear.

"That bonnet cost more than twice as much as we had allotted. If you had not already worn it, I should have insisted on returning it to Miss Crimpleton.'' Noting the fleeting satisfaction that crossed her sister's face, Alexandra's own eyes narrowed. "Since that is no longer an option, you are going to pay for half the cost out of your allowance.''

"But that is not fair, Sandy! I cannot do so out of my paltry allowance. Besides, I have already spent most of it for the month,'' Didi cried, gesturing toward the heap of purchases on the chair.

"Nevertheless, you will pay for half the cost of the hat. You may give me what is left of your allowance now and the rest next month.''

"No, I won't. I'll need my money to play silver loo at the Amberdales' card party next week. I won't give it to you. You cannot make me.''

For an instant, brown eyes blazed challengingly into blue before Alexandra said with unmoved calm, "I don't propose to wrest your money from you, Didi. I will convey your apologies to the Amberdales that evening for the sudden indisposition that prevents your accompanying us there.''

''You wouldn't do that! This is the first invitation we've had to an evening party since we've been in town.''

''You ought to know me well enough to believe I will do it if you force me.''

''Oh, very well.'' Didi's eyes fell and she retrieved her reticule from the pile on the chair. She pulled the strings apart and emptied the contents onto the table at which her sister sat, not bothering to pick up the coins that rolled off the tabletop as she turned on her heel and started to gather up her purchases with angry motions. ''You'd have been wiser to let me keep the money. I might have won enough at silver loo to pay for the wretched bonnet,'' she said nastily, but she was not allowed the last word, for Alexandra's voice stopped her as she reached the door.

''By the way, Didi, whatever possessed you to give your direction to a strange man who approached you at the theater?''

The sullen expression disappeared from the younger girl's face as she spun around. ''Oh, did Mr. Dane call? I thought he would. A pity I was out, but he'll call again.''

''Indeed he will not. I saw to that. I cannot believe you are so dead to propriety as to be striking up an acquaintance with a chance-met stranger. It is bad enough to encourage such men by replying to their overtures, but to be giving them your direction is the outside of enough. Where is your sense of fitness?''

''Oh, pooh! Must you be so stuffy? He was perfectly polite and respectful and he looked like a man of fashion.''

''Well, he looked like a counter coxcomb to me,'' Alexandra retorted. ''After you have met a few real gentlemen at Almack's and private parties you will be better able to discern the difference.''

Had she been less annoyed with Didi at the time, Alexandra would have taken care not to phrase her remarks in a manner likely to emphasize the difference in their respective experience of society. As it was, her careless remark brought a quick flash of resentment to her sister's face, and her chin angled upward.

"A lot of good it will do us to be presented to gentlemen of the first stare. As soon as they learn that we are situated in this out-of-the-way location and see this dreary hired house, they will know us for the provincial rustics we are."

Alexandra laughed, her good humor restored by the look of fastidious distaste on her sister's lovely face. "Well done, Didi, although just a trifle overplayed. Harley Street may not be the most fashionable address in London, but it is perfectly respectable."

"Respectable! Who cares for that?"

"I do, for one, and the people who will be calling here. Did you think to hide our circumstances from the world? I wouldn't dream of being so dishonest, even if it were possible, which it is not. I assure you, the only people who will shun us will be fortune-hunters and snobs, and we can have no wish to cultivate either group. I know you are disappointed not to be residing in Mayfair, but houses in those neighborhoods cost upwards of fifty pounds per week to rent, and we were able to obtain a six-month lease on this one for two hundred and fifty pounds."

"But it is so dull and gloomy here with these great ranges of houses all alike, all built of ugly dark brick with brown stone doorsteps and miles of spiked iron railings. Ugh!"

"Now, Didi," exhorted Alexandra, hanging on to her patience, "what is the use of all this complaining? Except for the odd mansion, which you surely could not have imagined we could ever afford, the squares and streets in Mayfair also feature rows of similar houses. That is, after all, the essence of a metropolitan area, and whether it is brown brick or coal dust, most of London looks dark. At least this area north of Oxford Street has wide straight streets, and you must admit there is less noise since we do not get so many street hawkers here-

abouts. The situation is pleasant, the rooms are adequate
in number and size, and the furnishings no worse than
one has to expect from a hired house. It will suit our
purpose admirably, I promise you.''

Didi had been looking increasingly impatient during
her sister's catalog of the supposed virtues of their temporary abode, and now she said with pure petulance,
''Well, I still say it is dreary in the extreme and we should
find another house immediately if we expect any true
gentlemen to visit us.''

''*Dammit* all, Didi, can you not get it through your
head that we cannot *afford* a better house!'' cried her
sorely tried elder sister. ''Believe me, our saloons will
be overflowing with gentlemen callers this spring unless
you are so unwise as to show them that unpleasant expression you are wearing at present.''

''Or you treat them to a display of profanity!'' the
younger girl flung back. ''At least *I* am never guilty of
using language unbecoming to a lady of quality.''

''Didi, get out of here before I really lose my temper,''
her sister advised in deceptively soft tones.

The younger girl departed with her head in the air,
satisfied that she had gotten some of her own back.

Watching her straight back and slightly swaggering
step, Alexandra conceded privately that her own conduct
had not conformed to the standard she set herself in dealing with her charges, at least not at the end of the trying
interview just concluded. Didi could sometimes provoke
her to the point where it would be a pleasure to throttle
her, but it was unfair to place the blame for her own
weakness at her sister's door. Alexandra was well aware
that her besetting sin was a quick temper and quicker
tongue. All right, a profane tongue, if she were being
honest. That's what came of spending most of her early
childhood hanging around the stables before her stepmother turned her over to the first in the series of genteel
governesses who paraded through Thornton Hall once her
own daughters emerged from the nursery. They had
drilled deportment into the rebellious adolescent that she
had been, but none had succeeded in eradicating the

memory of the free-and-easy speech obtaining in the stables. It was her safety valve, and she was guiltily aware that she derived great satisfaction from uttering the forbidden sounds. A fine one she was to be reading lectures to Didi about ladylike behavior. No, Alexandra decided in fairness to herself, that was carrying a guilty conscience too far. At least she knew what constituted propriety, while her sister didn't seem to have the least notion, despite her strict upbringing.

As her thoughts came round to her prime problem again, Alexandra's eyes lighted on the small pile of money on the table desk. As she bent to pick up the fallen coins, automatically totaling the amount in her head, she consciously reaffirmed her resolution to see that her too-beautiful sister navigated the hidden shoals of the social seas of London society without running aground or sinking herself beneath reproach.

2

~~~~~~

UNLESS THEY HAD CHANCED to fight beside him in the late war on the Iberian Peninsula, his acquaintances would have been hard pressed to recognize the suave Marquess of Malvern in the grim-faced man who strode up the shallow steps of a dark brick house in Harley Street. Even those more familiar associates who had boxed or engaged in other sporting contests with Malvern, and the still smaller number privileged to call themselves his friends, would have been startled at such intensity of emotion in one who seldom displayed any human feelings save amusement, and whose exquisite manners and worldly charm they would have unhesitatingly described as a not-quite-convincing disguise for a bone-deep cynicism about his world. No one who knew him was present, however, to mitigate the effect his unusually harsh aspect had upon the servant who opened the door to his lordship one late-winter morning.

Locating Leander Farrish had not proved the uncomplicated matter he had anticipated back in December when the echoing silence of his ancestral home following his sister's interment had played upon and augmented a furious melancholy until he could think of nothing but exacting payment from the person morally responsible for her death. Knowing there could be no rest for him until he had confronted the man Marielle had loved so tragically, he had set off early in the new year, undaunted by the prospect of traveling to Yorkshire in midwinter. Discomfort and inconvenience merely fueled his determination. The travel-weary hours were passed in trying to devise a way to call the man out without damaging his sister's memory. And in the end his quest had been stymied for a time despite his single-minded efforts.

The Standish estate, where his sister had been visiting when she met Farrish, lay between Leeds and Knaresborough. Her hosts professed themselves desolated at the thought that she might have contracted the illness that had proved fatal while in their charge, and it had been necessary to reassure them repeatedly that Marielle had been in fine health until she had developed pneumonia following exposure to a rainstorm after her return to Sussex. He had concocted a tale of carrying out a promise to his sister to deliver a keepsake to a Miss Farrish to account for his interest in that family, but it seemed the Standishes were personally unacquainted with the Farrishes, though knowing vaguely of their existence. Lord Standish, the father of Marielle's school friend, thought he'd heard of a family by that name farther north and west in the hilly country around Grassington. Miss Julia Standish recalled being presented to Leander Farrish and one of his sisters by the master of ceremonies at one of the Harrogate assemblies, but she could furnish no more precise direction than her father. Yorkshire hospitality being what it was, Malvern had been constrained to curb his impatience to be off again at once in order to accept the Standishes' pressing invitation to remain for a day or two. Thanks to a conspiracy of the fates in the form of a snowstorm which made travel impossible for several days, it was nearly a sennight before he was able to take his leave of his hosts. Many of the intervening hours had been employed in avoiding being alone with the vivacious Miss Standish, whose predilection for his society it had taken all his native and acquired social skill to fail to recognize. By virtue of an exhausting exercise in self-control, he won his release before his kind hosts tumbled to the true state of his emotions, but the accumulated frustration drove him to push his devoted coachman with less than his usual consideration over the next day or two as he resumed his interrupted quest.

The second phase of his search had been no more productive than the first. It was true that, after two days of

questioning innkeepers in the area, he had located
Thornton Hall, the longtime residence of the Farrish
family, whose present head he learned was Sir Thomas
Farrish. It was probably also true that the family included
a son named Leander, if the local version, Lee, referred
to the same person, but he ran up against a figurative
stone wall at Thornton Hall, which was currently leased
to a writer in search of solitude. Beyond informing his
uninvited caller that it was his understanding that the Farrish family had planned an extended stay in London, he
was unable to supply an address in that city. Moreover,
the agent with whom he had dealt had departed recently
for a month's stay in Bath without so far sending along
notice of the temporary location where he could be
reached. Stymied for the moment, Malvern had opted to
go on to London to try to locate the Farrishes on his own
rather than wait around a cold Yorkshire inn until their
agent deigned to acquaint the present tenant of Thornton
Hall with his direction in Bath.

Marielle had died in early December. It was mid-
February when Lord Malvern approached a house indistinguishable from its neighbors halfway down the
considerable length of Harley Street, where he trusted his
search would finally come to an end. Even in London it
had been no easy task to locate Leander Farrish. It seemed
he was unknown in the clubs, and it was not until last
night when he'd dropped into the Fives Court that a mention of the name had brought any positive response. One
of the younger men in the party he'd joined had admitted
to being at school with Lee Farrish. Luck had finally
swung in his favor, for, when questioned further, the
young man, the Honorable James Goldsmith, confided
that he'd accidentally run across his old classmate just
that afternoon and they had exchanged addresses. On
Malvern's remarking that he had not found Mr. Farrish's
name in the membership lists of any of the more popular
clubs, Mr. Goldsmith had laughed outright.

"And I daresay you won't, if it's left up to Lee. He
rides like he was born on a horse, but for the rest of it,
he's an odd one, interested only in science and astronomy

and suchlike. He's never to be seen at the races or the card tables, doesn't know what's going on around him, or even the time of day. Sandy runs that family, while Lee simply drifts along with his nose in a book.''

As he waited on the doorstep for his knock to be answered, Malvern recalled young Mr. Goldsmith's words. Last night he'd been too relieved to learn Farrish's direction to pay much attention to anything else, but now he found himself puzzling over Goldsmith's comments. The character given Lee Farrish by his old schoolmate was difficult to reconcile with a man who could lead a young girl on with false promises. And who was this Sandy who "ran the family"—another brother? No mention had been made of Sir Thomas or Lady Farrish.

His disturbed thoughts must have been evident on his countenance, for the servant who opened the door recoiled slightly before a professional blankness overspread his features.

"I wish to see Mr. Leander Farrish," Lord Malvern said, hastily rearranging his own features into an urbane mask.

"Who shall I say is calling?"

"Lord Malvern."

"If you will come this way, sir, I shall inquire if Mr. Farrish is at home."

A typical furnished town house, Lord Malvern concluded as he was conducted down the hall to a ground-floor room at the back, but at least the undistinguished furnishings were sparkling clean and the hall smelled faintly of something he remembered from his childhood, a concoction his mother had favored for polishing furniture. The small room where he was left to wait bore the stamp of someone with a flair for eradicating the impersonal air that clung invariably to rental property. The simple furnishings dated from the middle of the last century, but the elegant proportions of the mahogany tables had withstood the test of time and gleamed with polish. The few upholstered pieces had fared less well, their blue brocaded fabric sadly faded and showing signs of wear, but the eye tended to pass quickly over these items, attracted by a cheerful floral chintz in shades of rose, green, and blue that hung at the windows and was repeated in the cushions of two armless cane-back chairs and a woman's workbag reposing in the corner of the settee. A narrow table between the two windows contained an exuberant green plant and a small decorative porcelain box. Lord Malvern wandered over to inspect the rampantly growing plant and, by contrast, the winter-barren small garden outside. His idle fingers raised the cover of the box and released the tinkling sounds of mechanical music. Feeling like a trespasser, he hurriedly replaced it.

His eyes were drawn to a painting over the mantel as he turned back toward the room. That this had never formed part of the original furnishings of the house was instantly obvious. Lord Malvern's feet took him closer as his eyes remained glued to the half-length portrait of a young man. Executed in oils, it wasn't an accomplished work, the brushwork was amateurish and the colors were garish, even crude, but it was a compelling study for all its faults. The subject was a handsome young man seated at a plain table holding a variety of objects such as might be used in performing chemical experiments. He was gazing straight out of the scene, but with a faraway expression that indicated his attention had not yet left his own concerns. A lock of tousled black hair fell over his brow, and the portrait spoke clearly of a moment captured in time.

Lord Malvern was wondering if the subject of the painting could be the person he sought, when he suddenly realized he was no longer alone in the room. A dark-haired girl had burst in and come to a startled halt just inside the door.

"I *thought* I heard the music box—" she said, then broke off as though fearful she might have embarrassed the well-dressed stranger staring at her in the liveliest interest.

"Yes, I fear I was being nosy," he admitted, not at all put out.

The child, for she was still that despite the promise of future beauty, grinned widely, showing white, slightly uneven teeth that actually added to the unique appeal of her gamine features, dominated by a pair of large dark-lashed blue eyes. "I see you've been studying my painting of Lee. Do you like it?"

"Did *you* paint the portrait?" The man looked incredulous for an instant; then he said with deliberation, "I think it is a quite remarkable study."

"I'm listening to what you didn't say," the delightful elf replied seriously. "Sandy says it's a poor painting but a wonderful portrait. Do you know my brother, Lee, Mr. . . . ?"

"Lord Malvern," he supplied. "And you are . . . ?"

"How do you do, sir? I am Penelope Farrish."

"I am delighted to have the honor of your acquaintance, Miss Farrish." Lord Malvern made an elegant leg and smiled with great charm at the child studying him with reciprocal interest. Now she wrinkled a small straight nose.

"The other four are all 'Miss Farrish.' You may call me Penny if you like."

"Thank you, Penny, I do like," he returned, promptly accepting the favor conferred upon him. "Do you say you have four sisters?"

"Yes. You really don't know the family, do you? Who is it you have come to see, then?"

"Your brother, Lee. The servant who answered the door, your butler perhaps, said he would ascertain if he is at home."

"Yes, that was Edson. He moves with the speed of treacle. So does Lee, for that matter, unless he's involved with one of his smelly experiments. I'll get him for you," she offered, darting away on the words and leaving behind an impression of coltish grace and a rather bemused gentleman, if the odd smile on Lord Malvern's lips was an indication of his mental state.

None of his lordship's friends would have recognized that particular smile on the lips of one by repute notoriously unimpressionable when it came to feminine charms. The smile lingered for another few seconds until sounds coming from close by brought his attention back to his surroundings. The reason the movements to and fro in the next room were audible lay in the fact that the connecting door had been left slightly ajar. He was about to close the door when there came the unmistakable sound of breaking china, followed immediately by a feminine gasp and a furious *"Bloody hell!"* uttered in clear, distinct tones. He almost laughed aloud as the oath was followed by the sounds of more breaking china, though this time he would have sworn the incensed female in the next room had deliberately thrown two pieces against the wall.

He resisted an ignoble urge to peek around the door. The sight of a strange man witnessing her dilemma would be the last straw for the unfortunate maidservant, who would probably have her wages stopped to pay for the breakage. Noiselessly he closed the offending door, shutting it on a ringing *"Damnation!"* enunciated in those same clear tones.

With conscious rectitude, Malvern turned his back, literally, on the temptation to eavesdrop on the aftermath of the accident next door, returning to the middle of the room, where he resumed his puzzled study of the portrait of Leander Farrish. None of the recent confusion in his mind had cleared up when he heard the door behind him open and turned to find himself being inspected by another young girl.

Though a trifle smaller in stature, this one was a few years older than his brunette elf and very unlike Penny in appearance. She was as delicately fashioned as a fairy creature, with a short mop of honey-colored curls that framed a peaches-and-cream complexion and called attention to a delightful profile and a long slender neck. Both girls had blue eyes, but the ones staring at him now in surprise were the vibrant hue of forget-me-nots.

The flower eyes blinked. "I beg your pardon, sir. I did not know anyone had called."

That voice! Those oaths he had just heard had not come from an ignorant hulking servant girl but this exquisite creature. A jolt of pure rage rushed to Lord Malvern's brain.

"If I were your father, young lady, I'd soon teach you not to use language that would put a sailor to the blush, if I had to turn you over my knee and smack it out of you!"

"My father! Smack it out of me! I believe you're mad, straight out of Bedlam. Who let you in here? No, never mind that. Be so good as to leave this house immediately!"

She might be an obstreperous brat, but Lord Malvern granted her full marks for sheer toughness. She had not backed away an inch, nor called for help, but stood glaring up at a man twice her size, ordering him off the property with a haughtiness that would do credit to a princess of the royal blood.

His laugh held genuine amusement. "Now, calm yourself, Miss Farrish, if you are one of the Misses Farrish. We both know I am not mad—officious, mayhap, to stick my nose into what is not my business—but you may take it from one nearly old enough to be your father that a vulgar tongue will serve you very poorly in society."

"Thank you, I do not require lessons in conduct from a mummified dandy who knows no better than to eavesdrop in other people's houses. And what is this fustian about being my father? Why, you cannot be much over thirty!"

"I am two-and-thirty, to be precise, and the disparity in our ages must be sufficient excuse for my presumption in advising you, Miss Farrish," Lord Malvern drawled.

"You have the advantage of me, sir, in knowing my identity," she said, almost outdrawling him, "but I fear I cannot accept that a mere four years' seniority confers upon you automatic superiority in any quality I might wish to cultivate."

He knew by the wicked gleam in those fabulous eyes that she had reveled in seeing her antagonist's jaw drop before he regained control and snapped it up again. "If you think to gull me into accepting that you are eight-and-twenty years of age, my girl, you may think again, because I don't believe you."

"Your beliefs on this or any other subject are a matter

of the supremest indifference to me," Miss Farrish said
sweetly.

The pair were exchanging glares of mutual hostility
when the door to the hall opened and the subject of the
portrait walked in. Both pairs of angry eyes swung to his
attractive person, but his own gaze was fixed on the
stranger with a sort of puzzled eagerness.

"Edson said Lord Malvern was waiting to see me. Can
you be Lady Marielle Trent's brother, sir?"

"I *was* her brother," came the tight-lipped reply.

The healthy color receded from Lee's cheeks as he
croaked, "What can you mean?"

"My sister died in December."

Before Lee could react or Lord Malvern elaborate on
his bald statement, a small fury whirled on the latter.

"You *beast,* you sadistic *brute,* to break such tidings
to him in that unfeeling fashion!" In an abrupt change of
tone, the girl turned to her brother. "Lee, dearest, I am
so very sorry. Here, sit down."

Malvern watched unwinking as Miss Farrish pushed
her white-faced brother onto one of the cane-back chairs.
It had been his intention to discover Farrish's guilt or
innocence in his first unguarded reaction following the
terse announcement, but this female whirlwind had diverted his attention for a fraction of a second with her
screamed invective. It might have been pain that had
sprung to the young man's eyes in the first instant, but
he could not be sure, thanks to the interference of the
little termagant now tenderly placing a hand on her
brother's shoulder.

"Madam, will you leave us, please? This is between
your brother and me."

Both ignored his request. Lee Farrish seemed unaware
of his sister's ministrations. The glassy stare of incomprehension focused slowly and he whispered, "How
could it happen? An accident?"

"No. She developed an inflammation of the lungs after
wandering around in the rain, and it turned into pneumonia. She died with your name on her lips."

Lee's own lips parted and he caught his breath but made

no rejoinder. Watching him with the concentration of a scientist studying a laboratory specimen, Lord Malvern saw that he had withdrawn into his own thoughts, and he said sharply, "What was your relationship with my sister?"

Still the young man made no reply, but his sister cried, "Why are you doing this? What are you insinuating?"

Lord Malvern's inimical gaze left the silent young man and moved to confront the girl's fierce resentment. "My sister is dead because she was so unhappy over your brother that she took to wandering about the grounds in all weather, heedless of cold or rain. Do you think I can simply let the matter rest there?"

"I loved her."

Absorbed in the private battle of wills that had sprung up between them, Miss Farrish and Lord Malvern jerked their heads around at Lee's words. Lord Malvern recovered first.

"Then why is she dead?"

The raw pain in his voice, the first real emotion he had displayed thus far, penetrated Miss Farrish's defensiveness and softened her response. "Lord Malvern, it is indeed tragic that a sweet young girl like Lady Marielle should have died so . . . so wastefully, but can you not see that to try to assign culpability to my brother is merely to compound the tragedy?"

His eyes flickered briefly, but then the marquess turned a deliberate shoulder on her and addressed the man seated on the chair with his head in his hands. "Marielle loved you. If you loved her, why did you leave her?" he persisted.

"It . . . it wasn't like that." The younger man got to his feet awkwardly and faced the other, his face looking suddenly older and haggard. "There was nothing said . . ." His voice trailed off in the wake of the other's disbelief, and he made a helpless gesture with his hands.

Miss Farrish rushed into the breach. "Lee met Lady Marielle on two occasions only, both times at the assembly at Harrogate. They danced together several times.

That was the sum total of their relationship, as you termed it.''

"Let him speak for himself," snapped Lord Malvern.

"It's all right, Sandy." Lee raised unhappy eyes to his sister's mutinous face. "I'll tell his lordship anything he wishes to know, but that is essentially the whole story, sir."

"You and Marielle met but twice, and both times in public?" demanded the incredulous marquess.

"Yes."

"But you say you loved her?"

"Yes."

"Yet you never told her that you loved her?"

"How could I? I was told that her brother was a marquess and the family was rich and well-connected in the south. Our family is neither."

The simple statement seemed to incense the marquess's temper beyond tolerance. "That is the most sickening, mawkish tale I've ever had to swallow!" he declared.

"The truth is seldom cosmic or heroic," Miss Farrish said softly. "I am very sorry for your loss, Lord Malvern."

"You may keep your sympathy, Miss Farrish," he hurled back through gritted teeth. "Good day to you both."

Before either Mr. or Miss Farrish could summon the butler to show their uncivil guest out, he had spun about and stormed out of the room.

3

THE BLACK MOOD STAYED with Lord Malvern for several days. At the end of this period he penned a stiff apology to Miss Farrish for his rude rejection of her kind expression of sympathy. It rankled his pride to have to apologize to a female for whom he had conceived an instantaneous dislike, but it was also pride in the honesty of his self-dealings that demanded that he acknowledge the truth of the matter; only innate kindness on her part could have prompted her to offer condolences to one whom she perceived as trying to injure her brother.

Hours of painful soul-searching had gone into the difficult acceptance of the fact that he had wanted someone—Leander Farrish—to be culpable in Marielle's death. It was easier to deal with anger and vengeance than with grief and the unhappy knowledge that his sister's death had been just what Miss Farrish had termed it: wasteful. Marielle had been gentle, sweet, and lovely, the epitome of feminine virtue, but there had been no steel in her makeup, unfortunately. Had she possessed a tiny fraction of the mental toughness he'd come up against in Leander Farrish's unlikable sister, she'd still be alive today. Impossible to picture Miss Farrish going into a decline over unrequited love.

The aftermath of the unpleasant scenes in Harley Street and the pain of coming to grips with the loss of his closest relative was a period characterized by a dreary flatness. He was putting up at the Royal Hotel across from St. James's Palace, not having wished the bother of opening his town house when all his energies were concentrated on finding and punishing Leander Farrish. He didn't want it now, but neither did he relish the idea of returning to an empty house in Sussex. One place was as good or as bad as another in his present frame of mind.

He had spent three consecutive nights roving aimlessly from club to club, drinking deeply in each until he'd had to be put to bed by the hotel staff, but there was little satisfaction in that, and not much future. Another morning he woke up in the bed of a lightskirt with no recollection of how he'd gotten there. A servant had shaken him awake, handed him his clothes, and led him stealthily out the back entrance past the dining parlor, where the popular young woman, whom he wouldn't recognize again if he walked smack up to her, was entertaining her married protector, who had dropped in unexpectedly for a cozy breakfast à deux. There wasn't much future in that course either.

There did not seem to be any reason to look to the future at all as matters stood at present. He hadn't thought much about his own personal future in the years since he'd sold out of the military after the first victory over Napoleon in 1814. His father's health was failing at that time and there was much to learn about managing the estates that descended to him shortly thereafter. He naturally stood as guardian to his orphaned sister, and it was her future that had become his primary concern during the last several years. A year ago he'd invited his grandmother's sister to reside with them in the house in Hanover Square to oversee Marielle's come-out. Though she'd enjoyed her Season as much as an intrinsically shy personality ever could enjoy an unceasing round of parties and crowded events, she had not formed an attachment to any of the men who had paid court to her. If only she had met Farrish in London instead of in Yorkshire, when he had not been there to see her through the throes of first love! If only she'd written to him at the friend's hunting box in Leicestershire where he was staying, to say she was unhappy, he'd have come home and put a stop to that solitary rambling.

Regrets pursued Lord Malvern those first weeks in London and attacked him in every unoccupied moment. The problem was that there was nothing with which he particularly wished to occupy his time these days. No pleasures had more than a momentary effect, and he was doing nothing to produce a sense of lasting satisfaction or accomplishment with his days or nights. Obviously he could not simply drift along indefinitely, avoiding all decisions relating to the future—that word again! He knew this, but still seemed incapable of steering his thoughts into productive channels, let alone his actions.

Perhaps he should return home. There was nothing but an endless round of repetitive social events to look forward to in London, whereas he suddenly recalled an open invitation from an old friend from his school days, Dr. Gideon Mantell. Gideon's letter of condolence after Marielle's death had mentioned plans to do some archaeological excavating around Mount Caburn near his home in Lewes, seeking evidence from burial mounds, the long barrows or round barrows, of the small dark race of people that had inhabited the Sussex Downs during the Bronze Age. Like Gideon, he loved his native countryside and had roamed over much of it from the coast around Rye to Chactonbury Ring in the western half of the country. If he joined Gideon in his archaeological search, at least there would be some purpose to his activities beyond transitory pleasures. The rub was that there would still be that huge empty house to bear, for he could not impose himself on his dedicated friend, whose active medical practice would allow him precious little time to play host to one whom he delighted in apostrophizing as a member of the "idle rich."

The irony was that Malvern knew himself constitutionally unfit for a life of gilded leisure. During his eight years in the Army there had certainly been spells of enforced idleness, but it hadn't mattered so much when there were novel settings to explore and the constant companionship of similarly placed contemporaries to ward off loneliness. He hadn't missed the ubiquitous masculine camaraderie as much as he'd anticipated when he'd returned home. Even after his father died there had been Marielle to look after, and a satisfying number of his particular friends had returned safely to England after Waterloo. London was naturally rather thin of congenial company at this time of

year, but it would soon be swelling with members of the
ton settling in for the Season. He concluded that his spirits
were more likely to perk up amongst the crowds in the
city than back home alone in Sussex.

It came to Lord Malvern like a *coup de foudre* that
what he really needed was a wife. The idea was novel
enough to be disturbing, but he had oceans of time in
which to examine it in all its aspects for the future.

His first reaction was to retreat mentally. He'd never
met a woman he could bear to contemplate looking at
and listening to for the rest of his life; the very thought
induced a slight queasiness. He'd been glad while in the
military that no female had ever produced more than a
transitory aberration in his nervous system or heartbeat.
There had been no reason to rule marriage out once he'd
settled into the life of a landowner, but no attraction toward the institution either. He had his estates to manage,
his sister to look after, and friends with whom to enjoy
his leisure. He'd been aware that Marielle had tried to
play matchmaker for him last spring while he was acting
as escort during her come-out, but none of the pretty
girls she'd paraded before him had made a lasting impression. For one thing, they were all so young! By the
time a man passed thirty, there was not much the fair sex
could offer by way of novelty or interest.

This fact of life was no less true in the late winter of
1818 than in the spring of 1817, but some essential must
have changed within himself since the loss of his sister.
Perhaps his expectations had become more realistic with
the passing of time. He no longer thought to find a female
who would light up his life and fill all the empty corners
of his heart, but in the great city of London there must
be any number who could grace his house, bear his children, and provide pleasant society during the winter
months. Most important of all, he could hope that in time
his children would give meaning to a life that lacked all
significance at the moment.

Once he had taken the fateful decision, Malvern set
about preparing the scene with his customary efficiency
that so belied the air of indolence that characterized his

public persona. What had that frightful sister of Farrish called him? In the act of writing instructions to his steward to send people up to prepare the town house, Lord Malvern paused, frowning into space as he searched his memory. It had been something totally outrageous that would have tickled him had he not been so irritated by her. "A mummified dandy," that was it! Extraordinary creature! It was fortunate for the continuation of the species that Miss Farrish was not typical of the young ladies who came to London each spring to catch a husband. If she unleashed that excoriating tongue on all her acquaintance as she had on him, it was small wonder she was unmarried at eight-and-twenty—if she were telling the truth about her age—despite such obvious assets as a head of honey-colored curls reminiscent of a naughty choirboy, the face and figure of a pocket Venus, and eyes of the most intense blue he'd ever come across. If the other sisters Penny had mentioned were at all like the one her brother had called "Sandy," Mr. Thomas Farrish would have his hands full unloading any of them onto unsuspecting suitors. It might be amusing to watch the process from a safe distance, but if he had read the situation correctly, the Farrish family was unlikely to be established among the cream of society. The brother had not even considered approaching him for permission to pay his addresses to Marielle because he felt the difference in their stations so acutely. Not that he would ever have consented to see his only sister thrown away upon the son of an impoverished country gentleman, but if he'd been aware of the mutual attraction he'd have found a way to deal with the situation, and Marielle would still be alive. In this context he could strangle that handsome, romantic-looking young idiot, as much for his damned humility as for having the sort of looks that were evidently irresistible to young girls. It had been a fierce, compelling desire to do just that in the presence of the fool's loving sister that had made his hasty exit imperative that day. The desire to do a violence to a blameless young man had lessened with time and returning reason, but the residue of bitterness against an unkind Fate would not fade anytime soon. And that was another good argument in favor of turning his mind toward the more promising task of finding a wife.

While Lord Malvern was setting about preparation for wife-hunting in earnest, the family he had dismissed from his thoughts was steadily insinuating itself into that stratum of society for which he mistakenly believed them ineligible. Before ever undertaking the expenses of a London Season, Alexandra had written in great detail to her godmother, Lady Amberdale, describing her sisters and the family financial resources and asking her ladyship's advice on the best course to pursue in trying to establish the girls respectably. She had rather expected to be told to lower her sights and concentrate her efforts in one of the more popular watering holes for a month or so in the summer, but Lady Amberdale had done nothing of the sort. It was she who had suggested that the Farrishes rent their home for a six-month period to offset some of the expenses of a London sojourn, and she had backed her advice by producing the eventual tenant from her wide acquaintance. Nor had her practical assistance ended there. Lady Amberdale had found the house in Harley Street and negotiated the lease on more advantageous terms than the inexperienced Lee would have managed.

Lady Amberdale had assured her goddaughter of vouchers for Almack's and dissuaded her from considering a court presentation as too costly for their limited resources. She reiterated this advice when Alexandra brought her sisters to visit their benefactress soon after settling into their temporary home.

When the young ladies had been taken into the dining room for refreshments, their hostess seized a moment for a private word with Alexandra. "Now that I've seen them, my dear, I am more than ever convinced that a court presentation would be an unnecessary expense. The few doors that will remain closed will not prevent your sisters from taking the town by storm. The eldest will become all the rage, as you were, and the twins will attract every eye wherever they go. All three together will create a sensation."

"That is what I thought myself," Alexandra said eagerly, "but it might simply have been my own partiality. Dear Lady Amberdale, I do thank you so much for all your assistance in making this Season possible. You have always been so kind to me."

"Your mother was the dearest friend of my youth. Her early death was a tragedy for you and for your father. Marion would have known how to keep him away from the corrupting influence of the hardened gamesters. That woman he married afterward didn't have the brains of a goose. She was spiteful too. I had to beg and plead before she'd let me bring you out. She never would have exerted herself to do her duty by you. It was for you to shore her up and manage the household while she luxuriated in playing the invalid."

"Her health was precarious, dear ma'am," Alexandra reminded her hostess gently. "In the end it was necessary to return home when she became acutely ill, and she died that very summer, you know."

"Just when I had such hopes of seeing you well-married too. You had turned down at least three eligible offers, but I was so hopeful of Tony Hazelton. He never married, you know, even after coming into the title." The buxom matron achieved an arch look as she peered shortsightedly at her young friend.

"Well, I am persuaded it had nothing to do with me," Alexandra disclaimed hastily. "I liked Tony better than all the rest, but the situation at home was such that I could not have married in any case. They were all so young when their mother died."

"Nonsense. You could have married and had them to live with you."

Alexandra laughed outright. "Can you imagine any bridegroom being willing to take on a ready-made family of five? I cannot. It was all for the best that I had not accepted any offer."

"The best for your family perhaps, but not for you," Lady Amberdale retorted. "Though it's not too late yet. Now that I see you again, I feel sure you will still command a good deal of admiration."

Alexandra chuckled again. "Please, dear ma'am, if you feel an inclination to exercise your matchmaking talents, I would beg of you to direct your efforts in behalf of my sisters. Remember, I shall still have Penny at home for several more years."

Lady Amberdale heaved herself out of her chair. "If you are bent on a lifetime of self-sacrifice, I don't suppose I can stop you," she admitted, sweeping the young woman before her into the dining room.

It was not to be supposed that the decision to eschew a court presentation would be anything but disappointing, but the twins accepted that it was an expense they could not afford. There was a Drawing Room for the queen's birthday on February twenty-sixth, and Didi pleaded that they should all go.

"Lady Amberdale would sponsor us if you asked her, Sandy. You know she would."

"That is not the point, as you are well aware, Didi. Besides, even if we could justify the expense of hoops and full court regalia, which we cannot, there isn't time enough to have it all made up."

"There is bound to be at least one more Drawing Room during the Season. Please say we can go to that one. There will be ample time for you to make our dresses if you feel we cannot afford to have a modiste do it. You can design as well as any modiste anyway, Sandy."

"Thank you for the compliment, Didi, but I cannot undertake to chaperone you girls and act as couturière also. Our schedules are already becoming too crowded to make finishing the clothes we've cut out a comfortable proposition."

Didi had subsided sulkily, but thanks to their rapidly expanding social contacts, her family was not required to endure her sulks for long. As Alexandra had predicted, once her sisters had been seen at the Amberdales' card party, they were besieged with callers. Most were smitten gentlemen, but Lady Amberdale possessed sufficient social prestige to persuade some other hostesses to include the Farrishes on their visiting lists.

Alexandra saw to it that these calls were returned

promptly, even if Didi considered that the time involved might have been more enjoyably spent in the company of attractive men. It would be social suicide to alienate any hostesses who might provide occasions for her sisters to meet eligible gentlemen. The girls all had sweet voices and charming manners and they comported themselves well on these occasions. If mothers of marriageable girls tended to look askance at them and leave them off their guest lists, that was only to be expected and did not go unnoticed by other, more disinterested hostesses without daughters of their own in direct competition with the lovely Farrish girls.

Her sisters were having a wonderful time even before their first appearance at Almack's Assembly Rooms, where select twice-weekly balls traditionally served as the most productive venue for promoting suitable marriages among the *ton*. Admission was by invitation only, and the six society patronesses who controlled the issuing of vouchers enforced strict rules of propriety on the premises. To be refused admission was to cut oneself off from the best society, thus severely reducing one's chances of contracting an eligible alliance.

Alexandra impressed the importance of maintaining the level of decorum expected in that hallowed precinct upon her sisters, though she spoke mainly for Didi's benefit. Cassie and Arie were good-natured girls who, from living in the shadow of an acknowledged beauty all their lives, were nearly devoid of personal vanity. Content in their unique relationship, they were remarkably lacking in a competitive spirit, happy to follow along where stronger personalities led. On the other hand, Alexandra's dreams were made horrible by visions of where Didi's intense competitiveness could lead if there was a lapse in attentiveness on the part of her duenna. So far, the novelty of their situation and a plethora of admiring gentlemen vying for her favors had kept Didi in sparkling good humor, but Alexandra was not so simple as to expect this happy state of affairs to continue indefinitely.

Cassie and Arie had made friends with a few girls they had met during the rounds of visiting. Not so Didi, who collected men about her like flowers attracted bees but was on no more than nodding terms with any of her feminine acquaintances. It was beyond Alexandra's power to promote friendship, but at the risk of irritating her sister, she frequently reminded her to take care not to offend any of the young women in their circle by seeming to be standoffish. That would be bad enough, but it would be fatal to be caught voicing denigrating opinions of other females. These girls had brothers, and she would not like to earn a reputation as one who cared for nothing but masculine admiration at the cost of charity toward her own sex.

Whether Didi took any of her sister's strictures to heart was problematic, but Alexandra was too good a strategist to leave anything to chance during her campaign. There would not be funds for another London Season next year. This was her one chance to establish the girls more creditably than could be expected in their own limited local society in Yorkshire.

Lady Amberdale insisted on personally overseeing the initial appearance of the Farrish sisters at Almack's. She called for them in her carriage, arriving at an early hour for a final inspection before embarking on what she confidently expected to be an evening of vicarious triumph.

The four young women were coming down the white stone staircase as Lady Amberdale entered the foyer. Didi was in front, and the worldly matron, who had seen the beauties of the past quarter-century come and go, pulled up short in silent tribute to the enchanting picture she presented in a simply cut gown of white sarcenet that flowed over the beautiful lines of her slender figure. A wreath of orange blossom adorned her jet-black hair, pearls gleamed around her lovely throat, and long kid gloves completed the all-white ensemble.

Lady Amberdale tore her eyes away from the vision joining her in the foyer to assess the pair drifting down side by side in their sister's wake. It was not often that Cassie and Arie dressed alike, but at Lady Amberdale's request they were both attired in soft muslin gowns of the palest shade of blush tonight, set off with knots of satin ribbon in a deeper pink adorning the short puffed sleeves. The same deep pink satin was tied about their slim waists, the long ends of the sashes floating free as they moved. They too wore fresh flowers in their hair, but pink had been chosen instead of white to compliment their mahogany-hued ringlets. Both wore fine gold chains from which heart-shaped lockets hung above the modest décolletage that revealed smooth creamy shoulders. The tips of pink dancing shoes were visible as the twins descended, looking a trifle anxious under Lady Amberdale's thorough examination.

"Relax, girls. You look a perfect picture," that deceptively formidable-looking lady said with a throaty chuckle.

"Then, may I assume you are satisfied they do you credit, ma'am?" Alexandra followed her gay question down the stairs and joined the others, looking, did she but know it, scarcely older than her sisters.

"They do *you* the greatest credit, my dear," Lady Amberdale assured her goddaughter. "You have achieved just the look of tasteful simplicity that enhances their individual attractions, while creating a total harmonious picture that is going to rivet every eye on them. And I know you designed and made the twins' gowns, for they told me so last week. No one will suspect they did not come from a first-rate couturière."

"I thank you, ma'am," Alexandra replied, dropping a mock curtsy. "I do really enjoy designing and cutting patterns. The girls helped with the sewing, thank goodness. We find ourselves always on the go these days. There will be too little free time to make any more of their clothes, I fear."

"Oh, do not say that, Sandy," Didi begged. "You know you promised to make me another ball gown."

"I'll do my best, my dear, given the time. Here is Sally with our wraps, girls."

As the young ladies disposed their evening cloaks about them, Lady Amberdale complimented her goddaughter on her costume. "I like that figured lace over the blue slip, Alexandra. You have managed to strike just the right note with that little cap and your mother's diamonds, though I shouldn't be saying this if you did not look so absurdly young as to make your including yourself among the dowagers appear like a joke. Will you dance?''

''Definitely not at Almack's, ma'am, and you have just hit upon the reason yourself. We shall not always have you with us to lend us countenance, so I must establish myself as the girls' chaperone from the start.''

Lady Amberdale sighed as she climbed into the waiting carriage and said over her shoulder, ''Well, I cannot like it, but I must agree that it is the prudent course under the circumstances. People will talk so. It is too bad of you to have no suitable female connection who could accompany you everywhere this Season.''

''I shall make a very stern dragon, ma'am, I promise you,'' Alexandra declared gaily.

Cassie and Arie laughed at this absurdity, but Didi's expression was thoughtful as she subjected her eldest sister to a short study from under long curling lashes.

Lady Amberdale enlightened the girls about what to expect of Almack's, warning them that the rooms were not particularly elegant, nor the refreshments anything special. It was the company, as they were aware, that was responsible for its prestige. To ward off any nervousness on their first appearance, she predicted with confidence that they should score an immediate success, begging them only to stay together in the beginning so that as many people as possible should be impressed by the rare spectacle of three lovely girls so alike as to defy comparison.

The twins politely concealed their amusement at this unlikely situation so as not to wound their kind benefactress. Didi smiled with equal politeness to disguise her firm intention to distance herself from inclusion in a group effect at the earliest possible moment. Alexandra took a deep breath as the carriage slowed down as they entered King Street, preparing herself for the first real battle of the campaign for which she had planned so exhaustively for so long.

4

THE FIRST PERSON Lord Malvern spotted on entering the ballroom of Almack's was the last person he would have expected to encounter in that sacred locale. He recognized Miss Farrish—whose given name he still did not know—by her petite stature and pert profile. This last was presented to him as she stood at the edge of the dance floor talking with a stout matron and an attenuated pink-of-the-*ton* who was constantly fiddling with his cravat. The marquess's eyes narrowed as they lingered on the little Alexandrian cap covering the fair curls. She had not worn a cap in her own house. Why should she adopt this mark of the spinster now? It was absurd in any case, when she looked like a teenager.

As the music wound to a close, three couples left the floor and headed straight for the small group of which Miss Farrish was part. Lord Malvern stared. Triplets? It couldn't be. As the three young ladies came closer, he saw that two exceptionally pretty creatures were indeed twins and the third just happened to be the most beautiful girl he had ever set eyes on, at least from this distance. He couldn't wait to verify his judgment at closer quarters.

"Ah, Robert, I see you've wasted no time in discovering London's newest sensations." The loud whisper came from close behind him. "Incredible, ain't they? Each one more beautiful than t'other."

"Take care, Freddy, you are drooling," drawled Malvern, smiling quizzically at the fresh-faced man with the slightly fatuous expression.

"No more than you, old boy. You can't fool me. I

47

recognize the look in those steely eyes. Haven't seen it since Spain, but I recognize it. The hunt's up.''

"That's the trouble with old friends," Lord Malvern complained. "They never hesitate to express the most objectionable opinions, even in public.''

"Especially in public." His old friend produced a wicked grin greatly at odds with his boyish countenance.

"Have you had the good fortune to meet the young ladies?''

"Can you doubt it? I have the right connections," his friend boasted.

"Which connection might that be?''

"My mother is bosom bows with old Lady Amberdale, who seems to be sponsoring the Farrishes—that's their name. I apprehend they're from Yorkshire or some other godforsaken place in the north. It's no good your begging me to present you, though, Robert," the man called Freddy added with another of those unholy grins, "because you're much too old and far too dangerous to be paraded before such unfledged babes. My conscience wouldn't allow it, and I'd lose all credibility with the chaperones.''

Lord Malvern's eyebrows soared. "If you ever had any credibility, you mean. If memory serves, I am a mere three years your senior, Freddy. Besides, how can you presume to know that my intentions aren't all that is pure and honorable?''

"Well, they never have been so far," his friend retorted, but there was a gleam of aroused interest in his eyes. "Very well, if you intend to make it a condition of our continued friendship, I'll present you.''

"No need for such a wrenching sacrifice, old man. I have a connection of my own to call upon in this instance.''

"Who?" demanded his friend, suspicious of the bland expression on the other's face. "This is their first appearance, as far as I have been able to ascertain.''

"I just happen to be acquainted with the eldest Miss Farrish.''

"The little dragon? How did you meet her? No, never

mind. I wouldn't believe anything you told me anyway. For my money, she has more *je ne sais quoi* than the younger ones and is more my size, to boot.''

''Well, my advice to you is to cease salivating, my lad. That one is too old and dangerous for you.''

''That little darling?'' Freddy stared at his friend in the liveliest astonishment, alerted by the sudden brusqueness in Malvern's tones. ''She cannot be more than a year or two older than her sisters, and she has a smile that lights up her face.''

''I admit that I have not been privileged to see Miss Farrish smile, but I have it on the best authority, her own, that she is eight-and-twenty years of age. And now, I shall leave you, Freddy, or I shan't get to meet the fair ladies before the next set begins.''

Lord Malvern turned away on his words, leaving a perplexed and intrigued friend to stare after him.

From under her lashes Alexandra watched the approach of the marquess with mixed feelings. She had noted him in conversation with Sir Frederick Marlowe a moment ago and had marveled at how greatly a smile improved him. She had been too incensed throughout the inimical exchanges of their earlier meeting to appreciate or even acknowledge any good points in the man, but now in a calmer frame of mind she could find nothing to disparage in his appearance at least. In the black-and-white evening clothes and knee breeches that were *de rigueur* at Almack's, he was the epitome of masculine grace and elegance, with the broad shoulders and narrow hips required to do the costume full justice. She would not allow him to be handsome—his habitual expression was too coldly inhuman for that—but she had not noticed the extreme fairness of his thick hair or the regularity of his features on that other occasion. There was no gainsaying his acquaintance would be a feather in their cap, but Alexandra didn't like the man. Nor did she trust him.

Lee had been too devastated at the news of Lady Marielle's death to do more than absorb an emanation of hostility from her brother, but Alexandra had been well aware of Lord Malvern's ill-concealed desire to commit murder; indeed, she had sensed a need in him to do violence. When she heard the facts of the unfortunate girl's demise she could appreciate his feelings. She did not hold them against him, having gained some appreciation of his strong attachment to his sister. No, what was giving her an uneasy tingle at the base of her spine at present was the blandness of his expression tonight.

Not being stupid, Lord Malvern had been forced to accept Lee's innocence of any wrongdoing with respect to Lady Marielle, and he had been left with a huge load of anger that had to be contained. That accounted for his rudeness and abrupt departure, she was convinced. It seemed to her that those feelings were too strong to dissipate harmlessly in a man such as he seemed to be. He could have no very charitable feelings toward the Farrish family, so why was he approaching them now?

The obvious answer was her sisters' or, more likely, Didi's attractions, but he did not strike her as a man to be readily bowled over by feminine beauty. Perhaps he merely intended to acknowledge her with a bow and move on. Alexandra was unsure whether she would be relieved or affronted by such an action, but the question did not arise.

Lord Malvern pulled up in front of her, bowed, and said with the suave drawl she disliked, "Good evening, Miss Farrish. How delightful to see you again. May I be permitted to meet the rest of the family?"

He was smiling again, but she didn't care for this half-hearted version and did not trouble to return it. "Yes, of course, sir, but first you must meet a very dear friend of ours. Lady Amberdale, may I present Lord Malvern?"

Alexandra's critical eye could not fault the marquess's charming manner toward Lady Amberdale, though it was her uncharitable opinion that he probably polished off chaperones for breakfast. The three girls were agog with anticipation, their eyes all for the splendid gentleman their sister had produced out of thin air. "Girls, may I present Lord Malvern? My sisters, sir. This is Aphrodite, and the twins are Cassandra, beside me, and Ariadne, next to Lady Amberdale."

Beyond a swift glance to ensure that she was not making sport of him, Lord Malvern accepted the girls' improbable names without a blink as he made all the correct responses.

Lord Malvern's manners were impeccable, and Alexandra approved his faintly avuncular air when addressing the twins. She was unsurprised to detect no trace of this in his attitude toward Didi. Didi's inviting brown eyes had yet to produce an avuncular response in any man under sixty. It was obvious that he admired the lovely girl, but anyone with two eyes must do so.

After the initial amenities the marquess turned to Alexandra. "You don't dance, Miss Farrish?" he asked politely.

For the first time that evening, Alexandra regretted her decision. It would have given her pleasure to discomfit him by accepting what she knew was merely offered to appease the conventions and clear the decks for an invitation to Didi. "No, I don't," she said shortly.

"A pity."

The little smile with which he accepted her refusal told her plainly how great a lie was his conventional expression of regret, and she was fired with a desire to snub him soundly as he turned to Didi.

"Then may I hope to have the pleasure of a dance with you, Miss Aphrodite?"

"I fear you are too late, sir. All the girls' dance cards are full," Alexandra explained with acid sweetness, but Didi chimed in innocently, "I have one waltz free, but Sandy says we may not waltz until one of the hostesses has indicated her approval."

"I shall do my utmost to prevail upon one of that august body to present me to you as a desirable partner, but if I fail in this delicate endeavor, will you develop a sudden thirst that will permit me to escort you to the refreshment room, Miss Aphrodite?"

Alexandra remained unmoved by the charm of Lord Malvern's smile, but Didi dimpled enchantingly and said, casting down her eyes, "I believe that might be arranged, sir, if Lady Amberdale permits."

The minx. Was she deliberately bypassing her sister in the chain of command to challenge her authority as chaperone? This was promising indeed, but Lord Malvern was too seasoned a campaigner to gratify her whim at the expense of his standing with authority. "Then if your sister and Lady Amberdale have no objection, may I write my name in for this waltz, Miss Aphrodite?"

The ladies having no objections to put forth, he indicated the dance card hanging with her fan from her wrist, but was denied access to it by the black-haired beauty, who shook her head smilingly. "I shall remember, sir. It is the last waltz on the program. And I am never called Aphrodite, you know. We all have such impossible names. I am just plain Didi."

"I shall not allow you to term anything about yourself plain, Miss Didi," Lord Malvern replied with an obvious gallantry that gratified its object and nauseated her elder sister. He turned with an inviting smile to the silent twins. "And what are you two called instead of your lovely but admittedly unusual names?"

"I'm Cassie."

"And I am Arie."

"Charming, both. And may I be so bold as to inquire what 'Sandy' stands for?" He continued to direct his smiling regard at the twins.

"My name is Alexandra," said Alexandra briefly.

"Ah, the conqueror, of course. I shall not be so banal as to comment on the appropriateness of the appellation."

"You already have," Alexandra pointed out.

"But at least give me credit for resisting the obvious in Miss Aphrodite's case," he riposted, going her one better. He was studying her critically. "Having already met your brother and your youngest sister, one would not think to look at you that you come from the same family as all the others."

"How clever of you to guess," returned Alexandra, adopting his drawl.

Didi's laugh tinkled. "Oh, Sandy is only our half-sister. Her mother died before Papa married our mama.

Why, she is quite five·years older than Lee, and he is nearly three-and-twenty,'' she added artlessly.

"Thank you, Didi, but I doubt that my age is of interest to Lord Malvern. I see your next partners heading this way, girls. Lady Amberdale and I are going to sit over in that corner during this set. If you will excuse us, sir?''

Alexandra put a hand on her godmother's elbow and guided her away under cover of the natural confusion attendant on starting up the dance. She had a lot to think about before resuming her active duties as chaperone, not all of it pleasant where Lord Malvern was concerned.

Lady Amberdale was troubled with no such reservations. "I've not chanced to meet Lord Malvern, but he's from a very good family. Pity about his sister's death. I remember her as one of the more sought-after of last year's crop of heiresses, but she was too shy to make the most of her opportunities. A sweet gal, though. How do you come to know Malvern?''

Alexandra gave her godmother a greatly expurgated version of Lee's acquaintance with Lady Marielle and their meeting with Lord Malvern. Lady Amberdale gave it as her opinion that it would have been a coup to secure an alliance with the Trent family.

"Lady Marielle was a sweet girl, ma'am," Alexandra said earnestly, "but I do not believe she and Lee would have made a successful match. She needed someone who would cherish her, support her spirits constantly, and look after her closely. Lee is too young and too wrapped up in his scientific pursuits to provide that kind of support to a wife at present.''

"Hmmnn, perhaps you are right. You know your brother best, but all is not yet lost on that score, if I am any judge. Malvern was very taken with Didi, and she does not have to be wrapped in cotton wool like the Trent girl. In fact, I'd say she was awake on all suits. Did you notice she would not allow Malvern to see her dance card? Depend upon it, some poor soul who thought he was engaged to sit out a waltz with her is going to be disappointed when she gives him the slip.''

"I suspected as much, and can only trust it was not equally obvious to Lord Malvern."

"Why should it be? He don't know her, and if he did suspect, most likely he'd be flattered. With his sister dead he may feel a need to settle down and set up his nursery. If you play your cards right, you may be able to snag him for Didi, though it's early days yet. Most men will react as Malvern did initially, but it takes more than looks to hold the attention of any man who isn't a complete nodcock. Malvern certainly isn't that. You'll excuse my frankness, my dear, when I say that though Didi isn't as featherbrained as the twins, she's not precisely needle-witted either. However, I would not let that discourage you. It's amazing how stupid even the most intelligent men can be when it comes to choosing a wife, and Malvern was certainly smitten tonight."

Unaware that she had done a three-hundred-and-sixty-degree turnabout, Lady Amberdale continued to ramble on, pleasurably exploring possibilities in the mistaken impression that Alexandra was in agreement with her hopes of catching the marquess for Didi.

Alexandra could not explain her doubts on this head without divulging the essence of the situation between Lee and the Trent family, so she remained silent. She could not quite dismiss the hideous thought that Lord Malvern might decide to revenge himself on the Farrish family by raising their hopes that he meant to marry Didi and then backing off in a manner that would cover them with public humiliation. It was a terrible motive to attribute to anyone and she was disgusted with herself for entertaining it for even an instant, but banish it completely she could not. Not after reading his continued dislike of herself tonight. Would an experienced man like Malvern allow himself to be bowled over by a girl's beauty when he held her brother in contempt, disliked her sister intensely, and regarded the family as beneath his notice socially? It seemed nonsensical, but no one could ever claim that love followed the rules of logic or even common sense.

There would be no point in cautioning Didi. Once she

learned of Malvern's wealth and social position, she'd be hell-bent to captivate him, and such was her narrow concept of the world that she would attribute any warnings from her sister to mean-spiritedness or the simple jealousy of the less-favored toward the ideal. It would never occur to Didi that any other woman, given the chance, would hesitate to jump into her shoes. Nor, based on her experiences in Yorkshire, had she any cause to doubt her ability to make any man she met fall in love with her. It might be no bad thing for her to have a salutary lesson in that respect, but not, if her sister could prevent it, administered by a man like Lord Malvern.

Her own course was clearly indicated. Eternal vigilance was to be her role, ready to step in whenever quick intervention was needed to avert a situation that could produce the elements of a scandal. Meanwhile, she might at least try to enjoy this first evening of triumph without sitting here manufacturing problems for the future.

That her sisters were enjoying their first visit to Almack's was obvious by their sparkling looks as all three danced every dance save the interdicted waltzes. The twins could have accepted partners for twice as many dances and Didi for double that number again. Lady Amberdale proved a font of knowledge about the various men who approached the girls, for she was conversant with the family history and financial standing of most of her world after a half-century spent among the cream of British society. Once when Didi had gone off to dance with a young man whose handsome face had been matched by an equally pleasant manner, she leaned toward Alexandra and whispered, "Better drop a word in your sister's ear not to waste her time on Hexton, my dear. It's common knowledge that the family's all to pieces."

"But his father is the Earl of Caswell, ma'am, and I understand that Lord Hexton is his only son."

"That's as may be, but there are three sisters to establish, and rumor has it that Caswell has been selling out of the funds for over a year and is now selling off his blood stock. He is counting on getting an heiress for the lad to save the family. He may pull it off too. He's a likable boy, and the girls fall for those romantic dark types. If only he'd cultivate a brooding air like Byron, I'd say it was a dead cert.''

Alexandra smiled at the deliberately vulgar expression, guessing that her godmother wished to soften the realities for her. Still, there was a trace of wistfulness in her voice as she confessed, ''It is all so . . . so commercial, is it not, ma'am, but what else can I do? Please do not misunderstand me when I say that Papa will not lift a finger to see the girls fittingly settled. He is rarely at home these days. For the past few years his habit has been to pay long visits to congenial friends, never stopping off at Thornton Hall for more than a day or two at a time, and this once or twice a year at most. He has given me full power to manage the estate, which is why I was able to lease it without consulting him. I have no choice but to do the best I can for the girls, even if it means taking a hand in what should be an emotional attachment between two people only.''

''Don't talk romantic twaddle, Alexandra,'' her godmother bade her. ''Left to their own devices, young people would make more disastrous unions than have ever been forced on them by greedy parents. And there is no talk of force in any case. It is merely a matter of seeing that the girls meet the right sort of men. Once you have weeded out the ineligibles, you may let nature take its course.''

''That is a much more comfortable way to look at matters, ma'am, and I thank you for pointing me in the right direction. You know how grateful we all are for your invaluable assistance. I could never have undertaken this adventure without your guidance and support.''

''Nonsense, child,'' said Lady Amberdale gruffly, though she patted her goddaughter's knee in her pleasure at the tribute, ''I expect to derive a great deal of enjoyment from watching events unfold this Season. Why, I haven't felt such a delicious anticipation since I married off my youngest daughter five years ago.''

"How is Selina? Will she and Sir Harry be coming to town this spring?"

"Unfortunately, no. She is expecting to be confined in late June. Is that not typical of Selina? She never did have any sense of timing."

This time Alexandra let the laughter bubble up. She dearly loved this outspoken lady, whose astringent manner concealed an exceedingly kind heart.

"That's better." Lady Amberdale nodded with satisfaction. "For a moment you looked as though all the cares of the world had been deposited on your shoulders."

Entertained by her godmother's pithy comments on all and sundry, Alexandra succeeded in banishing concerns about the future for the remainder of the evening. Nothing was required of her in the way of chaperoning duty save the periodic administration of tactful commiseration to those disappointed seekers after her sisters as dance partners. When a distraught young man stopped in front of her demanding to know Didi's whereabouts late in the evening, she excused herself to Lady Amberdale and personally conducted the claimant into the refreshment room, murmuring soothing platitudes all the while. Lord Malvern having been unsuccessful in his suit to receive permission for Didi to waltz, the pair had put their alternate plan into effect, but it was really too bad of Didi not to have insisted on being returned to her sister before the start of the next set.

As she expected, the missing pair was *tête-à-tête*, completely engrossed in one another in a far corner of the room. Alexandra sent a cheerful call ahead of her approach to break the spell.

"Didi, darling, here is Mr. Mainwaring, concerned lest you had forgotten your pledge to dance this set with him."

To her credit, Didi responded with what sounded like sweet sincerity as she jumped up immediately and apologized to the worried Mr. Wainwaring, claiming not to have heard the music start up. She shot a flirtatious glance at the marquess and pretended to scold. "Naughty man, if you will be so fascinating, then you must keep your watch in sight so your partners can keep track of the time.'' She extended her hand to her impatient new swain, begging prettily for his forgiveness as the pair headed for the dance floor.

Alexandra had already started to return to the ballroom when a lazy observation from Lord Malvern brought her up short.

''Your sister has such pretty manners. I wonder where she learned them?''

Alexandra concealed a smile behind pursed lips as she glanced over her shoulder at the man who had risen earlier and now took a step toward her. ''If you think I am going to be so obliging as to provide you with an opening for your wit by claiming I taught her, you may think again. She got them out of the air,'' she replied blandly.

''Oh, so suspicious, Miss Alexandra Farrish. I admit that at our first meeting the thought did occur to me that you learned your manners at Billingsgate market, but upon reflection I fear I did not come out of that encounter resembling Sir Galahad either.''

The reference to Billingsgate, famous for its foul-mouthed female fishmongers, stung enough to keep Alexandra from accepting the olive branch offered, if indeed such a provocative speech could be so construed. She saw nothing in that suave, guarded visage to reflect an honest change of heart. Chin high, she said evenly, ''I apprehend that, having met my . . . the rest of my family, you now find your natural dislike of me somewhat inconvenient. Pray do not let that concern you, sir. I have lived with dislike all my life. A little more will not trouble me greatly.''

She knew she had angered him by the flash that came and went in long narrow eyes the color of pewter. Lord Malvern remained in full control of his temper, however, as he denied her charge. ''You are mistaken in believing I dislike you. Why should I? We are scarcely on intimate enough terms for so strong a word to apply. But apart from my sentiments, how can you who come from a large lovely family make such an outrageous statement?''

"Because it is true, and as you were quick to point out earlier, I do not really belong to that large lovely family."

"I should have said you were the heart of it," he declared, glowering at her. "It is obvious even to a stranger that they all depend on you. Who dislikes you?"

"Really, Lord Malvern, my relations with my family can be of no interest to you," Alexandra protested. "If you will excuse me, I must return to Lady Amberdale. She will be wondering what has befallen me."

"I thought as much. You spouted a cheap lie just now and choose to evade the consequences by running away like a coward."

"How dare you!"

"Who dislikes you? Either support your claim with evidence or admit you were lying."

Deep blue eyes clashed with steely gray; then the heat went out of the blue, leaving them quite deadened. Alexandra moistened her top lip with her tongue, hesitated another few seconds, and when his eyes didn't release her, said with quiet conviction, "Who dislikes me? My father for one. It is quite understandable when you know that my birth caused my mother's death. He cannot forgive me for that and he still cannot bear to be around me for more than a day or two at a time. I am told I look like her, which doesn't help. Even a later marriage to a very beautiful woman did not change anything in this respect. My stepmother disliked me also, simply because I existed, as my mother had existed before me. She did her duty by me, but my presence was a thorn in her side till the day she died.

"Do the children dislike me? Not actively, except for Didi, who would dislike anyone who tried to exert authority over her at present. I think Lee quite likes me when he remembers my existence, but he has always been a solitary sort of person, immersed in his studies as a child and in scientific pursuits now that he is grown. The twins do not dislike me but they are sufficient for each other, a unit complete in itself, which needs no other human companionship. And Penny?" A little smile ap-

peared in the deep blue depths, which was accompanied
by a softening of beautifully cut lips. "Penny still loves
me. I stand in the place of a mother to her, you see. And
now, sir, I must get back to Lady Amberdale. If you
found my explanation tedious and boring, you have only
yourself to blame."

Miss Farrish was gone before he could voice his
thoughts, which was just as well, because Malvern was
unsure of what he wanted to say. It was not that he had
found her tale boring; far from it. To be the recipient of
such disturbing revelations, told in a shockingly matter-
of-fact style, had rendered him acutely uncomfortable.
Though he had not doubted for an instant that she was
telling the truth as she perceived it, his impulse had been
to protest that she was wrong or at least exaggerating the
situation. He was annoyed with Miss Farrish for erasing
the social distance between them and furious with himself for the taunts that had provoked her into dropping
her guard and saying what she must surely regret when
her temper cooled. She would chalk up another mark
against him, and rightly so. They had met but twice, and
each time he had acted in a manner so far removed from
his usual adroit social style as to astound him and cover
him with shame. How could two supposedly civilized
adults strike such sparks of animosity off each other?

And yet, he no longer disliked her; she was mistaken
there, though his behavior gave her good cause for thinking so. It was as if some primitive sense of danger alerted
him in Miss Farrish's presence and roused all his defenses. Well, if the results of the first two meetings were
anything to go by, he'd be wise to limit their future contacts to situations where the presence of other people
would act as a safeguard.

He could not avoid Alexandra Farrish entirely if he
intended to pursue the promising acquaintance begun
with the gorgeous Didi, which he most certainly did.
Now, there was a girl to set a man's senses quickening
in the most pleasurable fashion. Those eyes of hers! Great
limpid pools of deep brown fringed by fabulous thick
curly lashes. It was an absolute delight to watch her face

sparkle and change with each thought. She was a born flirt, but that did not trouble him. The girl was young and testing her powers. Many a time he'd wished Marielle had been endowed with a trace of feminine coquetry.

As Lord Malvern headed back to the ballroom, he was filled with a distinct sense of anticipation and his thoughts had switched from the eldest Miss Farrish to the family beauty. If his dreams were going to be haunted by the presence of one of them, he knew which one he'd choose.

5

LORD MALVERN LET A DAY GO BY before paying a morning call in Harley Street. At his advanced age it went against the grain to pander to feminine conceit by vying for the favors of the Season's successes, but such was the price if he were foolish enough to fix his sights on a spectacular beauty. It was asking too much to expect to have a clear path to this newest wonder of the modern world.

Within seconds of attaining the modest entrance hall of the Farrish house, his expectations of competition were confirmed. His nostrils were assailed by the heady perfume of roses, which his seeking eye located while Edson relieved him of his hat and gloves. What appeared to be dozens of yellow and white roses were massed in an arrangement of baroque splendor in the center of a pier table under an ornate mirror halfway down the hall. Impressive tribute indeed, he reflected, his eyes following Edson's movements to a table where several other hats testified to the presence of male callers in the Farrish reception rooms. Voices and soft laughter drifted down to meet him as he ascended in the butler's wake.

In the seconds before Edson announced him, Lord Malvern saw that the roses downstairs represented but a small portion of the floral tributes received by the Farrish sisters since their maiden appearance at Almack's. Someone with an artistic eye and a sense of daring had combined various offerings into striking bouquets in a variety of containers distributed around the fair-sized saloon. Doubtless the five gentlemen scattered about the room with less artistic placement represented a partial list of donors of the botanical largess. His appearance was greeted by the masculine contingent with no very welcoming expressions, though the young ladies' smiles more than made up for the deficiency.

During the necessary shifting around to make room for Lord Malvern, that gentleman demonstrated the quality of his competition by ending up next to Didi Farrish, who had smilingly changed places with one of her sisters to aid this favorable rearrangement. Though initially stunned anew by her beauty, which daylight seemed to have enhanced beyond his feeble memory, he recovered his wits enough to assess the situation with the part of his attention he could spare from the delightful creature beside him.

After the eldest Miss Farrish had performed the necessary introductions, two very young gentlemen had begun a playful teasing of the twins, who protested in pleasurable confusion, identical dimples appearing in their cheeks. Malvern was on nodding terms with the other three callers, two of whom were vying for Didi's straying attention. The third had jumped up to assist Miss Farrish, who obviously had the intention of carrying the armless chair beside a table desk at the window to the group seated around the fireplace. It seemed to Lord Malvern, idly observing the scene from his favored position, that Miss Farrish would have preferred to accomplish the task by herself, but she relinquished her hold on the chair to her gallant assistant after a barely perceptible hesitation. The young gentleman, flush with virtue, promptly hoisted the chair in front of him, nearly knocking over an occasional table bearing a squat round vase of red, white, and pink blossoms in the process. Miss Farrish sprang forward to rescue the vase and its floral contents, narrowly averting a watery disaster. Lord Malvern waited in some anticipation for an explosion such as he had witnessed on his first visit, but though she winced and pressed her lips firmly together for an instant, Miss Farrish proceeded to direct the placement of the chair with the professional smile of a good hostess. Certainly the would-be Sir Walter Raleigh had nothing to

complain of in her sweetly expressed thanks as they reseated themselves.

"A delicate little lady like yourself should never be
lugging heavy furniture around, ma'am," he asserted,
well repaid for his gallantry.

Miss Farrish produced another smile and an inaudible
murmur which he was free to interpret as agreement with
this kind sentiment before she took up a piece of embroidery and resumed her stitching.

Lord Malvern assumed only a minor part in the various
conversations that morning, though hugely entertained by
the desperate maneuverings of Didi's admirers as they
sought to capture and keep her attention. Though generous with her smiles, she refused to be monopolized by
any of her court, distributing her favors with the adroit
impartiality of a seasoned belle. She listened with wide-
eyed interest to the tales and observations offered, responding with quick appreciative laughter to all the bon
mots and witticisms uttered by the assiduous entertainers.
Lord Malvern did not choose to compete in the story-
telling but he was in a position, having been present,
to confirm the rumor that all the guests at the Marchioness of Stafford's recent evening party had worn mourn-
ing for the death of Charles XIII, the former King of
Sweden. He could not help but conclude from the expression of keen interest on her lovely face that his acquaintance with such leaders of society as the Marquess
of Stafford enhanced his appeal in her eyes. This did not
bother him. He was realist enough to accept with equa-
nimity that any charm he might possess for the opposite
sex could not be divorced from his wealth and social
position. After all, was he not seeking for a wife exclusively among those females who could fulfill all the re-
quirements his own position demanded? Who was he to
command disinterested devotion to his person alone? He
noted with well-concealed satisfaction that his rivals
sensed a subtle shift in the atmosphere that all their best
efforts to entertain could not quite dispel.

Lord Malvern was aware that Miss Farrish had also
noted the slight increase of favor with which her sister

was regarding the man she herself had taken in dislike, but he gave her credit for possessing enough shrewdness and concern for her sister's welfare to put aside personal bias. She might look scarcely older than the other girls at first glance, but he could see now that her diminutive stature and that short curly mop of hair were largely responsible for this initial impression. True, there was still the freshness of youth about her complexion, but her eyes revealed an awareness of life that was not yet present in her sisters. Behind the startling beauty of their intense blue, they were knowledgeable eyes.

Miss Farrish's participation in the gay banter being exchanged in her drawing room was minimal, but Malvern was not fooled into thinking her mentally removed from the scene despite her busy fingers and generally downcast gaze. He had twice heard her ask a leading question of someone temporarily out of the main conversation, and once he intercepted a meaningful look at one of the twins, whose bubbling high spirits had led her to the brink of what might be considered by high sticklers to be unladylike pertness in her replies. The girl had subsided with a rosy blush and no one the wiser, though the youth who had been egging her on was momentarily disconcerted to come rather abruptly to the end of a promising avenue of amusement.

An altogether surprising person, Miss Alexandra Farrish. After their initial meeting, Malvern would have had no hesitation in describing her as one of those underbred creatures totally at the mercy of their passions, with an ungovernable temper and an intemperate, albeit articulate, tongue. She had been annoyingly calm, cool, and controlled at their second encounter at Almack's, at least until he had deliberately provoked her temper. Today he was being treated to yet another side of Miss Farrish, the understanding exerciser of maternal authority.

He suspected there was more to the beautiful Didi than met the eye also, and decided it was time to arrange more favorable circumstances for exploring the delightful prospect of discovering the person behind that exquisite face. He waited patiently, not surprised that the earlier visitors

made no move to depart when the time had come and
gone for ending a morning call. He expected that Miss
Farrish was fully capable of dislodging guests who had
outstayed their welcome and he was proved correct in due
course.

When a pointed blue-eyed glance at the mantel clock
went deliberately unnoticed by any of the stubbornly lingering gentlemen, Miss Farrish laid aside her embroidery
and rose to her feet in one fluid motion, saying briskly,
"Well, this has indeed been a delightful visit and I hope
you will all come again very soon, but I am persuaded
you all have other places you should be at the moment,
as have we, so we'll say good-bye for the present, shall
we?"

This astonishingly direct speech was accompanied by
an irresistible smile of pure mischief that robbed the
words of any intent to wound. The men laughed and rose
en masse to make their *adieux*. Not having any standing
to lose with Miss Farrish, Lord Malvern waited and then
strolled over to Didi when she had bidden the others
good-bye. He invited her to go for a drive with him the
following afternoon. She refused with what looked like
real regret on the grounds of a prior engagement and
made the same reply for his next proposed time.

"I really am most sorry to have to refuse, sir. I do
hope you will ask me another time."

"How does your schedule look for Monday afternoon?" he asked, bending a keen look on her.

"Monday? Why, I believe I am quite free then. Thank
you, I should love to go driving with you."

"Then shall I call for you at four?"

Didi hesitated. "Could we make it half-after four instead?"

"That's fine. I'll look forward to it."

Lord Malvern said his good-byes to the twins, who
were standing near the hall door, and glanced around to
locate Miss Farrish just as that young woman lifted the
armless chair shoulder-high and safely negotiated the obstacles to return it to its original position in an enlightening demonstration of delicacy and weakness.

"Good morning, Miss Farrish."

Lord Malvern had the distinct impression that the redoubtable Miss Farrish jumped and spun around with a guilty expression before regaining her poise and bidding him a cool *adieu*.

The door had barely closed behind their last caller when Didi turned on her elder sister. "How could you be so rude, ordering our guests out of the house as if this were a theater and the play was done?"

"That's an apt comparison, Didi," Alexandra said. "It was the only way to shake them loose from the bone they were guarding so jealously."

Didi ignored this unflattering analogy. "But it was so rude! What will people think of us, treating callers in so summary a fashion?"

"The rudeness was theirs in not abiding by custom in limiting their calls to the accepted length." Alexandra continued to restore the furniture to its original arrangement, unmoved by her sister's criticism. Didi's next words brought her up short, however.

"By the way, I have accepted an invitation to go for a drive with Lord Malvern on Monday afternoon," she said with elaborate casualness.

"But I thought Monday afternoon was set for your drive in the park with Sir Frederick Marlowe."

"It was, but Lord Malvern had already extended two other invitations for times when I was already committed, so I did not dare refuse a third. He is a much better catch than Sir Frederick, and taller and more handsome too."

"Be that as it may, I feel sure those 'people' whose opinions you value so highly would not consider this sufficient excuse for reneging on a prior commitment when a more appealing offer comes your way. I assume that is your intention?"

"Yes. Lord Malvern wanted to call for me at four, but that is when Sir Frederick is coming, so I asked him to make it four-thirty instead. When Sir Frederick arrives, you will have to tell him I have a bad head or something, Sandy."

"Not I, my dear. I refuse to be a party to this deception. I fear you will have to make your own excuses to Sir Frederick." Alexandra had been heading for the door as she spoke, but now she half-turned and tossed a warning over her shoulder. "I should take care what I was about if I were you, Didi. Even the most popular girl in the world will find her court diminishing rapidly if it becomes known that she treats her suitors with scant regard for their feelings. Also, unless I am vastly mistaken, Lord Malvern and Sir Frederick are friends."

Alexandra went out of the saloon, leaving her sister a prey to no very pleasant thoughts if the uneasy expression on her face was a true indication.

In the end it was Cassie who delivered Didi's apologies to Sir Frederick Marlowe when he arrived to take her driving on Monday afternoon. Edson led him down the hall past the now fully opened roses to the small morning room next to the dining room. There he announced the visitor and withdrew, leaving Sir Frederick alone with a lovely dark-haired girl, one of the twins, though which one, he didn't attempt to guess.

"Good afternoon, Miss . . . er . . . ?"

"Cassie," said the vision, laying aside her stitching and coming toward him slowly. She stopped about three feet away and cast him a diffident glance before bursting into rapid speech. "I am sorry to be the bearer of bad news, sir, but Didi asked me to tell you that she has a headache that will prevent her from joining you for a drive this afternoon. She desired me to convey her sincere apologies for disappointing you at the last moment like this."

"Naturally I am most sorry to hear of Miss Didi's indisposition and trust she will feel quite recovered by tomorrow, but as for my own disappointment, will you think very badly of me if I say that I shall leave here a disappointed man only if you refuse to give me the pleasure of your company in your sister's place?"

In the ordinary way Cassie was not a victim of shyness, but this gallant speech coming on top of the unpleasant task of covering up for her sister, if not by actual lies, at least with a lying intention, mired her in confusion for the moment. She could only stare at the gentleman's pleasant countenance and stammer, "You . . . you wish me to go with you? But . . . but it was Didi you wanted to take driving."

"And I should have enjoyed it immensely, but that doesn't mean I shall find your company one degree less pleasing. Will you come?" he added with a coaxing smile that brought a blush to her cheeks.

"Oh, but I am not dressed to go out," she reminded him, looking down at her light cotton dress. "You will not wish to keep your horses standing about on such a raw day while I change."

"Ten minutes or so won't hurt them," he assured her. "Please come."

"Then I'll find Sandy and ask her. Pray be seated, sir."

Sir Frederick made himself comfortable as the young girl whisked herself out of the room. He was not left long to his own devices, however, for Miss Farrish entered the morning room a few moments later, saying with an easy smile, "Good afternoon, Sir Frederick. Cassie tells me that, having taken out your horses, you are determined to have your drive and have asked her to go in Didi's stead."

Sir Frederick had risen on her entrance. Now he said with a pained expression, "I trust you will accept my fervent assurances that never in my life have I been guilty of such an infelicitously worded invitation."

Miss Farrish chuckled. "I absolve you, sir. It is I who am guilty of infelicitous wording. Do sit down again. Cassie will be down in a moment."

The five or six minutes before Cassandra appeared dressed for driving were spent in comfortable conversation. Alexandra had liked Sir Frederick immediately at their first meeting at Almack's and she had seen nothing since to alter her favorable impression. There was a genuine friendliness beneath the polished address that appealed to her. Obviously he was a victim of Didi's beauty along with nearly every other man who crossed her path, but if Sir Frederick were in the same besotted state as some of the other moon calves who camped out in her reception rooms day after day, he managed to conceal it admirably as he said all that was proper in wishing Didi a quick return to her usual state of health. Sitting here today after receiving what might be considered a crushing disappointment, he carried on a desultory conversation with the ease of a man at home in all social situations. A few minutes later his attentive attitude toward the slightly flustered Cassie, utterly appealing in a burgundy velvet pelisse trimmed in matching satin and set off by a flattering bonnet of the same two fabrics, was everything her eagle-eyed sister could wish. If he were laboring under the strains of a broken heart, no one could have guessed his condition. He might be a bit older than she would have chosen as an ideal match for the girls, but there was time enough to worry about that if he showed any intention of fixing his interest with one of her sisters. At least she need not have concerns for the girls' physical safety with a man of Sir Frederick's experience and driving ability. Unless her memory was playing tricks on her, that ridiculous spotted cravat he was wearing was the insignia of the Four Horse Club.

The front door had scarcely closed behind the departing pair when Didi swept into the morning room looking magnificent in her blue gabardine walking dress and the blue velvet bonnet. She said through clenched teeth, "Wait till I get my hands on Cassie. What was she thinking of—accepting an invitation to go with Sir Frederick in my place? It is no thanks to her that he and Lord Malvern did not meet in our entry hall! I can only pray that Lord Malvern is not a few minutes early and doesn't pass Sir Frederick on the street."

"Oh, what a tangled web we weave . . ." Alexandra declaimed unsympathetically, barely glancing up from Cassie's discarded piece of embroidery that she had picked up and begun working on.

"It would have been perfectly simple if Cassie had kept her head, not to mention her pride, and refused Sir Frederick's invitation. Now I shall have to make sure we do not go near the park and we shall have to stay out longer than they do. Oh, I could slay her!''

''Slay whom—Cassie?'' inquired Penny from the doorway. ''You should be grateful to her for getting rid of Sir Frederick without his becoming suspicious. *I* would not tell lies for you.''

''No one asked you to, Miss Pertness. This child,'' Didi continued, turning her back on Penny and addressing her elder sister, ''is being very badly brought up, in my opinion. You have made a pet of her, and the consequence is that she minds everyone's business and does not know her place. She should have been put in a seminary in Yorkshire while we are in town. Her education is being sadly neglected.''

Alexandra paid no attention to this harsh sentiment, correctly attributing it to Didi's annoyance at the situation that had developed from her decision to renege on her appointment with Sir Frederick. Penny, however, was justifiably resentful, and the two younger girls were engaged in a hearty quarrel when Lord Malvern was ushered into the morning room by Edson. The disputants whirled around to find him regarding them in amused surprise.

''That will be enough, children,'' Alexandra said unnecessarily, for the sisters had fallen into an abashed silence. She held out her hand and welcomed Lord Malvern with her best lady-of-the-manor air.

Lord Malvern replied to Miss Farrish, complimented Didi on her promptness, and aimed a charming smile at the youngest member of the family. ''I am delighted to see you again, Penny. You dashed away without even giving me the chance to say good-bye last time.''

''When was this?'' Didi demanded of her sister. ''I was not even aware you had ever set eyes on Lord Malvern. Why did you not tell me?''

''Why should I?'' retorted Penny, still smarting from her sister's earlier gibes. ''You never tell me anything that happens to you. I have to find out everything from the twins or Sandy.''

''That will do, Penny,'' her eldest sister said in firm

tones before turning to the visitor. "I must apologize for
my sisters' conduct, sir. They are not usually so contentious."

"I did not mean to be contentious, Sandy," Penny said
with conscious dignity. "In fact, I came in here a minute
ago to tell Didi that Lord Malvern's curricle had just
pulled up outside. I think your grays are the most beautiful pair I have ever seen, sir, and so well-matched, complete to a shade. You are so fortunate to be driving behind
them, Didi. Everyone will stare at you. How I should
love to drive such a pair."

"And so you shall—well, perhaps not drive them the
first time, but certainly ride behind them," Lord Malvern
promised, smiling at the wide-eyed youngster. "Just
name the day, provided your sister approves, of course."

"Thank you, you are very kind," Alexandra said,
casting Lord Malvern a glance of warm approval, certainly the first he had ever earned in that quarter.

"Is there any place in particular you wish to go?" he
asked Penny when a day had been decided upon for their
outing.

"Well, I have been longing to see the Apollonicon,"
Penny said hopefully. "Lee promised to take me there
ages ago, but he keeps forgetting."

"You must excuse my little sister, sir," Didi put in
sweetly, having been standing in disbelieving astonishment at finding herself ignored during this interval. "Being the youngest, I fear she has been long indulged
beyond what is proper. You must not tease Lord Malvern
to take you to see ridiculous exhibits, Penny."

"The Apollonicon it shall be, then," that gentleman
promised the child, accepting her excited expressions of
gratitude before turning his most charming smile on the
annoyed beauty, who hastily rearranged her features into
a more pleasant expression. "And is there any particular
destination you had in mind today, Miss Didi, or shall
we just head for the park for the afternoon strut?"

"No, not the park," she said quickly. "That is, I have
always wished to visit St. Paul's Cathedral, but for some

reason or other have not yet done so.'' She raised melting brown eyes to his in a look of sweet supplication.

If Lord Malvern was surprised at such an unusual request, he betrayed none of it, assenting readily to her wish. As they prepared to leave, Didi reached for the parasol she had leaned against the tea table earlier.

"That is a vastly fetching parasol, Didi, but you would do better to take an umbrella," Alexandra advised, glancing out the window. "I fear we shall have some rain within the hour.''

"Nonsense, the sky has looked like this all day. In any case, a little rain won't hurt me," Didi declared gaily.

"It will ruin that parasol," Penny pointed out reasonably. "You know Sandy is always right about her weather predictions.''

"Nonsense, my pet. No doubt we shall be long back before it starts to rain." Didi kept a determined smile on her lips as she led her escort out the door, cutting short his leave-taking of her sisters.

The smile was nowhere in evidence, though, when she returned to the house an hour and a half later, holding at arm's length the bedraggled remains of a once-elegant blue-and-white parasol. When her opinion was sought, Alexandra reluctantly pronounced it beyond salvaging, but she held out more hope for the restoration of the costly blue velvet bonnet.

"The parasol protected the hat from the worst of the rain. We may have to replace the satin ribbons, which have been sadly spotted, but I am of the opinion that we might be able to raise the nap of the velvet with some judicious steaming in the places where it is a trifle crushed.''

Didi thanked her elder sister but made no bones about placing the major share of blame for her ruined items on Cassie's shoulders.

"I had to allow plenty of time, did I not, for Sir Frederick to deliver that wretched girl back here before I returned, lest we run smack into them. Therefore, I had to pretend to Lord Malvern that I considered a little rain no very bad thing, and assure him I did not at all regard seeing my new parasol ruined,'' she said furiously, and nothing Alexandra could say served to mitigate her annoyance with the twin who had exceeded her commission in delivering her sister's apologies to the rejected swain.

"The way of the transgressor is indeed made hard,'' Alexandra murmured.

"Thank you, I have had quite enough of your moralizing quotations, Sandy, but I will concede that in future it will be less trouble to go through with an appointment, even if I receive a better offer. There are too many unknown factors that can intervene. However, it all worked out very well in the end, for now Lord Malvern believes me to be a prodigious good sport, and you know he might not have asked me again for ages if I had turned down a third invitation.''

And with that complacent summarization, Didi went off to her room, her good humor nearly restored, though she had much to say to Cassie when they met at dinner. Alexandra was forced to intervene sharply on behalf of the innocent Cassie, whose actions had been motivated solely by concern for Sir Frederick's feelings. Not by nature a devious personality, she had not even considered the possible consequences of accepting that gentleman's invitation. She did possess plenty of spirit, however, and was not loath to return Didi's harsh words in full measure.

Alexandra called a halt to all further discussion of the event on the grounds that it was over and done with, and even went so far as to forbid any future requests between sisters to deliver lying excuses to anyone.

"For, although there were no embarrassing repercussions this time, girls, this sort of dishonest dealing is never justified. There could be serious consequences that you would deeply regret, not the least of which would be to earn a reputation for playing fast and loose with other people's feelings.''

Alexandra was a bit premature in assuming they had brushed through the episode with neither of the gentlemen involved being the wiser.

In the timely, almost incidental way Nemesis has of

overturning the best-laid schemes of mortals, Sir Frederick Marlowe and Lord Malvern happened to be sparring together at Jackson's a few days later. For some reason or other they had not chanced to meet since both had been present at Almack's on the occasion of the Farrish sisters' first appearance.

They were getting dressed at the end of their session when Sir Frederick glanced at his friend over the cravat he was adjusting and observed idly, "I saw you haring over to the Farrish girls at Almack's that night. Since I heard nothing of your being tossed out in disgrace, I assume you succeeded in gaining an introduction. How goes the acquaintance with the Beauty?"

"Progressing nicely, thank you, Freddy. Your concern touches me deeply."

"Dare I ask where?" The unholy grin flashed across Sir Frederick's boyish countenance for a second before he explained, "I inquired because I expected to trip over your big feet in Harley Street before this. Or perhaps you have decided to hold yourself aloof from the fray in the hopes that she might grow bored with the eager attentions of the rest of us and decide that your godlike indifference is irresistible. Is that the plan?"

"Your Machiavellian mentality is a continual source of amazement to me, Freddy. Now, I am a simple soul at heart and I rely more on quick footwork than guile." Malvern ignored the rude noise emitted by his old friend and continued, "As a matter of fact, I have already had the pleasure of taking the lovely lady driving. Have you done better?"

"I might have known," his friend said with a groan. "All I can claim is that I *almost* took the lady for a drive. She had the headache that day, so I settled for one of her sisters instead."

"And have you switched your allegiance in consequence?"

"Sorry to destroy your hopes, but though she is a charming girl, she is too young for me."

"Didi Farrish is scarcely a year older than the twins."

"Some things are not measured in calendar terms,

Robert. In my estimation, Miss Didi was born with the knowledge of Eve at her fingertips.''

"I would not argue with that, but there are other aspects of life, you know." Lord Malvern smiled reminiscently. "I arrived in Harley Street to find her squabbling with her youngest sister, which must be an indication of her tender years. And later I was pleasantly surprised to find her less concerned about her appearance than is common among accredited beauties. It rained the afternoon we went driving, but she did not turn a hair about receiving a wetting, even though her pretty parasol was completely wilted.''

"When was this?"

"The last time it rained, Monday afternoon. In fact, if you have nothing better to do in the next hour, you may like to help me select a parasol to replace the one that was ruined in the rain. Well," he prodded a moment later when his friend had not replied, "have you an engagement in the next hour?"

"No," said Sir Frederick, seeming to come out of a deep study, "I am as free as the air and can think of nothing I would rather do than help you choose a parasol for Miss Didi Farrish—as long as you promise to acknowledge my assistance when presenting it to her."

6

IF MOST PEOPLE meeting Lord Malvern for the first time wondered what lay behind the civilized but uncommunicative exterior he presented, the same could not be said for those newly meeting Sir Frederick Marlowe. A man of moderate stature and compact build, he was blessed with regular features assembled into an open, pleasant aspect that was every bit as deceptive as his friend's more intriguing mystery. For one thing, most people tended not to seek beneath the surface amiability. They accepted the good nature and charm and didn't trouble to probe for hidden depths. Such shortsighted folk would never discover the active intelligence or the keen sense of the ridiculous that were basic to Sir Frederick's character. In a flash he had reevaluated the events of Monday afternoon in the light of his friend's unknowing revelations.

Not being burdened with a romantically acute sensibility, Sir Frederick could recognize without heart burning the fact that Cassie's acceptance of his invitation had been motivated by pity for his plight. He could even appreciate what must have been Didi's feelings when her sister innocently complicated the situation she had arranged to suit her own preference. While deriving a piquant satisfaction from her well-deserved discomfort on that day, he could still empathize with the frustration and fear of discovery that had driven her to pretend that she didn't mind being caught in a rain that ruined her possessions. Ordinarily Sir Frederick would have been grateful to have gained a revealing glimpse into the person behind Didi's beautiful facade at so little cost to his feelings. He'd have merely put the episode behind him, for

the surface good nature was genuine and he was not one
to interfere lightly in his fellow creatures' pursuits.

In this case, however, Miss Didi Farrish had presented
him with a problem. For the simple truth was that his
friendship with Robert Trent went back a number of years
and had been forged on a battlefield. He suspected that
Robert was in a peculiarly vulnerable state because of his
sister's recent death. There was a distinct possibility that
his generally highly developed sense of self-preservation
where women were concerned was in abeyance at present.

Sir Frederick examined his own motives with scrupu-
lous honesty while he watched Robert set about choosing
a silly item of feminine frippery with all the care he'd
exercise in selecting a pistol. The upshot of the process
was a decision not to intervene actively between the pair
in case the attraction proved mutual and deepened into a
true attachment. Therefore, Robert should not learn of
Monday's little deception from him. On the other hand,
it would do Miss Didi no harm to wonder if he were
aware of her deceit. Thus the jokingly expressed promise
he had exacted from Robert to let the beauty know he
had been involved in the selection of the new parasol. He
briefly considered accompanying Robert to Harley Street
when he presented the gift, but dismissed the idea. For
one thing, he did not intend to cause the girl public embarrassment, nor did he wish Robert to get wind of anything. Less admirably, it suited his purpose to let Miss
Didi worry and wonder if her trick had been discovered,
and by whom.

This admittedly unchristian motivation led him to continue to seek out Didi Farrish at each affair he attended,
though he ceased calling in Harley Street. He made it a
point to ask her to dance just once each time. If he were
fortunate enough to secure a dance, he proceeded to entertain her with a smooth flow of unexceptional chatter,
never once harking back to their abortive drive. His mild
blue gaze could become singularly penetrating, however,
and the beautiful Miss Farrish developed a faint uneasi-
ness in his company that did not displease him. He was

unsurprised to find his petitions for dances refused more often than not. He knew instinctively that Didi would be relieved if he removed himself from her immediate circle, so he was careful to maintain amicable relations with all her sisters.

This was scarcely a hardship. The twins were delightful dancing partners even if too newly fledged to hold his interest for long, and the eldest Miss Farrish could match wits with the most accomplished women of his acquaintance. He had liked her at once, but it had been Robert's surprising warning against her that had transformed what might have been a passing interest—after all, she buried herself among the dowagers most of the time—into a genuine wish to know her better. It had not taken long to discover a questing and well-informed mind beneath the matter-of-fact practicality she assumed in guiding her sisters' footsteps in society. She did not affect any formal mannerisms, nor was she one to stand upon ceremony with persons she liked; in short order they were comfortably upon first-name terms. He considered himself well rewarded in their growing friendship but was no closer to satisfying his curiosity about Robert's attitude after a half-dozen meetings with Miss Farrish than at the first.

Sir Frederick had thought he detected a touch of caution in her greeting to him at the first evening party they both attended after the replacement of the ruined parasol, but his manner must have settled any fears she might have entertained of public disclosure, because the reserve had not been present since. However, if he were given to making comparisons, he'd have to say that Alexandra Farrish seemed to regard Robert with the same sort of wariness Didi reserved for himself. The natural spontaneity that was one of her attractions chilled to impeccable civility in Robert's presence. For his part, Robert seemed to have forgotten his dire warning against her; certainly there was no hint of animosity in his manner toward Alexandra Farrish now. From his own observations, Sir Frederick estimated that his old friend's interest in this lady was almost as intense as in her beautiful sister, but

of a scientific rather than amatory nature. The choice of
the word "scientific" struck him as odd, but how else
describe Robert's air of regarding Miss Farrish as some
sort of interesting specimen worthy of detailed study? All
in all, the part of his nature that took keen delight in his
fellow humans' idiosyncrasies kept Sir Frederick hover-
ing at the edges of the developing situation.

Alexandra would have been chagrined to learn that her
antipathy to Lord Malvern was perfectly apparent to his
closest friend. A decade of being in sole charge of her
family had matured her beyond her years. Combined with
an active concern for her fellow beings, and the total lack
of self-consciousness that was the result of always putting
the children's needs before her own, it lent her a poise
that was nearly invincible in most circumstances. Though
it killed her to admit it, Lord Malvern threatened her
armor of poise in some obscure way. Her brain told her
to ignore his disturbing presence, very sound counsel that
she found nearly impossible to follow for equally obscure
reasons. She had to go on trying, though, because, as
she had anticipated, Didi was determined to have him.
The clear-eyed girl had looked over the field of contenders for her favors and decided that Malvern was the premier catch of the season. He was a bit too old for her,
and she actually preferred the smiling dark good looks
of Lord Hexton to the cold Nordic coloring and unfathomable visage of the marquess, but the latter's wealth and
social consequence made him much the more eligible of
the two. The marquess represented a greater test of her
powers of enslavement too. Though obviously and artic-
ulately admiring, he displayed none of the eagerness to
do her bidding or fall in with her every whim that some
of her other suitors did. It would be a real feat to bring
him to heel, and she was exhilarated by the challenge.

Didi would not have dreamed of confiding any of her
intentions or rationalizations to her elder sister, but she
did not need to. After nineteen years of exposure, her
mind was an open book to Alexandra. Her sister operated
on the simple principle of determined self-interest. Her
behavior was perfectly consistent and true to this prin-

ciple and would probably remain so unless she ever complicated her life by loving someone else enough to make the other person's welfare a factor. So far, this situation had not arisen. Didi loved no one but herself.

Standing with her brother watching her sister drifting about in the arms of Lord Malvern as the pair waltzed at the Ingrahams' ball in late March, Alexandra thought them the most striking couple in the ballroom. The gentleman's fair hair, appearing almost silvery under the two great chandeliers, made a dramatic foil for the night-dark ringlets of his partner. His height and impressive physique lent her slenderness an ethereal quality as their steps matched effortlessly. They were grace in motion and drew admiring glances from scores of people on the perimeter of the dance floor.

Both were smiling as they came off the floor a moment later, and Didi said with flattering frankness, "That was wonderful. Never do I feel so safe from possible collisions during a fast waltz as when I am partnered by you, sir."

"Well, I am known far and wide for my fleet footwork," Lord Malvern replied with an amused smile and a quirked left eyebrow.

Didi giggled and then said quickly, "Oh, dear, here comes that crashing bore Sir Martin Rosswell. I was forced to accept his invitation to dance or refuse him in front of several others, but he stepped all over my feet the last time we danced." She grabbed her brother's arm. "Dance this next one with me, Lee. Quick, before he reaches us. Sandy may tell him you pulled me onto the floor or something." She hauled her grumbling brother away before her indignant sister could protest this breach of good manners.

Alexandra's eyes darted blue fire at the backs of the departing couple before she composed her features into a welcoming expression as Sir Martin came up to the pair remaining. It was necessary to exercise all the tact at her command and blacken her brother's reputation for mannerly conduct into the bargain before she succeeded in smoothing down the knight's feathers. For once she was actually grateful for Lord Malvern's presence as he did his bit to help Sir Martin forget his grievance. This took the form of offering the irate gentleman a pinch of snuff from a gold-and-malachite box of French origin that took Sir Martin's eye and sparked a discussion of these miniature works of art that Alexandra was happy to abet with an occasional comment or question. When after a few moments someone beckoned to Sir Martin and he excused himself, Alexandra turned to thank Lord Malvern for his timely assistance.

He was not looking at her, and she followed the direction of his sober gaze to where her brother and sister were gracefully executing a figure. She closed her lips on the remark she had intended.

"Your brother and sister are the most attractive couple on the floor," Lord Malvern said a few seconds later, unconsciously echoing her earlier opinions about himself and Didi. "He is as handsome as she is beautiful."

There was a quality of heaviness in the even tones that caused Alexandra to cast a swift look at him and discover a brooding expression that prompted a quickening sympathy. "It was not surprising that your sister should have tumbled into love with Lee, sir, he is so very good to look at, but I am persuaded a match between them would have been a mistake," she said quietly.

His surprised regard switched from the couple on the dance floor to the earnest face of Miss Farrish. "What? Do you not believe then that true love was thwarted just by the mere contemplation of the harsh guardian's probable refusal?"

"Stuff and nonsense," she replied, ignoring the bitter undertone. "They thought themselves in love, no doubt, but neither was a positive enough personality to fight for what they wanted. What I truly believe is that had Lady Marielle been granted time to know Lee better, she would have realized that he is too young and absorbed in his scientific pursuits to provide the steady source of emotional support that a woman hopes to find in the man who will be her husband."

Lord Malvern appeared to consider this opinion for a

moment with narrowed eyes. "Steady emotional support. Is that what you would hope to find in your husband?" he asked unexpectedly.

"I? Certainly not, I was speaking generally."

"Well, speak specifically, O Evasive Miss Farrish. Would you look to find steady emotional support from your husband?"

"At my age I would not look to find a husband, even were I free from family responsibilities, which is obviously not the case."

"Must marriage and your responsibilities be mutually exclusive, Miss Farrish?"

"Must you always be so provoking, Lord Malvern? However did we get onto this ridiculous subject anyway?"

"If you consider marriage a ridiculous subject, I fear you will not be very helpful to your sisters."

She grinned at him, briefly displaying pretty teeth, and proceeded to enunciate each word with the care people reserve for addressing the mentally defective. "I consider marriage a ridiculous subject only as it pertains to myself. Is that speaking specifically enough?"

Lord Malvern was given no chance to reply, for Miss Farrish's attention was diverted at that moment. "Oh, look, here comes Freddy, and he has someone with him."

Piqued by her casual use of his friend's Christian name, Lord Malvern fixed his eyes on Miss Farrish. Thus he was in a position to witness her little smile of welcome freeze for an instant as her eyes widened in amazement before a radiant, transforming smile lit up her face.

"Here is someone who says he knows you, Alexandra," Sir Frederick began.

"Hello, Alexa. I always knew we'd meet again," said a deep-voiced man whose hungry gaze devoured the smiling woman.

"Tony Hazelton, my dear friend. It has been so long." Alexandra's voice was not quite steady as she eagerly extended her hands to the tall thin man, who grasped them strongly and proceeded to raise first one and then the other to his lips while his eyes never left her face.

"Too long. Ten whole years. And to think that I nearly didn't come here tonight on my first night in London. But I'd have found you, Miss Mischief, never fear, once I'd settled in and put my ear to the ground."

Alexandra laughed outright but protested, "That was a lifetime ago. I beg of you not to resurrect that dreadful appellation, Tony, especially since I am bringing my sisters out this spring. If we are to renew our friendship, you must not threaten my authority," she warned half-seriously.

"I say, this is most promising," Sir Frederick put in with his devilish grin as his eyes traveled back and forth between the engrossed pair. "Robert, are you acquainted with Lord Callum?" he asked the man who had stood silent and unmoving throughout the happy reunion.

"Oh, I do beg your pardon, Lord Malvern. I was so overwhelmed to see a friend from the past that my wits and my manners have been scattered." Alexandra performed the introduction and the two men bowed and exchanged a minimal acknowledgment. Lord Malvern wore his most unrevealing expression, and Lord Callum's eagerness to get back to Alexandra was patent.

"The music is winding down," Alexandra said into the tiny pause that ensued. "Tony, you must meet my brother and sister, who are coming toward us now, and I believe I see the twins approaching from the other end of the ballroom."

Lord Malvern stood silently observing the scene as an unusually animated Miss Farrish made her dear old friend known to her family. Lord Callum produced all the correct responses and did not bat an eyelash at the string of Greek names. He complimented Miss Farrish on the distinction of her beautiful siblings, but even someone as self-centered as Didi Farrish must have seen that his interest never strayed from the eldest member of the family for long.

When the music started up again, Lord Callum held out a hand to her. "We have never waltzed together, Alexa. Will you do me the honor?"

"Oh, but I never dance anymore, Tony," she explained, hanging back.

"With me you do. Come."

Lord Malvern had to acknowledge himself bested in fleet footwork as the newcomer overrode her demur and swept his old friend into the circle of whirling dancers. In less than a minute Alexandra's petite figure was lost to sight, blocked out by other twirling couples.

Lord Malvern took no part in the brief buzz of reaction that sprang up among Miss Farrish's sisters before their next partners arrived to claim them. Leander was lost in his own thoughts, as usual, but the girls' collective astonishment soon gave way to individual reactions.

"My goodness, I never expected to see anyone literally sweep Sandy off her feet," Cassie exclaimed, atwitter with pleasurable shock.

"No," agreed Arie, always the quieter of the twins. "Lord Callum was most masterful. And he called her 'Alexa.' Isn't that sweet?"

"Well, I think it quite improper of her to go dashing off with a strange man when she is supposed to be acting as our chaperone," Didi declared with a toss of midnight curls.

"But, Didi, did you not understand? They have not seen each other in *ten* years," Cassie pointed out. "Besides, chaperones often dance, you know they do."

"They can if they are married ladies, but Sandy told me she did not intend to dance lest it jeopardize her position as our only protector."

Cassie looked ready to rebut this argument, but three eager gentlemen arrived at that moment to put an end to all discussion of the propriety of a spinster chaperone of eight-and-twenty electing to dance at a ball.

"How glad I am that I am not an unmarried woman," said Sir Frederick, removing his thoughtful gaze from the departing young ladies and their escorts to his comrade's uncommunicative features. "What a bore it must be to be forever hedged about by conventions and restrictions." He shuddered delicately. "I do not envy Alexandra her role this Season."

"She seems to be enjoying herself at the moment," Lord Malvern remarked dryly, his eyes on the small smiling young woman in sage green who danced past the spot where the three men were standing at that moment.

"Yes, that will make a total of fifteen minutes of personal pleasure so far this Season, barring the play. I know she enjoys the theater. Who in her situation could ask for more?"

"I am engaged for this dance with Lady Milliken. I see her entering the ballroom now. Excuse me, please." Lord Malvern nodded to his friend, glanced briefly at the unconscious Lee, and removed himself from the scene.

Two days later, when he arrived in Harley Street to collect Penny for the promised trip to the Apollonicon, the faint air of reckless gaiety, as recent as his acquaintance with Didi Farrish, was absent from Lord Malvern's manner. His narrow eyes passed over the calm-faced man very much at home on the brocaded settee, to rest with more than ordinary penetration on the attractive person of Miss Alexandra Farrish as she came forward to greet him in the ground-floor room where they had first met more than a month before.

"Good afternoon, Lord Malvern. Penny will be here directly. She managed to get her gloves dirty and has gone upstairs to change them." Her little smile of welcome faded at his formal greeting and she said coolly, "You remember Lord Callum, sir?"

"Of course."

The men exchanged acknowledgments and Miss Farrish said with more warmth, "It is exceedingly kind of you to give Penny this treat, sir."

"Not at all. It just so happens that I had not gotten around to visiting this mechanical marvel myself. Penny has done me a favor by recalling it to my attention, and I anticipate she will provide companionship of a suitable mental compatibility," he assured her solemnly.

His reward was a sudden glowing smile that began in deep blue eyes and spread all over her face. "Then you must have a most interesting mind, sir," she said with a little chuckle. "But pray do not allow her to tease you to take her to any other marvelous shows of London. She has an insatiable curiosity for all things of an extraordinary nature, so be warned.''

Penny's entrance at that moment saved him from responding. She looked sweet and appealing in a blue pelisse and bonnet the exact shade of her eyes, but he guessed she cared little as yet for that. Her big eyes reflected a trace of uncertainty when they first met his, but were reassured by his smile and a courtly offer of his arm.

Miss Farrish cut into her sister's breathless apology for keeping him waiting to say meaningfully, ''You will remember what we discussed, Penny.''

''What did your sister intend by that cryptic remark as we left?'' Lord Malvern asked idly when, having crooned over and petted his grays, Penny was at last settled beside him in the curricle and they were headed for St. Martin's Lane.

''Oh, nothing important. I'm not to tease you to take me other places or say anything to mortify the family,'' she recited as if by rote. ''What is the greatest speed your grays can attain, sir?''

''Over sixteen miles per hour, and no, we shall not be attempting anything of the sort in city traffic. I fear dash and style shall have to compensate for speed today.''

''Yes, of course.''

Glancing at his passenger sitting decorously with hands folded, her face resigned, he laughed and queried shamelessly, ''What sort of things would mortify your family?''

''I shouldn't think anything would embarrass Lee. He's impervious to what other people think of him—not like Didi.''

''Didi is not impervious to what others think of her?''

''Heavens no. She hates having to live in Harley Street, you know. She doesn't want her friends to know we are not wealthy. It is simply ludicrous to my way of thinking, for if it matters to your friends whether or not you are rich, then who would wish such creatures for one's friends in the first place? Do you not agree, sir?''

"I would certainly agree that wealth is not an adequate yardstick with which to evaluate friendship, and those who employ it would in all probability not be missed as friends."

"That's more or less what Sandy said when Didi first complained about living in this neighborhood."

"What did Sandy say exactly, do you recall?"

"She said the only persons who would refuse to call on us in Harley Street would be fortune-hunters and snobs, and we did not wish to cultivate either group anyway."

"That sounds like a direct quote."

"Well, I was listening outside the door when Sandy was reading Didi a lecture about sneaking back—" His confiding companion halted abruptly, flushed to the roots of her hair, and finished somewhat lamely, "That is, when she and Didi were discussing it."

"Eavesdropping! Miss Farrish, I am appalled at your complete lack of delicacy or ethics."

Penny slanted a peek at her escort's profile and was reassured by his twitching lips. "I do not think you are," she said boldly. "Neither is Sandy really, though she says I am a precocious brat who will surely come to a bad end."

"You do not seem unduly worried about such a dire prediction."

"No," she admitted with unimpaired cheerfulness. "If I did not listen when they have all forgotten I'm there, I'd never know anything about what is going on. Didi never tells me anything, and the twins are always giggling together about the people they meet. They don't want me around when gentlemen come calling—not that I have any desire to listen to a lot of besotted men sitting around paying ludicrous compliments to my silly sisters. It is not my idea of intelligent conversation," she concluded with dignity.

Beneath the amusement her prattling afforded him, Lord Malvern experienced a twinge of sympathy for this curious child whose normal routine had been totally disrupted while the family deployed itself in a strange environment for the benefit of her sisters. He'd try to plan another outing for her in the near future, he decided. Meanwhile he changed the subject as he neatly feathered a corner and passed a slow-moving barouche.

"Where is the rest of the family today?"

"Didi is driving with Lord Hexton in the park, and the twins are spending the afternoon with the Debenham girls, who are even sillier than Cassie and Arie. They twitter and gossip about everyone who attends their parties. I find them extremely—"

"Ludicrous?" he suggested.

"Yes," she replied, happy to find him so quick of understanding. She continued her report. "Since she was not busy with the others for a change, Sandy planned to fit my new dress before you came, but that Lord Callum arrived. He called yesterday too. All they do is sit and talk about what happened years and years ago. It is excessively boring."

"Well, they have a lot to catch up on. Your sister and Lord Callum are old friends who have not seen each other in many years," he said, addressing the hint of resentment coloring the clear young voice. "Does Sandy make your clothes?" he asked to give her thoughts a new direction.

"She was used to design and makes most of our clothes before we came to London, but now she is generally too busy with the girls' social activities. She doesn't have much time for her garden either, but I help her with that."

"A garden in London?" Lord Malvern was astonished.

"It is just the small area at the back of the house, but Sandy has already prepared the ground and planted flowers and herbs. She is an avid gardener at home. In fact, she belongs to the Horticultural Society and corresponds with other members about developing new varieties and breeding in desirable characteristics and other things I do not really understand."

"A woman of parts, your sister Sandy," he said lightly. "Where does she find the time to accomplish so much?"

"She goes to bed late and rises early," Penny said

quite seriously before calling a fine team of matched bays
to his notice.

Lord Malvern was well-entertained by his young companion during the drive to St. Martin's Lane. She possessed a more inquiring mind than her beautiful sister
and her conversation was governed by none of the inhi-
bitions or prohibitions that produced a boring sameness
in young ladies just entering society. Thanks to her in-
tellectual brother she was aware of the upcoming polar
expedition and quite prepared to discuss its goals and haz-
ards. He gathered that she was a voracious reader and
concluded that the proximity of libraries and booksellers
in London was her chief compensation for having been
pulled up by the roots, as it were, in the process of
launching her sisters into society. In view of her own
considerable talent for drawing and painting, he was not
surprised to find her eager to discover where the best
paintings might be seen.

"It is the opinion of Sir Benjamin West, the president
of the Royal Academy, that the best works of art are in
private collections, the most notable being those of Lords
Stafford and Grosvenor. There is not much worth the
name in any public place, unfortunately, but cheer up,
the annual exhibition of the Royal Academy at Somerset
House is coming up in a few weeks. I hereby and forth-
with extend to you an invitation to view in my company
this prime collection of the latest productions of our own
most renowned artists."

Since he was looking at her while delivering this grandiloquent invitation, he saw the eager glow in the blue
eyes that were just a shade or two lighter than her eldest
sister's, but for once Penny was less than articulate as
she stammered, "Oh, you are t-too kind, s-sir. I should
like it above anything, b-but I was not hinting—indeed I
promised Sandy I would not plague you to take me anywhere."

"Let us leave Sandy out of this if you please, Miss
Farrish," he said firmly. "I trust you do not wish to
wound my tender sensibilities by rejecting my offer. I
tendered the invitation in the expectation of having con-

genial company with which to view the latest offerings of our preeminent artists, and I am further counting on you to enlighten my ignorance where necessary. Now, it is all settled and we will speak no more about it.''

"Thank you so much," she replied, recovering her composure. "I shall be delighted to mark it on my calendar, but as for enlightening your ignorance, that is simply ludicrous. I am persuaded you are a person of wide and varied knowledge; indeed, Sandy told me so.''

"Your sister said that about me?'' Lord Malvern asked, startled.

Incurably truthful, Penny qualified, "Well, she actually said you were the only one of Didi's suitors who could converse on any other subject than court gossip or sporting events.''

"Rather a free translation," was his dry comment.

"Oh, I knew what she meant," Penny assured him sunnily.

The Apollonicon, five years in the making, happily came up to Penny's expectations when Lord Malvern had paid the admission fee at the rooms of its builders, the organ manufacturers Flight and Robson, where it was exhibited. Built at a cost of ten thousand pounds, it was a huge chamber organ with forty-five stops and nineteen hundred pipes. It had six keyboards and could be played manually as well as mechanically. Its mechanical repertoire included the overtures to Mozart's *The Magic Flute* and *The Marriage of Figaro*, Weber's *Der Freischutz* and *Oberon*, and Beethoven's *Creatures of Prometheus*.

After listening to a mechanical concert for nearly a half-hour, Penny gave it as her opinion that the manufacturer's claims in the handbills that the music was executed "without omitting a single note of the score, and with all the fortes and pianos, the crescendos and diminuendos, as directed by the composers, with an accuracy that no band can possibly exceed" were probably quite valid.

"It seems quite marvelous to me, but then, I am not at all musical. What do you think, sir?''

Lord Malvern, who was musical, and who had been

wishing himself elsewhere since the first few minutes of
the concert, agreed that whatever deficiencies a true music lover might detect in the performance, the invention
was certainly a formidable accomplishment and well
worth a visit.

They left Messrs. Flight and Robson's premises in perfect amity, each very well satisfied with the afternoon's
expedition, though not necessarily for the identical reasons.

7

~~~~~~~~

IT WAS ON THE WAY HOME that disaster struck.

The pair waited on the pavement for several minutes, Penny chatting away about the wonders she had seen and the marquess listening with an indulgent smile until his groom drove up in the curricle and jumped down. Lord Malvern, having a word with Bostwick about the condition of his horses, did not notice when Penny started to climb up into the vehicle.

At that instant there was a deafening clatter as an iron-rimmed barrel fell off a passing cart, bouncing and rolling about on the cobblestones. Lord Malvern's high-bred pair reared up in fear and protest just as Penny had one foot in the curricle and one in the air. Lord Malvern grabbed the cheek strap of one of the grays and Bostwick leapt for the other. They had them quieted in a matter of two seconds, but it was too late to save Penny from losing her grip and falling backward onto the street.

"My dear child, I am so sorry. Are you hurt?" Lord Malvern was at her side in a flash, reaching his arms down to assist her to her feet.

Dazed blue eyes blinked up at him. "I . . . I don't know."

She came up with him willingly, but when her left foot touched the ground she sagged in his arms with a little moan.

"What is it, Penny, your foot?" He slipped his arm behind her knees and lifted her bodily.

All color had fled her face and he was looking into twin pools of pain as she stared beseechingly up at him.

Game to the end, Penny whispered, "Sir, I fear I have broken my ankle," and promptly fainted.

His face set like grim death, Lord Malvern lifted her into the curricle and braced her against the seat. "Hold them steady, Bostwick," he commanded. "I am going to remove her shoe before she regains consciousness. It will spare her more pain later."

"Is the ankle really broken, sir?"

"I'll leave that for the doctor to determine. I want to get her home before she comes to, if possible. You drive them and I'll hold her on my lap to keep the jolting to a minimum. Look lively, we are already attracting a crowd of the curious.

"A fine protector I turned out to be," he said bitterly as he scooped the unconscious child onto his lap and made room for the groom on the seat beside him. "Her sister will have my head on a platter, and I don't blame her."

"It was a pure accident, sir," Bostwick ventured. "That diabolical barrel."

"She was in my care," Lord Malvern insisted, ending all conversation.

Penny's color was just beginning to return as they pulled up in front of the dark brick house some fifteen minutes later.

"She is starting to come around. Ring the bell, Bostwick, then hold on to her while I climb down. Quick, man, before she's fully conscious."

As it happened, Miss Farrish was crossing the hall as the door was opened by Edson. Her eyes flew from the child's ashen face against Lord Malvern's shoulder to that gentleman's equally colorless visage. Her hand went to her throat involuntarily, but her voice was controlled as she asked, "What happened?"

"An accident. The horses bolted as she was climbing into the curricle and she fell back into the street. Her ankle might be broken. She fainted, which was a small blessing, because I was able to remove her shoe before the swelling advanced very far."

"Edson, find Elsie and send her to fetch Dr. Walsh at once," Alexandra said, having grasped the essentials.

"My groom will go for the doctor if you'll give him the direction, Edson," Lord Malvern put in. "I can't tell you how dreadfully sorry I am about this, Miss Farrish," he continued when the butler had gone out to speak to the groom. "You cannot blame me more than I blame myself."

"Nonsense, it was an accident, regrettable but certainly not malicious."

"I should have taken better care of her. I was speaking to Bostwick and did not notice that she was climbing up unassisted." Lord Malvern seemed bent on heaping coals of fire on his head.

"It wasn't Lord Malvern's fault, Sandy," came a weary little voice from within his arms, "or the horses' either. Something made a horrible noise that frightened them and they bolted."

"It was a barrel falling off a dray," Lord Malvern said, smiling with surprising tenderness at the pinched little face against his shoulder.

Alexandra, observing this, said briskly, "Well, now that we have established that the loose barrel was at fault, do you think you could carry Penny up to her room, sir? It will save her a trip later after the doctor has gone, by which time I daresay she'll be utterly spent."

She preceded him up two flights of stairs, her small figure marching with a resolute step. Toiling along behind her with a silently suffering Penny—he could tell by the tenseness with which she held herself—Lord Malvern was convinced that his delightful elf could not be in better hands. He suspected that the rest of the Farrishes might prove rather ineffectual in an emergency, but the eldest and youngest members of the clan certainly kept their heads. He followed Miss Farrish into a small but charmingly furnished bedchamber and gently deposited Penny on the narrow bed while her sister lighted a lamp on the mantelshelf and brought it over to the bedside table.

Penny's eyes were closed as she bravely coped with the

increase in discomfort caused by the inevitable jouncing, though he had moved as smoothly as he could on the way upstairs. He could see that the left ankle had swelled considerably in the half-hour since the accident. She reminded him of a broken doll as she lay there limp and unmoving. His heart went out to her, remembering the sunny chatter he had found so entertaining a mere hour since.

Alexandra interrupted his musings as she held out her hand. "Thank you for carrying her upstairs, sir, and for the outing, which I am persuaded Penny enjoyed prodigiously—"

"Oh, I did," came a faint echo from the bed. The child's blue eyes opened and she managed a shadowed smile at her anxious escort.

"Lie still, my pet. I'll take over now, sir," Miss Farrish continued, edging him toward the door as she spoke.

"I'd like to stay—downstairs, of course—until after the doctor has seen her," he said, resisting her obvious intention of speeding him on his way.

She frowned a little; then, as voices ascended the stairwell, the frown cleared. "Oh, the girls have returned. They will see to your comfort, sir."

Women were strange creatures, he reflected in the hallway a moment later as Miss Farrish rapidly acquainted Cassie, the first to appear, with the situation. Their sense of hospitality must be appeased even when heartily wishing the guest elsewhere, as he was convinced was the case with his reluctant hostess.

The twins uttered shocked exclamations of sympathy, but they were not permitted to enter their sister's bedchamber.

"I cannot have Penny disturbed any more than is necessary, and I have no time to deal with vapors or hysterics," Alexandra said with brutal candor. "Send Elsie up to me. She can help me get Penny undressed. Take Lord Malvern into the drawing room and have Edson bring up some sherry for him and tea for the rest of you," she ordered before vanishing into the bedroom at the sound of her name being called by her injured sister.

Wondering uneasily if he would now be the one to deal with hysterics or vapors in Miss Farrish's stead, Lord Malvern trailed the twins down to the first floor, where they med Didi, who had just returned, bright-eyed and vivacious, from her drive.

"Oh, the poor little thing!" she said when the twins, speaking at the same time, told her about Penny's accident.

"Sandy wouldn't let us see her," Arie said plaintively.

"Of course not." Didi shuddered. "I could not bear to see her when she is in pain."

Cassie, who had dashed down the next flight with instructions for Edson, reappeared at the top of the stairs to inform her sister in a slightly breathless voice that they were to give Lord Malvern sherry while they waited for the doctor.

"How delightful," said Didi, becoming the gracious hostess. She led the way into the drawing room and smilingly accepted Lord Malvern's assistance in removing her pelisse. In their concern for Penny, the twins had cast off their outer garments in the upper hall and draped them carelessly over the railing.

The next half-hour had a quality of unreality about it for Lord Malvern as he went through the motions of a tea party, drinking the surprisingly good sherry Edson brought presently while the sisters had their tea. In the interim, before the arrival of refreshments, he recounted the circumstances of the accident, patiently answering all the girls' questions.

Didi had tut-tutted on hearing of Penny's attempt to climb into the curricle unaided. "That child is becoming a hoyden. Sandy allows her too much freedom. In my opinion she would benefit from a year or two in a good seminary."

"Oh, no, Didi, you are too harsh on her," both twins protested in unison.

"Did you all attend a seminary for young ladies?" he had inquired. When all three denied any schooling outside of the home, he pointed out with a tolerant smile, "And yet you have all emerged as elegant, well-behaved

young women. I daresay Penny will in her turn become
a model of grace, charm, and decorum.''

The twins laughed appreciatively, but Didi made no
bones about disagreeing with him. ''Penny is different,''
she insisted coolly. ''Her interests are not those of a normal female. Sandy has permitted her to tag after Lee and
assist him with his strange experiments. I daresay she
knows the names of more stars in the heavens than words
in the French language, and she refuses to learn to play
the piano or harp. Her stitchery is abominable, and—''

''But she shows great promise as an artist, and I understand that she assists Miss Farrish in her garden.
Surely these are also accomplishments worthy of any female. For my part, I find her quickness of understanding
remarkable and her person a rare delight.''

Didi's beautiful brown eyes flickered as they met uncompromising gray ones. She took in a breath and said
sweetly, ''On behalf of her family, may I say we are all
grateful that a gentleman like yourself finds something to
admire in our little sister, who is very dear to us?''

The wisdom of her about-face was immediately clear
in the approving smile Lord Malvern turned on her.

The simultaneous arrival of the refreshments and the
doctor, who was glimpsed through the open door as he
started up the second flight of stairs, brought a return of
anxiety to those in the drawing room. The brunt of the
conversation fell on Didi and Lord Malvern, for the twins
were too distraught with listening for returning footsteps
to hold up their end properly. Indeed, Arie was looking
increasingly distressed as the minutes dragged by.

''What can be happening up there? Oh, I do hope the
ankle is not broken. Penny so hates to be cooped up
indoors.''

Her twin immediately murmured soothing platitudes,
but she was nervously biting her nails herself.

At last those in the saloon heard the sound of light
footsteps on the upper stairs, and a moment later Miss
Farrish entered ahead of the doctor, a short rotund man
of middle years and congenial aspect. ''Dr. Walsh says

her ankle is not broken,'' she announced brightly, but the flower eyes held strain.

"Thank goodness,'' said the three girls in unison.

"It is a cause for relief, naturally, but the child has suffered a bad sprain,'' the doctor warned in a wheezing voice that had Lord Malvern reaching for the sherry decanter. His eyes sought Miss Farrish's in mute questioning and she gave a faintly perceptible sign of assent as Dr. Walsh went on to say that his patient would not be doing any walking for at least ten days.

"So long?'' asked Cassie, her eyes opening wide.

While the doctor explained about the necessity for allowing nature sufficient time to repair the damage, Lord Malvern poured out two glasses of sherry, one of which Miss Farrish offered the physician. The other was for her, he insisted.

"Thank you, but I'd prefer a cup of tea.''

"You shall have that too, but this pot is cold by now. Drink the sherry while you wait for fresh tea to be brought up,'' he urged, and his recommendation was reinforced by the doctor, who assured her sherry was a fine restorative after the strain of coping with her young sister.

"The child showed remarkable fortitude, but you were suffering with her the whole time,'' he added with a shrewd look at her wan features.

"I really should get back upstairs to her,'' Miss Farrish said worriedly as she accepted the glass Lord Malvern continued to hold out to her.

"She'll sleep soon,'' Dr. Walsh predicted, "but a cup of well-sweetened tea will send her off in comfort. Do not worry about food tonight. She needs rest more than nourishment. She'll make up for any missed meals tomorrow.''

Edson appeared then, having been summoned by an alert Cassie while her sister was being persuaded to the sherry.

Lord Malvern retrieved his hat and gloves from the table where he had tossed them earlier while the doctor was taking his leave of Miss Farrish. She turned from the physician to find him at her side just inside the door.

"I know you have been wishing me gone for ages, and I do apologize for abusing your hospitality, but I had to know about Penny," he said simply. "I should like to call on her if I may."

"Yes, she was fretting just now because she did not thank you properly for her wonderful excursion," Miss Farrish said with a faint smile as she gave him her hand. "Not tomorrow, though. The doctor warned that she will have considerable discomfort for a day or two."

He gave her hand a friendly squeeze and said unexpectedly, "Do not try to do all the nursing yourself or you'll be worn to a thread. Let the girls help."

There was a startled flash of gratitude in her amazingly blue eyes but she said merely, "Penny is not really sick. In a day or two when the pain diminishes it will be more a question of keeping her entertained than actual nursing."

"Well, there should be enough of you to do that," he agreed with a teasing smile. He headed for the stairs, tossing a general farewell over his shoulder.

As he climbed into his curricle and relayed the doctor's verdict to the patiently waiting Bostwick, Lord Malvern realized suddenly that he was emotionally drained. He wondered if this was how it felt to be a parent, moments of acute anxiety followed by relief that left one limp. He spared a thought for Miss Farrish's probable state at the moment. He could go home and sink himself in the soothing care of an expert staff until he had rallied enough to plan his evening. He guessed that Miss Farrish at this moment was mentally reorganizing her time and household to accommodate this sudden development. Though her brother and sisters would no doubt assist in the task of keeping Penny amused during her enforced convalescence, the primary responsibility would rest with Alexandra, where, he gathered, all responsibility for the Farrish family's daily affairs had rested for some considerable time.

Lord Malvern knew from Didi that her mother had been

dead for some years. How many years? For perhaps the first time since he had met her and been dazzled by her quite astonishing beauty, his thinking apparatus was re-activated as he considered the Farrish family as a whole. Where, he wondered, was Sir Thomas Farrish, and what role did he play in the life of his family? Not one of the six Farrish children had ever let drop a mention of their parent in his hearing, except for Alexandra's soon-regretted confidence at Almack's. He found that he was suddenly consumed with curiosity to learn more about a man who could be so little in the collective consciousness of his large family.

Lord Malvern had to contain his curiosity for the next two days, since Miss Farrish had made it abundantly clear that she would not welcome callers until Penny was over the worst of the discomfort accompanying a sprained ankle. Accordingly, he sent flowers the day following the accident, kept to his plans to spend the evening at the Daffy Club in strictly masculine company, and generally exercised patience until the next afternoon, when he ventured to present himself on the Farrish doorstep to try his luck. Somewhat to his surprise, the stiffly correct Edson unbent to the degree of graciously allowing that the family would be pleased to receive him in the drawing room.

There was only one beaver hat on the hall table today, Lord Malvern noticed as he followed the butler up the stairs. He won a mental wager with himself as to the identity of its owner when his sweeping glance discovered Lord Callum seated at his ease on a gold sofa beside Miss Farrish. All the family was present except Leander. The accident victim was ensconced on a daybed that had been brought into the room and set near the fireplace. She was beaming at him and beckoning as he paused to speak to Miss Farrish, who had come forward to greet him.

"Wherever did you find lilacs this early in the year?" she demanded in lieu of a more conventional greeting.

His nose had already located the tall crystal vase containing white roses and an artistic shower of the fragrant purple blooms. The vase was placed on a table near Penny's couch. Since he had no intention of admitting that he had scoured London for flowers that would remind the child of the country, he merely smiled as he took the hand Miss Farrish extended.

Miss Farrish's eyes fell on the box under his arm and she leapt to a correct conclusion, saying in admonishing tones, "You should not, you will spoil her abominably. She has already acquired an inflated idea of her importance these past two days."

Since her radiant smile, the one she had seemed to reserve exclusively for Lord Callum, was turned on for his sole benefit at the moment, Lord Malvern could not really consider himself reprimanded. He kept her hand a moment longer, asking in low tones, "How is she progressing? She looks a trifle peaked still."

"That is to be expected, sir, under the circumstances," Miss Farrish replied, keeping her own voice lowered as she sought to erase the hint of concern in his eyes as they dwelt on the child. "Recollect that it is not yet forty-eight hours since the accident. Although she is much easier at present, she has had to bear considerable discomfort these past two days. I promise you Dr. Walsh is quite satisfied with her medical progress."

"What are you two whispering about over there?" Didi called, her gay question efficiently severing the momentary intimacy that had sprung up between Malvern and her sister.

"Are you talking about me?" Penny wanted to know.

"Why should you think your sister and I have nothing to discuss save yourself, Miss Importance?"

Lord Malvern smiled lazily at the eager child as he approached her couch and held out the colorful package. "For you to share with your faithful attendants," he said, widening the smile to include her three sisters. The twins were perched on footstools drawn up to the daybed, and Didi sat in a gold bergère chair at a little distance. He exchanged civil greetings with Lord Callum while Penny tore off the wrappings.

"Oh, lovely! My favorite sugar plums!" squealed the

excited child. "Thank you very much, sir." She had the box open and passed it immediately to Cassie, who circulated it about the room while Arie dragged an armless chair over to the daybed for Lord Malvern. He dropped onto it, smiling his thanks at Arie, and continued his appraisal of her little sister.

In the glow of sudden excitement, Penny looked more herself, the wan image he had noted on his entrance erased, at least temporarily. Although dark-haired and with the promise of good height like all the offspring of the second Lady Farrish, Penny was not quite in the same mold as the others. For one thing, her eyes were blue like those of her half-sister, and she did not possess the oval-shaped face and classically regular features shared by the other four. He watched her take back the box of sugar plums onto her lap. After he made a negative movement of his head, she popped a whole one into her mouth and grinned at him unself-consciously.

Another Miss Mischief, he thought, and realized that Penny was more akin to Alexandra in personality, though her looks were original to herself. Her face was rather like an inverted triangle with a wide brow, large wide-set eyes, high, pronounced cheekbones, and a pointed chin. Her brilliant white teeth were slightly irregular. She would never be classically beautiful, but he knew with sudden conviction that she would exude an irresistible attraction for the male of the species one day, like her eldest sister when she was not consciously playing the singularly unsuitable role of duenna. Like Alexandra's, her appeal would be partly physical but mainly owing to a vital intelligence and an eager acceptance of life's challenges that was grounded in bedrock integrity of spirit.

Lord Malvern was not granted time in which to become cynically amused at himself for the grandiloquent conclusions he had somehow drawn from watching a charming child greedily enjoying sugar plums. At that moment Lord Callum indicated his intention of departing, citing an appointment in the City. The next few minutes were taken up by the formalities of leave-taking. At the end of it, sated for the present with sweets, Penny turned to her visitor and exclaimed contritely:

"I have not yet thanked you, sir, for taking me to hear the Apollonicon or for my absolutely gorgeous lilacs and roses. No one ever sent me flowers before," she added in naive explanation. "It was almost worth hurting my ankle for, though I do sincerely beg your pardon for spoiling our outing at the end. Didi says no one will ever ask me anywhere again until I acquire a little conduct."

"I trust then that you will have acquired this magical commodity by the end of the month," Lord Malvern said, looking solemn. "Have you forgotten we have a date to visit the exhibition at Somerset House? If your sister is willing to give me another chance, that is."

"What is all this?" asked Didi, and Alexandra, coming back from seeing Lord Callum into Edson's hands, echoed the query as she reseated herself on the sofa.

"Did not Penny tell you that we are engaged to view the annual exhibition of paintings by the Royal Academy together?" He turned to the child and inquired with mock humility, "Miss Farrish, are you about to depress any pretensions I may cherish of being a moderately desirable escort for a lady by declaring that you have forgotten our appointment?"

"No, sir, but I did not mention it to Sandy in case you no longer wished to take me after I embarrassed you in public."

"You did nothing of the sort, my dear child," he said with a sincerity no one could doubt. "I am looking forward to it, but you must take care to obey all the doctor's instructions so your ankle will be strong enough by then for an hour or two of standing and walking."

"Oh, I will, sir, even though I hate having to stay indoors all the time. Cassie and Arie have been reading to me and playing games, and when Edson told Lord Hexton why we were not receiving callers yesterday, he sent me some very clever puzzles that will take hours of time to work out."

"It was exceedingly kind of Lord Hexton," Didi said.

"Indeed it was," Lord Malvern agreed smilingly. "By

the way, does your father know of the accident that has befallen his youngest child?''

The casual question produced a moment of dead silence. Glancing around the circle of suddenly blank faces, Lord Malvern wondered for an instant if Sir Thomas Farrish even existed, though he had certainly heard him spoken of in the present tense and he had not forgotten Miss Farrish's disturbing claim that her father disliked her and did not like to be in her company for long.

Penny was the first to recover her tongue. ''Papa? Why would Papa care about my ankle? Do we even know where he is, Sandy?''

''I believe he may be visiting Lord Sturgis at present,'' her sister replied after a barely perceptible pause, ''but of course I would not think of alarming him unnecessarily about a minor mishap.''

''Fortunately a sprained ankle may be considered to fall in the category of minor mishaps,'' Lord Malvern agreed cordially. ''Would you consider a broken ankle serious?''

''Naturally I should, for Penny's sake,'' she declared, her recent friendliness vanishing as she met his bland look with stony calm, ''but there would have been nothing my father could do for her that we could not. Men are generally out of place in a sickroom anyway.''

Whether to break the intimate though faintly inimical contact between her sister and Lord Malvern or simply because she was used to being the focus of all attention in the drawing room, Didi spoke up then. ''Papa is scarcely ever at home, sir. Sandy has run the estate for as long as I can remember.''

Lord Malvern's eyes skimmed her briefly and returned to Alexandra. ''Not your brother?'' he asked.

''Lee has been of age for less than two years,'' she replied with the same stony calm. ''So far my father has not seen fit to make any changes in an arrangement that suits all parties.'' Her eyes told him she resented his questions but, driven by an inexplicable need to understand the situation, he continued his impertinent inquisition.

"How long has it been since your stepmother passed away?"

"Ten years," Miss Farrish said with tight-lipped brevity.

"I do not even remember Mama," Penny piped up in a small voice.

Miss Farrish wrenched her eyes away from the man's intent pewter regard and looked at her youngest sister. Her voice softened immediately. "Your mama was very beautiful, tall and graceful like Didi, and she was inordinately pleased that you had inherited Papa's blue eyes. And now, my pet, I think you have been up quite long enough for the first time out of your bed." She ignored Penny's automatic protests and turned back to Lord Malvern, keeping her voice light. "Lee carried her downstairs at lunchtime, sir, but he has gone out. May I impose upon your kindness once again to carry her up to her room before you leave us?"

Anytime within the next thirty seconds, for preference. Lord Malvern mentally finished her unspoken wish and acknowledged to himself that she had every right to throw him out, and with much less tact than she had employed. He had been unpardonably personal and prying, very unlike his usual self, but there had been no other way to find out what he wished to know. Apart from Lady Amberdale, no one in their current circle was remotely familiar with the inner workings of the Farrish family. He did not regret his presumption, however much he regretted losing the pleasant sense of being liked by Miss Farrish that he had briefly enjoyed. She was not one to harbor a grudge, he concluded with a happy conviction that should have struck him as unjustified, given his slight acquaintance with the lady.

Penny nestled confidingly against his chest as he transported her to her room a few moments later. He had gotten a little of his own back with a prolonged and gallant leave-taking of the other three girls, designed to annoy her bossy sister. Miss Farrish was right: the child was tired. She was too thin as yet for her height, which was already two or three inches above that of the deceptively doll-like Alexandra. Being blessed or cursed with an energetic nature, she was the type to overtax her strength, again like her eldest sister. Once more he experienced a curious rush of anxiety for this endearing child as he laid her on her bed and smilingly accepted the shy kiss she pressed on his cheek. Alexandra must see to it that her sister did not damage her ankle permanently by trying to do too much too soon.

Out on the pavement a few moments later with Alexandra's prim and insincere thanks ringing in his ears—she was obviously still annoyed with him—Lord Malvern was inclined to jeer at his seesaw reactions to the Farrish clan. If he was going to start acting ridiculously paternal and protective of a child who was not his own, then it was indeed high time he got himself a wife and set up his nursery.

Considering the events of the past few weeks, he thought he could say without conceit that he had the inside track with Didi Farrish, though she was having a wonderful time being seen in the company of most of the town's eligible bachelors. He begrudged her none of her success and was content for the moment to remain one of the main contenders for her hand. He realized, of course, that this sanguine attitude would not be true if he were already in love with her. How very odd that though he spent much more time with Didi, and very enjoyably too, it was her youngest sister he had fallen in love with, in a sense, and the eldest he found most stimulating. His last thought, before he unexpectedly met an old friend who engaged his attention in Oxford Street, was not of any of the attractive Farrish offspring but of a man whose selfishness was of such a magnitude as to permit an almost literal abandonment of his children to raise themselves. Small wonder she was bossy!

8

PENNY'S RECOVERY PROCEEDED SMOOTHLY, if more slowly than was acceptable to an active child. Lee carried her downstairs each morning to the daybed, which became a permanent part of the decor of the drawing room. There she was permitted to reign, if not quite as queen, at least as a pampered princess while all the family's visitors made much of her and showered her with books, novelties, and games to keep her amused during the period of enforced inactivity.

When there were no callers, the twins constituted themselves her willing handmaidens within limits. The irrepressible Cassie kept her in a state of mirth with her blundering attempts to solve some of the puzzles that arrived, and Arie was never too busy to fetch and carry or keep the invalid company during her solitary meals. If Didi confined her ministrations to those moments when visitors were present to admire her in the role of doting sister, no one minded, least of all Penny, who was unused to receiving any benevolent attention from this source. And if, when no visitors were present, Didi complained more than once that the child was being ruined by overindulgence, Penny did not mind that either, for no one else paid any heed to these dark predictions.

Alexandra was privately much relieved as she witnessed the beneficial results of what might have been a serious injury. Her conscience had been uneasy about her youngest charge ever since the family had established a hectic social routine that left the child too often to her own devices. Although the other girls were her main priority this spring, she was aware that their pleasures had come at the cost to Penny of the companionship she had hitherto enjoyed within the family, without introducing any new attractions to make up for the deprivation. This had been brought home to her forcibly by the child's rapturous response to Lord Malvern's invitation. The fact that Penny had accepted her solitude so uncomplainingly only added to the weight of guilt Alexandra carried with her. She was determined, once the child was on her feet again, to spend more time with her, if it was only in the nature of running errands together or doing chores about the house. She had automatically taken care of the flower arranging, a task she loved and for which she found more scope in London than she had anticipated, thanks to the generosity of the girls' admirers. From now on she would enlist Penny's aid in this labor of love.

Another suggestion for Penny's benefit came from Lord Malvern. This gentleman, initially disliked and distrusted for his possibly insincere designs on her most beautiful sister, had insinuated himself into Alexandra's good graces with his devotion to the youngest member of the family. She was no fool, and unlikely though it seemed, given Lord Malvern's worldliness and cold demeanor, she recognized the sincerity of his affection for Penny and forgave him all his annoying traits, even including the perverse and inexplicable sense of delight she was convinced he derived from baiting herself. She still could not tell from watching the couple together if he was in love with Didi or meant to marry her, but she no longer feared that any harm would come to her family at his hands. Under that air of slightly inhuman detachment there was real kindness—perhaps not for everyone, but wonderfully comforting for those who touched his heart or aroused his sympathies.

Penny had done both. If there was any danger of her becoming spoiled, the blame would be laid properly at Lord Malvern's door. He visited her daily during her convalescence, even when he could spare only a few minutes from his schedule. It was not done to curry favor with Didi, for she was sometimes out driving with one or another of her admirers during his visits to Penny. Until

Alexandra took him sternly to task for overindulging his little friend, he never arrived empty-handed either.

It was on the day Lord Malvern brought Penny some of the discourses of Sir Joshua Reynolds on the arts that he and Alexandra fell into a discussion of the child's talent and the ramifications of her gift. At first pleased to find that a man of taste and culture shared her opinion that Penny's natural talent placed her work well above the level of a feminine accomplishment, she was subsequently rather disconcerted to hear him advise training on a scale much beyond the services of a drawing master, which she had been considering as a partial solution to the problem of the child being too much on her own. It seemed Lord Malvern would like to see Penny accepted into the studio of a skilled painter for instruction on a regular basis while the family remained in London.

"Oh, but she is much too young and it would not be seemly for a girl, and even if I were able to persuade an established artist to accept her as a pupil, his fee would be bound to be prohibitive," she said, marshaling a platoon of objections to such a radical suggestion.

"You disappoint me, Miss Farrish. I never expected to find you missish or conventional. How is Penny to learn the techniques of painting without sustained contact with someone able to teach the skills she lacks? Naturally you would require that the lessons be private so that she should receive as much instruction as possible in the remaining weeks of your stay, and you might wish to be present for propriety's sake. As for the cost of such a program, it would give me great pleasure to assume that responsibility, since I feel she is in some small way my discovery."

"Good heavens!" she said, her eyes widening in shock. "Can you possibly believe that I could allow anyone outside the family to pay for something like that? It is unthinkable!"

"Why?" he asked with unmoved calm. "Most great artists have had the support of a patron in the beginning, or if you find this rationale unacceptable, could you not consider me practically a member of the family by now? . . .

By adoption,'' he added smoothly as her eyes swung to Didi for an instant before returning to meet his with a question in the blue depths.

"Oh, you were only funning." Relief sounded in Alexandra's voice and the uncertainty cleared from her face as the pucker between her brows faded. She smiled at him.

There was no answering smile on Lord Malvern's lips as he opened them, but whatever he might have replied was lost in limbo, for Didi, who had been engaged in conversation with Lord Hexton, chose that particular moment to ask the marquess a question. By the time he had satisfied her, someone in the room had distracted Alexandra. There was no further opportunity to clarify the matter before the callers departed. Didi saw to that by keeping Malvern's attention focused on her own charming self. Penny pouted a little at that, but Alexandra was grateful to escape from what had turned into an embarrassing situation.

Alexandra was somewhat preoccupied that afternoon as the puzzling conversation with Lord Malvern refused to stay banished from her mind. Had his offer to pay for art training for Penny been the generous impulse of the moment that he then felt compelled to defend, or had he purposely led the conversation around to her talent? If it were the first case, then the incident was over and could be safely forgotten. If he had actually given the subject prior thought, however, it raised one or two questions. He could not have expected her to be simple enough to swallow whole a tale about extending the offer in the guise of a patron of the arts, but what of his remark about being almost a member of the family? Was she to take it that he had a firm intention of marrying Didi? His quick qualifying addition, "By adoption," would seem to rule this out; certainly it precluded her asking him his intentions—not that she would! It was understandable that he would not wish to discuss his intentions with Didi's sister until he had made his feelings clear to the object of his affections.

The idea of Lord Malvern as a brother-in-law was a

little unsettling somehow, and Alexandra paused in her
preparations for dinner that evening to consider her own
reaction as, hairbrush arrested in mid-stroke, she gazed
soberly into the small mirror on her dressing table. To
borrow Penny's favorite adjective, it was ludicrous to be
any less than thrilled at the prospect of an alliance with
such a notable family. Why, it would crown the success
of the girls' Season to have Didi capture one of society's
most eligible bachelors. She smoothed out the little pleat
between her brows with the middle finger of the hand
holding the hairbrush and resumed her brushing. Of
course she would be delighted if such a stroke of good
fortune came their way. Lord Malvern's hint today, if it
had been a hint, had caught her by surprise, that was all.
It was merely prudent on her part to delay any mental
celebrating until the betrothal was a *fait accompli*.

There was no point in trying to lead up to the subject
with Didi in the hope that she might let fall a hint that
she was in the expectation of hearing a declaration from
Lord Malvern in the near future. No one had ever succeeded in prizing information from the secretive girl until
it suited her to reveal it, and the last person to whom she
would choose to bare her heart was the sister whose authority she so resented.

Consequently, when Lord Malvern was announced the
next day, Alexandra looked at him a little uncertainly as
she gave him her hand.

"Do not look so concerned," he said, obviously doing
a bit of inspired guesswork. "I am not here to plague you
about what we discussed yesterday. I apologize if I was
a bit premature. We'll say no more on that head for the
present."

Nonplussed by his unwonted gentleness, Alexandra
found herself wondering if this was the side of him Didi
saw. With an effort she turned to the smiling man who
had entered a half-step behind Lord Malvern. "Freddy,
welcome; it has been a long time since we've had the
pleasure of a visit from you."

"Yes, hasn't it? Too long." Sir Frederick responded
to her brilliant smile with a twinkle in his eyes that alerted

Alexandra to her slight display of gaucherie. If anything had been wanting to confirm her suspicion that he knew about the trick Didi had played on him, that knowledgeable look spoke volumes.

She laughed at the shared joke and turned to include her sisters in the greeting. Arie and Didi were attending to Lord Malvern's initial salutations to Penny, but Cassie was facing them, a smile lighting up her pretty face. Cassie was as friendly as a puppy, by far the most outgoing of her sisters, but there was an unguarded quality of delight in this welcome for Sir Frederick that gave Alexandra pause. A lightning side glance showed her the gentleman's startled awareness of the honor, though she would wager her mother's diamonds that he had no idea which twin had so favored him. One or two of the twins' feminine friends could tell them apart within a few seconds of meeting, but so far their masculine acquaintances seemed to find them interchangeable. Perhaps, she thought whimsically, that will be when we shall know a suitor is serious—he'll be able to tell the girls apart.

Alexandra subjected Sir Frederick to a surreptitious study during his stay, but he was as adept as Lord Malvern at concealing his true feelings. The affability that made him a welcome guest anywhere was very much in evidence, but if he favored anyone with a greater share of his attention, it was herself. This was no surprise, since they had become friends over the past weeks and enjoyed a bantering camaraderie. No, she could discern no partiality toward one of the girls upon which to build any hopes. It was entirely possible that Sir Frederick simply was not in the market for a wife at present. No matter, he was a charming companion and could be counted upon to keep the girls in a constant ripple of laughter with his drollery and apparently endless supply of absurd stories.

It was Lord Malvern who held center stage today, however, by virtue of having been among the guests who had witnessed the marriage of the Regent's sister, the Princess Elizabeth, to the hereditary Prince of Hesse-Hamburg the evening before in the throne room of St.

James's Palace with the Archbishop of Canterbury performing the ceremony. The Duke of York had given the bride away, Lord Malvern informed the fascinated young ladies, in place of the Regent, who had been prevented from attending by a painful flare-up of his gout. The queen had been present, though she had at first refused permission for her daughter to wed until it was agreed that this most faithful of her attendants should not leave for her husband's country immediately. Everyone knew that most of the royal princesses had spent their youth in lingering and confining attendance on their parents, denied permission to marry or even participate in anything resembling a social life of their own; thus there was a genuine feeling of pleasure abroad that this princess would eventually secure an establishment of her own, though Didi remained unimpressed.

"I fail to see why everyone is in raptures over this wedding. There is something ridiculous, almost improper about a forty-eight-year-old woman and a forty-nine-year-old man desiring to marry at all."

"You feel perhaps that persons in that advanced stage of decrepitude should quietly sit back and prepare for the coming of the Grim Reaper?" Sir Frederick asked with a smile.

"No, of course not, but to be making a great fuss over an arranged marriage between persons who, far from languishing for love, do not even know each other, is almost indecent, to my way of thinking."

"Not your typical hero and heroine of gothic novels," Sir Frederick agreed amiably.

"Oh, but, Didi, that is what makes it so romantic," Cassie argued. "The poor princesses have spent their whole lives in a gilded cage, as it were, without ever being free to meet ordinary people or choose their own friends or suitors. Naturally everyone is happy to see that Princess Elizabeth has at last escaped this fate."

"Well put," said Sir Frederick, smiling at the earnest girl.

"Was it a very splendid affair, sir?" Penny asked Lord Malvern.

"Not quite that perhaps, though the altar was covered with a red velvet cloth upon which was placed an abundance of plate including a huge salver with the Last Supper depicted on it," he added, seeing her deflation. "With a guest list largely composed of cabinet ministers, foreign ambassadors and ministers, and members of the suites of the royal dukes and princesses, I think the adjective I would apply is 'staid.' The bridal pair left almost immediately for Windsor, but the rest of the royal family did its royal best by its guests. The Queen, who was the only person seated during the ceremony, circulated about most graciously afterward. She was wearing a miniature portrait of the king hanging around her neck. By ten o'clock it was all over."

"But surely there were refreshments?" Penny was scandalized.

"Yes indeed, modest refreshments, and tea was handed from urns and kettles of fretted gold, along with glasses of king's cup, which is served only at royal weddings."

"It sounds a horridly flat affair to me," commented Didi, wrinkling her perfect nose.

Since Lord Malvern could not in truth argue with this summation, the subject was allowed to drop.

The talk in the Farrish drawing room the next day centered upon the attempted assassination of Lord Palmerston, the Secretary of War, who had been shot and wounded going into his office at the Horse Guards the day after the royal wedding. Coming just two months after an attempt on the life of the Duke of Wellington in Paris, it gave rise to concern over an increase in lawlessness in the wake of twenty years of nearly constant warfare, but evidently the perpetrator of this latest atrocity was thought to be mentally deranged and therefore, it was predicted, would escape the retribution of the courts and judicial system.

Though patriotically concerned for Lord Palmerston's recovery, the young ladies were actually more interested in snippets of news of the upcoming Drawing Room brought by their female visitors. In the face of Didi's periodic arguments and pleas during the past weeks, Al-

exandra had stuck to her guns in refusing to subject the
family's finances to the strain of a court presentation of
the girls. The twins were wistful but resigned; Didi was
a simmering caldron of resentment under the mask of
amused indifference she assumed when the topic was introduced by one or another of the more fortunate young
ladies of their acquaintance. Though her performance of
a delicate creature relieved to avoid the fatigue, nervousness, and discomfort that invariably accompanied this delicious ordeal was quite brilliant, none of the female
visitors was taken in by it. It was galling in the extreme
to her to have to suffer an exchange of knowing looks or,
even worse, tacit pity. Sympathy for her sister's deep chagrin enabled Alexandra to control her impatience with
Didi's sulky behavior within the family circle, but she
went about in dread of hearing the subject mentioned and
longed for the event to be safely behind them.

In order to pacify Didi, Alexandra agreed to take her
shopping for fabric to make up a gown that would complement the set of topaz jewelry the girl had from her
mother. Her white gown would not do; she had it fixed
in her mind that a shade somewhat deeper than the color
of a pumpkin would make an exciting contrast to the jewels. In a desire to appear as accommodating as possible,
Alexandra kept to herself any reservations on this unusual choice and she willingly conceded that her sister
generally knew what best suited her dark beauty, even if
she chafed at the unwritten restrictions custom placed on
the styles and colors deemed permissible for girls in their
first Season.

The twins volunteered to keep Penny company while
their elder sisters accomplished this errand. Didi's mood
had miraculously improved once she realized Alexandra
was ready to comply with her wishes on this vital matter.
Accordingly, the two set off for Oxford Street on a delightful mid-April afternoon, in perfect charity with each
other.

Many of the better drapers' shops that had proliferated
in Ludgate Hill and Cornhill in the last century had gradually moved westward over the years, and now there were

several large emporiums along this thoroughfare within walking distance of home. As Alexandra had privately feared, however, the unusual color her sister had set her heart on was not to be easily obtained. They had exhausted the possibilities of the neighborhood within a couple of hours and Alexandra ventured to suggest that Didi might consider a *cafe-au-lait* shade or even some pretty cinnamon-hued sarcenet they had seen in the first store they had visited.

"No," Didi replied flatly with a stubborn tilt to her chin. "At least not until we have tried everywhere possible. One of those silly Debenham girls mentioned a shop in Cheapside, David Barclay, I believe it was. Let us go there, Sandy. She said it is a very well-established store which royalty has often patronized."

"By the time we return home and send for the carriage, it will be getting rather late. Perhaps we should leave it for another day, tomorrow if you like."

"I have an engagement to go driving with Lord Hexton tomorrow. Please, Sandy, there is time to do it today. Look, here is a hackney cab coming toward us. We can hire that."

In the interest of prolonging the rare mood of harmony that had existed between them that afternoon, Alexandra allowed herself to be persuaded, and the girls hailed the cab and gave the jarvey the address. Having gotten her own way, Didi was at her most agreeable, chatting merrily of this and that during the long ride to Cheapside. She had several ideas to propose about the design of the gown, and was pleased to see that her sister was willing to give them careful consideration.

"What color gloves do you think I should wear with it, Sandy? Do you not agree that white seems too ordinary?"

"Let's wait until we find the fabric. Time enough to worry about gloves when we have accomplished that much."

"Yes, of course you are right," Didi agreed, deferring sweetly to her elder. "Something tells me we'll find just what we are seeking in this shop."

Happily, Didi's intuition proved an accurate predictor in this instance. They came across a lovely gossamer silk in a deep burnt-orange shade that looked glorious against her glowing skin. When she heard the price, the girl's beautiful brown eyes grew apprehensive as they turned pleadingly to her sister. Alexandra's frugal instincts, developed over years of making do on a meager allotment, were affronted, but she made an instant decision that it was worth the exorbitant cost to reconcile Didi to her exclusion from the Drawing Room.

When the young women left the draper's a few moments later with Didi clutching the precious fabric, their satisfaction evaporated rapidly at the discovery that the driver had left with the money they had paid him to wait for them.

"Well, we cannot simply stand around on the pavement waiting," Alexandra said in disgust. "Let's begin walking until we see another hackney carriage."

Actually it was Lord Malvern who was the first welcome sight they encountered when they had walked for nearly a half-mile in the gathering dusk without seeing an empty cab. He was coming from the City in his curricle and he pulled up just past them, tossed the reins to his tiger, and jumped down.

"I thought my eyes were playing tricks on me," he said by way of greeting. "What are you doing so far from home at this hour, and where is your carriage?"

When Alexandra had explained the situation, he said, "I would gladly take you home, except that we should all be crushed in the curricle, but I shall stay with you until we find a hackney."

The trio continued to walk westward, with a young woman on each of Lord Malvern's arms. Didi prattled away, describing their afternoon and her purchase, though she declined to relinquish her precious package into his care. It was Alexandra, glancing around at their surroundings, who noticed an altercation taking place as they passed a narrow street that was not much more than an alley. Down the street a dozen or so paces a man and woman were arguing, until the woman broke away suddenly and hurried toward them. Alexandra had time to see that she was actually a very young girl before the man caught up with her and jerked her back by the arm. Alexandra stopped abruptly, her fingers digging into her escort's arm.

"That man is trying to force the girl to go with him."

It was Didi who answered as they gazed down the alley. "It is probably just a quarrel between husband and wife."

"That girl is little more than a child," Alexandra retorted, taking a step into the alley with a startled Lord Malvern in pursuit.

Before he could reach her, the girl's protests escalated into full-scale cries as she struggled frantically in the man's grasp. "No, no, I don't want to go wi' you! Please, no!"

"Release that girl!"

Lord Malvern's voice came like a pistol shot past Alexandra's ear as she reached the struggling pair.

A burly, unshaven individual looked back over his shoulder as he tried to haul the protesting girl along with him. "Mind your own business, toff! It was 'er what came up to me. I'm only takin' 'er up on 'er offer, that's all."

"Do you wish to go with him, miss?"

"No, oh no!" the girl whimpered.

"You heard her. Let her go."

"Or what?" The man stood his ground, glaring back at his well-dressed antagonist.

"Or you'll wish you had. Please return to your sister, Miss Farrish."

With no intention of obeying, Alexandra stood stock-still. Lord Malvern looked utterly relaxed, and she experienced a stab of fear as the hulking stranger dropped the girl's arm and advanced on them.

It was over before she quite knew how it happened. One second the enraged man was leaping at Lord Malvern with both fists raised; then in the next he was lying on his back in the street, his eyes blank with shock. Lord Malvern, standing over the prone figure, was massaging the knuckles of his right hand and waiting. Alexandra,

her arm about the quivering girl's shoulders, held her
breath while the man scrambled to his feet, evidently still
of a mind to have another go at his silent opponent. She
released a breath as she saw the fight drain out of him
when he met the calm, dangerous regard of the waiting
marquess.

"Next time, make sure the woman is willing," Lord
Malvern advised him as, with an inarticulate snarl directed at all three, the man stumbled off, nursing his jaw.

"You'd best go home now," Lord Malvern told the
frightened girl, not unkindly.

"I . . . I can't," she whispered.

"Where do you live, child? We'll see you home if you
are afraid the man will come back," Alexandra offered,
glancing around to check on Didi, who was standing just
inside the alley.

"I can't go home," the young girl replied miserably.
"Mam and Pap can scarcely feed the little ones. I came
in from the country on the stage yestidy to work in a
milliner's shop, but I lost the paper that said where it was
at. All day yestidy I walked around the streets until a
lady wi' bright clothes found me and said as how I could
stay wi' her for a while. She said she had other girls what
worked for her." At this point in the recital Lord Malvern tensed and the girl glanced at him from fearful eyes
in a comely but unwashed face. She stopped, her eyes
dropping under his stare.

"Go on," said Alexandra. "Was it a milliner's shop?"

"I don't think—" began Lord Malvern.

"No," said the girl, shivering. "She fed me and took
me bundle and put it away. There was more girls there,
and they laughed when I ast was they hat makers. And
. . . and later, men came in . . ." The girl faltered, and
Alexandra, enlightened, said:

"Never mind, child, you need not go back there."

Lord Malvern pressed some money into the girl's hand.
"Find yourself a room for tonight, and tomorrow you
can look for work in a milliner's shop."

"Thankee, sir," the girl said doubtfully, "but me bundle's still at Mrs. Harris'. She let me sleep there last

night, but she said I couldn't come back today without I brought a man wi' me. That's why I . . . But I couldn't!'' she wailed, starting to cry again.

"Keep your money, sir. She will be in even worse case when it is gone. She is plainly unfit to be on her own in London.'' Alexandra had been studying the girl while she told her tale. She pulled a pocketbook from her reticule and wrote something on a leaf. "What is your name, child?''

"Mary . . . Mary Fenton.''

"Well, Mary, do you think you might prefer to work in a family home instead of becoming a milliner's assistant?''

"Oh, yes, ma'am. Me mam taught me to clean and cook, and I'm ever so strong, and she says I am better nor her wi' the young 'uns—''

"That's fine,'' Alexandra said, smiling at the eager girl. "I am going to give you some money to take a hackney carriage to my house at number forty-nine Harley Street, off Oxford Street. Can you remember that?''

"Yes, ma'am.''

"Good. When you get there, give this paper to the person who opens the door, and he'll see that you are fed and have a bed for the night, and I shall see you tomorrow when you are rested. But, Mary, I fear you will not be able to retrieve your bundle from Mrs. Harris. If you go back there, she will try to get you to stay. Do you understand?''

"Yes, ma'am, I won't go near the place again, but I don't have no clothes nor nothin'.'' She was looking fearful again, and Alexandra said bracingly:

"Do not worry about your belongings. We'll soon find some clothes for you. Good-bye until tomorrow, Mary.''

As Lord Malvern and Alexandra walked back to the main street, the gentleman inspected his silent companion's serene profile.

"If she goes back there for her belongings, she will be lost,'' he remarked just before they rejoined an impatient Didi.

"Yes,'' she agreed. "I suppose I could have brought

her home with me and depended on your kindness to see
Didi home, but this is something Mary has to do for
herself. After last night, she knows what's involved. If
she really wishes to establish herself respectably, she'll
show up in Harley Street.''

"You sound very confident."

''Not that, really,'' Alexandra said, meeting his glance
with serious eyes, ''but Mary has to make the choice to
improve herself. There is only so much other people can
do. I believe she will come.''

Gray eyes held blue ones for a seemingly endless moment before Alexandra looked away. As though the words
were being pulled from him, he said slowly, ''You are
very wise for one so young.''

Didi, on hearing an edited version of the incident in
the alley, was not so approving. ''Not another of Sandy's
lame ducks,'' she groaned. ''We have the most ill-trained
household in Yorkshire because she is forever trying to
reform miscreants or rescue girls who are headed for the
Magdalene.''

''They are ill-trained in the beginning, naturally,'' her
sister pointed out. ''Mary seems very willing to learn.
By the time we leave London, she'll be able to secure a
good position in a large house.''

''If she doesn't run off with the butcher's boy first. I
have not forgotten that dreadful Polly, whom you had to
marry off to the second groom.''

''Polly and John were very much in love and the marriage has prospered,'' Alexandra amended calmly.

''If you call three squalling brats prospering,'' Didi
retorted.

She was allowed the last word, for Lord Malvern spotted a hackney carriage at that moment, which he flagged
down for the tired young women. Alexandra thanked him
warmly for his intervention and Didi flickered her spectacular lashes at him and expressed a demure hope of
seeing him soon at Almack's.

9

~~~~~

As it happened, it was indeed at Almack's that the Farrish sisters next saw Lord Malvern. He wandered in on Friday evening just before the doors closed at eleven and sauntered over to the side opposite the orchestra to join the small group of spectators that included Alexandra Farrish and Sir Frederick Marlowe.

"Servant, Miss Farrish. Greetings, Freddy."

Alexandra favored him with a warm smile but did not interrupt her conversation with Mr. Godfrey Balings, a man of mediocre but determined conversational skills, whose habit it was to ensure his listener's unflagging attention by physically decreasing the space between himself and his victim by stages until he was nearly nose to nose with the transfixed object of these maneuverings.

Lord Malvern, seemingly engaged with Sir Frederick, had grasped the situation at a glance and now he winked at his friend and took an unobtrusive step backward so that Alexandra, defensively edging away from the advancing Mr. Balings, bumped squarely into him in the next moment.

"I beg your pardon, sir," she said, looking confused as she spun around. "I had not realized you stood so close. Did I hurt your foot?"

"I daresay I shall in time recover from the agony of having a fairy weight attempt to pulverize my foot," he drawled.

"I had no such aggressive intention, sir, as you must know," she protested, mustering a fair quota of mock indignation in the face of his teasing impertinence.

"Mr. Balings, I have been wishing to ask you whence

you had those handsome bays you were driving in the park t'other day,'' Sir Frederick interposed, casually taking that gentleman's arm and leading him a little aside just as Lord Malvern did the same with Miss Farrish.

As she found herself suddenly several feet away from her previous partner, with another group of people between them, Alexandra said on a laugh, ''As neat a rescue as I have ever witnessed.''

''And a demonstration of real nobility on Freddy's part. Balings is a crashing bore who substitutes physical intimidation for the charm and wit that is totally lacking in his conversation.''

''I was not in the least intimidated,'' Alexandra insisted with a touch of real indignation that caused her companion's lips to twitch, ''but I acknowledge that it is a rather disconcerting experience to find one's normal . . . space, for want of a better term, gradually invaded by a person with whom one is conversing on the most superficial level.''

''Your objection is hereby noted and I fervently disclaim any intention of impugning your courage, O Brave Miss Farrish,'' he declared solemnly. ''Shall I return you to Mr. Balings?''

She laughed again. ''Such nonsense you talk, but perhaps we should now rescue Freddy.''

''That would be to deprive him of the satisfaction of performing a good deed, which is, after all, the best reward of nobility, do you not agree?''

''I do indeed,'' she said, adopting his solemn tone.

''I hoped to see you tonight,'' Lord Malvern went on, ''to inquire the outcome of our little adventure in the alley. Did Mary ever show up on your doorstep?''

Alexandra's expressive countenance took on an added eagerness as she replied, ''Yes, she did eventually, though I had almost given her up by the time she arrived. I had not taken into account a newly arrived country dweller's unfamiliarity with public transportation. It took her literally hours to screw up her courage to summon a hackney and perform the daring act of commanding the driver's services. Poor child, she has had a sad welcome to the city, but I am persuaded she will do splendidly once she finds her feet. I have very good reports of her from Edson. He says that she is a willing worker and quick to learn." The glow faded as she gazed earnestly into the attentive face of Lord Malvern. "These girls are too young to be on their own in London, or indeed any city, but in many cases their families simply cannot afford to keep them if there is no work locally. I do not know what the answer is."

"Well, you have provided the answer in Mary's case. She owes her deliverance to your interest and concern."

"You overstate my part," she replied, a trifle discomposed by his praise. "Any well-intentioned person would have done likewise for the girl, who is little more than a child actually—only fifteen! One shudders to contemplate the life she would have led in that place—Mrs. Harris'."

"I beg to differ with you," he said slowly, holding her glance. "Many so-called well-intentioned persons would have given the girl a trifling sum of money and promptly forgotten her, as I was about to do, to my eternal shame."

"You are too hard on yourself, Lord Malvern. Gentlemen are more removed from the domestic scene than women, and they are concerned with larger issues. It is my observation that they tend not to think of individual lives unless a specific case is brought to their attention."

"You are very generous, Miss Farrish, more than I deserve."

"Goodness, how solemn we have become. This is scarcely ballroom conversation," Alexandra declared with a shaky laugh, throwing off the strange intimacy that had enveloped them momentarily. "Tell me, sir, were you at the Drawing Room last night?"

He followed her lead, pulling a rueful face. "Yes, for my sins. I promised Stafford I'd show up to support his daughter, who was among the fair damsels presented. Have you met her?"

"Lady Elizabeth Leveson-Gower? Yes, Cassie and Arie are slightly acquainted with her. She seems a charming girl. I believe Miss Seymour was also present, and Lady Emily Bathhurst?"

"They may have been," he answered carelessly. "Among nearly two thousand guests, I may have missed a few, though I assure you it seemed I was literally elbow to elbow with most of them. It was so hot the men's shirt points were wilting; one actually felt for the Regent in his creaking corsets and skintight finery."

Alexandra grinned. "The Drawing Room was in celebration of the Prince's birthday, was it not?"

"Yes, officially, though his birthday is in August. The rooms were crowded and airless, and more than one young lady succumbed to the vapors while minding her posture, balancing her headdress, and awaiting her turn to be presented to the queen. In short, it was exactly the ordeal Didi predicted it would be. I imagine she is congratulating herself on having escaped the experience."

The expressive face of the young woman beside him went curiously still, except that dense gold-tipped lashes fluttered down to veil her eyes for an instant before she smiled brightly at him and made a noncommittal rejoinder. A sudden conviction seized him that her remarkable eyes had held secret laughter. At his expense? Before he could question her, Lord Callum came up to them and extricated Alexandra with an adroitness that Malvern was fast coming to dislike.

Though a memory of her fleeting expression bobbed to the surface of his mind periodically, there was no opportunity that evening to seek out the meaning behind Miss Farrish's curious reaction to his mild observation. He was too late to secure a dance with any of the Farrish girls, and because the hostesses had recently relented and permitted them to waltz, he was not even granted the necessary privacy for an agreeable interval of flirtatious nonsense with Didi, since there was now no reason save fatigue to sit out a dance. He sought her out between dances, but though she bestowed what he had come to think of as her special smile on him in the midst of dealing superbly with a coterie of admiring petitioners, he came away thoroughly disenchanted with the time-honored courting ritual prevalent among the *ton* during a London Season. The stylized game of advance and retreat under the avid eyes of all one's own acquaintance plus society's most notorious gossipmongers was meant for youngsters, and he was no longer a youngster. He did his duty by the daughter of his father's old friend the Marquess of Stafford, and suffered through a dance with a tongue-tied damsel presented to him by Sally Jersey before making his escape to the card room, where he was equally unsuccessful at whist, a game at which he usually enjoyed better fortune.

Lord Malvern smiled emptily at Mrs. Drummond-Burrell and Maria Sefton, two of the eagle-eyed patronesses who were casting about for partners for several wallflowers as he left the premises, and he was rewarded with darkling looks from both. While shrugging into his gloves, it came to him suddenly that the only redeeming moments of the evening had been spent in the company of Miss Alexandra Farrish. That this should be the case at a ball when Miss Farrish did not even dance was doubly strange and another indication that he was getting too old for this sort of entertainment. The last glimpse he had had of Miss Farrish before his departure had included the ubiquitous Lord Callum. His brows snapped together as a picture of that gentleman's smug countenance flashed before his mind's eye.

At least she had not relaxed her self-imposed discipline and succumbed to her old friend's exhortations to dance while acting as her sisters' chaperone, he thought with savage satisfaction as he turned up his collar against a freshened wind and strode north toward Piccadilly. If the fellow truly had Miss Farrish's interests at heart and not just his own gratification, he would not place her in a position to attract the censorious notice of the matrons ranged around the walls watching all the proceedings and hoping for infractions of the unwritten rules. The selfishness of a certain type of person occupied his thoughts for quite a block until a hail from behind him proved to be from Sir Frederick hurrying to catch him up.

The result of Lord Malvern's frustration at Almack's was a stepped-up campaign of pursuit of the beautiful Didi. He presented himself in the Farrish drawing room

the next morning and succeeded in obtaining that wily
young woman's agreement to embark on two pleasure
excursions in his curricle during the next sennight. There
had been a thoughtful pause before she accepted the second invitation, and it occurred to him that he could not
recall a single instance until today when she had accepted
more than one invitation from any suitor in such a short
span of time. Miss Farrish must have noticed this abrupt
change of policy also, for she looked rather searchingly
at her sister when she sought her elder's sanction of the
appointments. During his visit he had the additional fe-
licity of seeing the petitions of two late-coming rivals
gently refused by the sought-after beauty.

Lord Malvern went away well pleased with his morning's work. The look Didi had sent him from beneath
demurely lowered lids after she had turned down Hexton's invitation to drive in the park had spoken of secrets
shared. Everything that had happened before this morning was merely prologue. He had greatly enjoyed teach-
ing her to perfect her natural talent for elegant flirtation
at balls and parties and had found her attempts to appear
sophisticated and knowledgeable about society amusing
and more revealing about her wholesome background
than she would probably wish. Now he would begin to
learn what she was really like behind the social facade,
what made her tick, to borrow a phrase from the clock-
maker's vocabulary. It was odd that though he had spent
most of his time in Didi's company, he should feel that
he actually knew more about the minds and characters of
her oldest and youngest sisters. The next sennight should
begin to remedy that situation.

Some ten days later an impatient Lord Malvern was
seated in lonely state in a corner of his town carriage
while his coachman inched his way through the press of
traffic that was unavoidable when the residents of one of
the mansions in Grosvenor Square gave a large evening
party. Ordinarily he'd have walked the short distance from
home, but the rain that had started as a light patter two
hours before was now a steady downpour. He watched it
sheeting down in the glow of the carriage lamps for a

moment; then his thoughts returned as they invariably did of late to the enigma that was Didi Farrish.

Lord Malvern was frankly baffled. With the clarity of hindsight he could now see that his recent confidence that he was on the path to a deeper understanding of the lovely girl and his own feelings toward her had been premature, to put the case no higher. His eyes were still directed out the window of the carriage but he was engaged in a mental review of the week's events as they pertained to Didi.

He was never bored in her company, he assured himself. Her astonishing beauty was a constant visual treat to him, and she possessed a charming, well-modulated voice and the confidence to use it. Her manners were refreshingly natural compared with the stiffness bred into some of the new buds by their overbearing mamas. For this blessing he could thank Miss Farrish, since she had had full charge of her sisters for most of their lives. Didi had more quickness of comprehension than the twins, he noted, resuming his catalog, and displayed a flattering appreciation for his own jewels of wit and wisdom. This was not the least of her attractions, he conceded with a self-mocking quirk of his mouth. But, and he kept returning to this point, what did she really think about the important political and moral issues of the day? Which artists and musicians did she prefer? In retrospect, their conversations seemed to have been all froth. At least he could not say with any confidence whether she held any opinions that differed from what was considered acceptable for girls newly entering society. She had never favored him with an exposition of any views that ran contrary to popular opinion.

In point of fact, he was no closer to a knowledge of the workings of Didi Farrish's mind after enjoying several hours of her exclusive company these past days. Though she seemed to find his attentions acceptable, even pleasurable, he had no idea of how deeply her heart was involved in her reaction to him. What was even worse, he was still unsure of the extent of his own feelings. Not since he was a brash young ensign had he pursued a girl so singlemindedly, but unless memory was playing him false, he had believed himself madly in love in those days, more than once actually. The objects of his short-lived passions had been most unsuitable and he had recovered too quickly to dignify the episodes with the word "love," but he had been deeply involved while the affairs lasted, he recalled with disturbing clarity. Though he told himself this rational courtship was a natural consequence of achieving a desirable maturity, memories of the wooer he had been yesterday mocked the calculated pace of today's suitor.

Why, he hadn't even kissed the girl yet! Even a very proper young lady might well question the ardor of a suitor who was content to do all his courting with words. Expressions of high-flown sentiments were a poor substitute for two hearts racing to the same heightened beat. To hell with the conventions!

Fortunately, the rush of reckless elation that followed this conclusion coincided with Lord Malvern's arrival in Grosvenor Square, so he was released simultaneously from physical and mental captivity. As he bounded up the stairs to join the queue of arriving guests, an unbidden memory tugged his lips upward. Here he was actually plotting to kiss Didi Farrish when he had already kissed her little sister twice. Properly speaking, it was Penny who had kissed him impulsively this afternoon when he returned her to her guardian after the promised tour of the exhibit of the Royal Academy. They had spent a delightful couple of hours viewing the latest works of the most recognized artists. He had been startled and impressed anew by his young companion's mature judgment and keen eye for quality, and enchanted as always by her uninhibited chatter.

Lord Malvern was unaware that his somewhat austere aspect softened markedly when he recalled the warmth of Penny's unconditional affection for him.

"You look like a man whose long shot has come galloping past the finish line five lengths ahead of the odds-on favorite," murmured a well-known voice in his ear.

"Good evening, Freddy. I was merely recalling a pleasant memory. Nothing of earth-shaking importance."

"We'll need a brace of pleasant memories to sustain our spirits if this mob is an indication of the crush upstairs," grumbled his friend as he rescued his outsize buttonhole from an encroaching elbow as they moved in the press of humanity toward the magnificently carved oak staircase in Lord Belfort's town house. "I abhor the smell of wet wool, especially wet wool mingled with French perfume."

"Why so gloomy tonight, Frederick?"

"Perhaps I envy you your pleasant memory. Don't mind me, Robert. I always get a bit jaded by mid-Season. Too much riotous living perhaps. I've been thinking I'd pop down to Kent and spend a few days with my grandfather. The old codger is a proper antidote to this bunch," he added, wincing visibly at a shrill artificial peal of laughter emitted by an overrouged woman with predatory eyes who was clutching her escort's arm in pretended nervousness at the crush of people. "Care to come with me?"

Malvern hesitated. "Not just now, I think, Freddy, though I do enjoy Lord Cathcart's unbridled tongue."

"Other fish to fry, Robert?"

"It's just that there are a number of commitments and engagements I've promised to fulfill in the next fortnight," his friend replied, not quite holding the other's gaze. "Oh, good, I believe this line is beginning to move more quickly."

One of Sir Frederick's most valued qualities in the eyes of his many friends was his unfailing instinct for the right moment to change the subject. This talent did not desert him now as he said amiably, "Another time, then. I wonder if Lady Belfort will deck herself out again in the complete set of the Belfort ancestral diamonds," he mused as they ascended another stair, "or if a more discriminating taste will prevail tonight. Care to wager a guinea on the outcome, Robert?"

His reward for this tactful ploy was a warning scowl and a sharp jab in the ribs as they came within earshot of the footman who would announce them.

* * *

In combination with Penny's recovery, the purchase of Didi's burnt-orange silk had seemed to mark the beginning of a hectic period of activity that threatened to leave all her sisters completely done up, Alexandra reflected on the morning of the Belfort ball as she swiftly tacked up a seam in the promised ball gown before Didi came in for the first fitting. The girl had pouted when told that the dress could not be finished in time for what promised to be one of the Season's most glittering occasions, but she had not been willing to curtail any of her own pleasures this past week to assist in the initial stage of construction. Consequently Alexandra had hardened her heart against all pleas to let other chores lapse in order to devote more time to dressmaking. Didi's essential selfishness was too well-established in her family to be called into question, but she was generally willing to negotiate an exchange of favors in order to gain an objective. This time she had flatly refused to give up any of her afternoon outings with members of her court, nor, on the grounds that she daren't risk breaking a nail or roughening her hands at present, would she agree to take over some of her elder sister's household duties to free her for sewing. Since she always spent her allowance before she received it, she had no money with which to hire a seamstress to do the initial sewing after the dress had been cut out, and Alexandra not only refused to finance such an unnecessary outlay but also forbade the twins from making their sister a loan for this purpose. With no avenue left to her, Didi had resorted to creative cajolery and promises of future favors. To both of these litanies Alexandra had turned a consistently deaf ear.

The result had been a predictable air of ill humor emanating from the thwarted beauty of late. Having invited it, Alexandra was impervious on her own account but sadly guilty at having brought down this cloud on the rest of the family. She was a bit snappish herself as Didi finally joined her after two separate messages had been sent up to her room.

She came in complaining.

"I was trying out that new composition for the complexion that Miss Singleton was singing the praises of the other day. After taking all week to get this far, could you not have waited a few minutes more? I had to wash the cream off before the time required for it to work, or chance getting it on my gown.''

''If you consider experimenting with questionable mixtures guaranteed to cure your nonexistent skin problems to be more vital than getting on with the making of this ball gown, Didi, I shall be more than willing to lay it aside for the time being,'' Alexandra said in the overly polite tone that meant she was controlling her temper. ''There are a number of tasks awaiting my attention elsewhere.''

''No, no, you know it isn't vital. I was simply explaining why I had to keep you waiting, that's all.''

''In view of the fact that I told you at breakfast approximately what time I should be ready for your fitting, and since I sent Edson to call you within ten minutes of that hour, I should prefer an apology to an explanation.''

Alexandra sat with her hands idle in her lap while her sister mastered a natural resentment at being taken to task and finally tended a grudging apology. ''Thank you, we'll say no more about it. Now, if you'll remove your wrapper and raise your arms over your head, I'll do the rest.''

The next few minutes passed in industrious silence except that Didi let out a loud ''Ouch!'' when a stray pin went through two layers of fabric and one layer of her skin. At one point Alexandra exhorted her sister to ''Stop slouching,'' but these were the only words exchanged until with a sigh of satisfaction she rose from her knees and stepped back to view the result of her labors thus far.

''How does it look? Let me go over to the mirror,'' begged Didi in one breath without waiting for her sister's opinion.

''Stay a moment. I want to hold up the skirt when you move, so you will not step on it and undo my hard work.''

The sharp-eyed Didi had one or two suggestions to make after examining the fall of the gown from every possible angle. When these had been attended to, both ladies agreed that even in this early stage of construction the gown promised to be something quite out of the ordinary. Didi's volatile spirits had begun to climb from the moment the whisper-soft silk slipped over her head, and when she left the room she was humming to herself.

Alexandra's eyes following her sister's departing figure reflected no corresponding lightening. If questioned, she would have to admit that her own spirits were not of the same high order as Didi's, though she was at a loss to pinpoint the cause. The Farrish family affairs were going extremely well at present. The girls were all enjoying a social success beyond her wildest expectations, and Didi had already received two offers of marriage. Neither was eligible, but both were from very young gentlemen who could be expected to recover rapidly from their disappointment.

Perhaps this edginess she was experiencing was a response to the sense of heightened expectation she had detected about Didi this past week. She could not help but connect it with a recent increase in Lord Malvern's attentiveness. Once the matter was decided, she would be able to relax and possibly even derive some personal enjoyment from the Season, for if Didi were to marry Malvern, ninety percent of Alexandra's concerns for the future would vanish. It would not signify if the twins failed to make a match this spring. Didi would be able to bring them to town again next year and chaperone them. It didn't occur to Alexandra to concern herself with Didi's willingness to be saddled with this responsibility. Lord Malvern had already demonstrated an avuncular interest in Penny, apart from any pursuit of Didi, and somehow she had no doubts of his accepting a role in settling the twins creditably.

No wonder she was becoming nervy about the status of his courtship. So much depended on it. As a brother-in-law, Lord Malvern would be by far the most useful of all the candidates for Didi's hand, not to mention being the only one who stood a chance of controlling her. Alexandra had noted that in the marquess's presence her willful sister was at great pains to say and do nothing that would detract from the image of demure sweetness she had evidently determined on maintaining in her quest for the best catch of the Season. It must be wearing to be continually playing a false role, but so far Didi had been equal to the challenge she had set herself. For the most part she had successfully hidden the narcissism and self-ishness that were at the core of her being. Her future husband was in for a shock at some point, Alexandra feared, but she could scarcely take it upon herself to warn the contenders off. Not only would this constitute a hei-nous act of family disloyalty, but such a shocking senti-ment would not be believed by the besotted gentlemen who worshiped at the shrine of Didi's undeniable beauty. When it came to shopping for a bride, *caveat emptor* must be the order of the day.

It was raining steadily when the Farrish girls de-scended to their carriage that evening, and Cassie and Arie emitted squeals of distaste as they hastily gathered their cloaks more closely about their bodies.

Didi pooh-poohed their qualms. "A few drops of wa-ter won't spoil your outfits," she said, settling into her corner of the carriage. "You'll dry off by the time we get to Grosvenor Square."

"Just in time to get wet again dashing into the house," Arie grumbled.

"Nonsense, it will preserve your flowers," countered Didi, referring to the wreaths of fresh flowers that crowned the twins' shining ringlets.

Listening to Didi rallying her sisters' spirits and con-tributing bright remarks about the expected guests on the drive to Grosvenor Square, Alexandra thought she had not seen the girl in such a state of controlled excitement before, not even on that first occasion at Almack's. She must be anticipating more than another pleasant evening of being the reigning belle at a ball. A prickling in her thumbs told Alexandra her hunch that Lord Malvern was getting close to the sticking point was not so far off the mark.

In consequence, Alexandra found herself in a state of heightened awareness that evening. Her disguised inter-

est was so concentrated on Didi and Lord Malvern that
she feared the various people who engaged her in conversation over the next hour or two must have gone away
with a poor impression of her ability to concentrate on
the spoken word, judging by several baffled looks occasioned by her vague replies to conversational overtures.

On the surface it was just another ball, though more
elegant than most by virtue of its setting, which was a
perfectly proportioned ballroom painted scarlet and gold
that had been added on the back of the Belfort mansion,
rather than the more common series of smaller rooms
thrown together for the purpose by less-fortunate home
owners. The music too was of the finest quality, since no
expense had been spared in hiring the best musicians to
be had.

Alexandra examined Lord Malvern's aristocratic countenance more closely than was her wont, but it was unrevealing of his state of mind as always—almost always,
she corrected herself. She had seen him anxious and
tender with Penny by turns, but tonight he wore his usual
social mask as he came up to claim the two dances with
Didi that were all an unmarried young lady could bestow
upon a man without raising eyebrows. He also claimed
the beauty for his partner at supper. Was there just a
shade of the proprietorial about his calm assumption that
his request would be granted? Alexandra couldn't be sure,
but the more she considered the situation, the less likely
it seemed that a man would choose a crowded ball as the
ideal place to propose marriage. To her mind at least,
privacy would seem to be the primary requisite for such
a delicate undertaking. There was a large supper room
set up with tables at one end of the ballroom and a small
antechamber at the other end which contained a sofa and
two or three chairs for the comfort of those persons who
might wish to get away from the music for a while, but
the doors remained open and any guest could wander in
at any time. Except for a fortuitous moment or two
snatched in the midst of a circulating mob, she decided
the Belfort ball was a dangerous place to look for privacy.
The chance of being overheard was always present.

By the time they went in to supper, Alexandra had relaxed her vigilance somewhat. Didi and Lord Malvern had already had their two dances and they were now seated with Arie and her partner at a table somewhat removed from where Alexandra sat enjoying a marvelous array of culinary delicacies in company with Lord Callum, Cassie, and Sir Frederick. Freddy was listening to Cassie's artless prattle with an indulgent air that endeared him to her sister. Alexandra eyed the attractive pair fondly, wishing that this dearly loved sister possessed a few more brains so that she might permanently attract a man of Sir Frederick's caliber. Not only would she love to acquire him for a brother-in-law, but she strongly suspected that Cassie preferred him to any of the younger men who made up the twins' court for the most part.

Alexandra looked up with a smile as Arie and her partner joined them. "Hello, angel. What happened to Didi?"

"Didi said she was stuffed with food, and Lord Malvern suggested they should walk off that sated feeling," Arie explained as she dropped onto a chair next to her twin, unaware of the enchanting picture they presented to the three appreciative males in attendance.

There was the briefest pause before Alexandra smiled brightly and said, "Would you all excuse me for a moment, please? There was something I wished to say to Didi. I'll be back directly."

She glided away before anyone could react to her announcement, and headed for the corridor that led past the ballroom and anteroom to the main part of the house. She couldn't have said quite what prompted her sudden action. Certainly she had no desire to eavesdrop on an offer of marriage, but in the unlikely event that the missing pair had been indiscreet enough to seek the doubtful privacy of the anteroom, she could at least stand guard outside and delay anyone who approached long enough to alert those inside.

It was slightly anticlimactic to find the antechamber completely deserted. Alexandra could hear murmurs of conversation from the ballroom as well as the sounds of the orchestra members tuning up, but in here all was silence. She was about to step back into the corridor when the heavy green velvet drapery across the window rippled with sudden movement.

Alexandra froze in her tracks for an instant. They couldn't be so stupid! She leapt forward and pulled aside one drapery panel. Her sister's eyes, dilated with alarm, met hers from within the three-foot window bay where she stood, obviously having just pulled back from Lord Malvern's embrace. Alexandra didn't even glance at him as she snapped at the girl.

"Honestly, Didi, have you no sense of decorum at all?"

Fury had replaced alarm in her sister's face as she accused, "You've been spying on me!"

"Be thankful it was I who came into this room and not someone who would delight in spreading a description of this scene all over the ballroom," Alexandra replied softly, once again in control. "Go out through the corridor, Didi, and join your sisters in the supper room. *Now*," she added as the girl hesitated, "before someone comes in here. And retie your sash, which is sadly crushed."

Not until the girl had left the room with a venomous glare at her sister did Alexandra turn her attention to Lord Malvern, urbane as ever, watching her with an unfathomable expression as he made a minute adjustment to his cravat.

"If you are about to complete your performance of an outraged parent by demanding to know my intentions toward your sister, may I beg of you to desist and save us both embarrassment?" he said in his most hateful drawl. "I don't yet know my intentions."

Alexandra stared at him dumbfounded for a second. She hadn't been outraged, only concerned lest their indiscretion be discovered. As she absorbed the meaning of his last words, however, anger rushed to her rescue and loosened her tongue. "Do you mean me to understand that you do not seek the status but only the privileges of a fiancé, Lord Malvern?" she asked hotly.

"No, I do not mean you to understand any such thing, O Disapproving Miss Farrish," he replied with an odd little smile. "Only what I said—I do not yet know my intentions toward Didi."

"And when will you know them, sir?" she demanded scathingly. "After you have kissed every eligible girl in London?"

In response to her sarcasm, he gave an exultant little laugh. "An excellent suggestion!"

Before Alexandra had any inkling of his intention, Lord Malvern swooped on her. One arm went around her shoulders, nearly lifting her off her feet as he caught her close to his chest. The other hand went under her chin to raise it to an angle where her mouth was accessible to his. He took full advantage of his superior size and strength and the element of surprise to kiss her thoroughly before Alexandra's defensive movements gained enough momentum to make the continuation of the exercise decidedly dangerous to the state of his appearance. At this point he released the wildly struggling female and judiciously stepped back out of slapping range.

"Damn you, you b-bastard!"

Lord Malvern smiled at the tiny virago blazing up at him. "You shock me, O Profane Miss Farrish," he chided.

He didn't look shocked, he looked exhilarated, Alexandra thought irrelevantly as he smoothed back his hair and readjusted his cravat.

"I . . . I could kill you!" she hissed between her teeth, aware of the disheveled appearance she must present after such a contested assault upon her person.

"You could try," he agreed as he walked past her toward the ballroom door. She was glaring after him in speechless rage at being denied an opportunity to further vent her spleen, when he paused and said over his shoulder, "By the way, I can now answer your question. I am not going to marry your sister."

10

"STOP SQUIRMING, DIDI, or I'll never get this hem even."

"I'm not squirming. I have an itch behind my knee."

"Well, scratch it and then stand still."

"I have been standing here for hours. Why is it taking you so long?"

"There are miles of skirt to pin up, that's why, and it has been no more than fifteen minutes since you came into this room," Alexandra said. "Turn to your left a little."

"How much longer will it take? This is our at-home morning. It would be extremely uncivil to keep any visitors waiting."

"I'm nearly finished." After the briefest hiatus, Alexandra said gently, "Edson knows we are in here and will tell us at once if Lord Malvern should call."

"Who said anything about Malvern? He is not our only caller." Didi gave a pettish shrug of her shoulders that pulled the diaphanous silk from Alexandra's light grasp just as she was about to set a pin, which ended up going into her own fingers instead.

"No, of course not." Alexandra offered the placating phrase as she sucked her pricked fingers before resuming her task.

Didi did not even notice the interruption. After a moment of fraught silence she exclaimed, "In another minute he would have made me an offer. He was just about to do so when you burst in on us at the crucial moment like a jealous wife in a bad farce."

Stung by the injustice of this view of the situation,

Alexandra cried, "That's unfair, Didi. I was only concerned lest you lay yourself open to gossip or criticism."

"There was nobody about, I tell you. If it had not been for your untimely appearance, Malvern would have come to the point then and there."

Alexandra said nothing for a moment as she continued pinning up the hem of the burnt-orange silk. She had been anticipating this conversation for two days, ever since the Belfort ball, and had agonized over what to say to her sister, but Didi had avoided her and had made no reference to the interrupted scene until this bitter outburst today.

"Well, have you nothing to say?"

Alexandra looked up into angry brown eyes and sat back on her heels with her hands loosely linked on her knees as she selected her words with care. "You are old enough to know that stolen kisses do not invariably lead to a proposal of marriage, Didi."

One slender hand made a gesture of dismissal. "Of course I am, but Malvern is not like a lot of the others, who only wish to take advantage of a girl. Why do you think I have led him along so slowly? If all I wanted was masculine embraces, I could have them any day of the week, just like that."

Alexandra stared nonplussed from the slender fingers that had executed a disdainful snapping sound to her sister's proud, angry face.

"Why don't you say something, instead of looking so dumbfounded?" Didi demanded. "Surely you are aware that most men like to kiss pretty girls. They all wish to kiss me!"

"Do you let them?" Alexandra asked with real interest.

"Of course I don't let them! Do you think I am so stupid as to get myself talked about while I have been bringing Malvern to the sticking point? And then you barged in and undid all my work in an instant."

"You cannot seriously believe that my interruption will put him off if Lord Malvern really wants to marry you,

Didi. Indeed, it should spur him on,'' Alexandra suggested dryly.

"Oh, I know you and your tongue! You probably lost your temper and said something horridly vulgar that has put up his back for the moment. Haven't you done pinning that hem yet?''

"Yes, yes, it is all finished,'' Alexandra said, aware of the prophetic nature of the words as she rose to her feet and silently helped her sister off with the gown.

Alexandra's expression was deeply troubled when she sank onto a chair with the unfinished dress draped across her lap after her sister had gone. What should she have said? How could she tell Didi that Malvern had confided in her that he did not intend to marry the girl he had distinguished with his attentions almost from the moment of her appearance on the social scene? How could any woman convey such information to another? Didi would hate her for it; she already blamed her sister for the fact that an offer had not been immediately forthcoming. Two days of thinking of little else had not produced an answer to Alexandra's dilemma. She had gone about her usual duties in a state of total absence of mind while her sister's situation and the scene in the antechamber revolved endlessly in her memory.

Could Didi be correct in laying Lord Malvern's failure to propose at her sister's door? Her petulant accusation just now had been perilously close to the mark, and had she not been immediately smothered in billowing folds of orange silk she could not have failed to note her elder's hot cheeks as she helped her remove the gown. It had not been until after her own lamentable lapse into hot-tempered maledictions that Lord Malvern had declared that he was not going to marry Didi. Not that he had not deserved her righteous anger after such despicable conduct, but she was consumed with mortification each time she considered her own regrettable mode of expressing her fury. Had her unladylike reaction forcibly recalled to him the way they had met and decided him against aligning himself with a family that contained a female of whom he thoroughly disapproved? If that were the case, though, would he have continued to pursue Didi all these weeks? The answer must be negative unless he always had the intention of leading Didi on to make her the object of general gossip and speculation before dropping her, as a means of avenging the wrong he once thought Lee did him, and this base motive she refused to assign to him. Despite his faults, she would take her oath that Malvern was a man of honor.

Alexandra's countenance took on a puzzled cast as she reviewed her acquaintance with Lord Malvern. Thanks to the unfortunate circumstances of their initial meeting, she had disliked him heartily at first and had continued to eye him askance for several weeks, wary of the cynicism she sensed beneath the surface amiability. But his sincere friendship with Penny had disarmed her completely, and in recent weeks she had come to like him very much and to consider him a friend. Now she did not know what to think. Didi had stated with confidence that Malvern was not like the majority of her court, who were always eager to take as many liberties as a girl would permit. Her own days of being courted were so far in the past that she must needs bow to Didi's superior knowledge on the subject.

Then why had he done it? What had caused a rational man conducting a rational courtship to behave suddenly in a manner completely out of character? She had not been able to comprehend that forced kiss when her initial rage had cooled at the ball, and two days later she had still not come up with a more convincing explanation than attributing it to a momentary aberration, one of those quirks of the masculine psyche that females could never understand.

The more vital question obviously was what would happen next. It was not unreasonable that Didi should have been expecting Lord Malvern to turn up on their doorstep seeking a private interview with her at the earliest opportunity following the interrupted embrace. Given his style of courtship, her expectations were eminently justified, apart from her natural conceit arising from the knowledge of the effect her beauty had on men.

Up to now, Didi had had ample reason to believe she could attach any man she set her sights on.

If Lord Malvern had been speaking the truth when he left Alexandra so cavalierly in the Belfort antechamber, Didi's hopes of marrying him were not going to be realized. Alexandra bit her lip and absently stroked her fingers over the lovely silk dress in her lap, wondering what she could do to soften the blow to Didi's pride when it inevitably came. And that was the most nerve-racking uncertainty of all. Did Malvern intend to simply disappear from their lives? That would send a clear message but it would also expose Didi to the unkind tongues of the so-called cream of society. On the other hand, if he gradually cooled his attentions to her sister, they might avoid the worst of the gossip, but Didi's agony of uncertainty would be prolonged until she finally accepted that her hopes would not come to fruition.

A shiver ran through Alexandra's slight frame. Either way, the Farrish family seemed to be heading into a patch of heavy weather. Her sister was never one to cut her losses philosophically or resign herself to failure. She was single-minded to a fault, and no one could throw a household into total confusion more rapidly than Didi when she was frustrated in her endeavors.

Alexandra took her time putting away her sewing materials and making herself presentable for morning callers. She did not know whether she hoped to see Lord Malvern in her drawing room or not. She was still too infuriated with his capricious behavior to find the sight of that cold, imperturbable face anything but an incitement to her temper, but for Didi's sake perhaps the best thing would be to bring this period of uncertainty to an end as quickly as possible so she could get on with her life. It had been a relief just now to realize that her sister's feelings were not greatly involved. She had determined to marry him, certainly, but she would have acted in a quite different manner had it been her heart instead of her pride that had been wounded by his nonappearance these past two days.

There was a satisfying parade of visitors passing

through the Farrish house over the next two days, but Lord Malvern was not among their number. Though Didi seemed her usual responsive self, blossoming in the light of masculine admiration, she refused all immediate invitations to go out driving with any of her callers on the vague grounds of a prior commitment. In the bosom of her family, however, her disposition disintegrated as a function of the elapsed time since the Belfort ball. The twins, who knew nothing of the events of the ball, were not slow to relate their sister's increasing testiness to the failure of Lord Malvern to put in an appearance. Their tactful attempts to discover whether a quarrel had taken place availed them nothing beyond a measure of uncomfortable exposure to the rough side of Didi's tongue. When they complained to their eldest sister about such Turkish treatment, they found her less ready to take their part than was her habit, and observed additionally that Sandy seemed determined to take no notice of Didi's bad temper herself, all of which increased their curiosity but not their knowledge.

When Lord Malvern did not show up at Almack's ball on Wednesday evening, the atmosphere of their happy home suffered even further disintegration, prompting the twins to seek escape by accepting an invitation to drink tea with Lady Georgiana Fane, one of their new friends. What made the occasion memorable beyond the scrumptious cream cake that was served was the intelligence imparted by another guest that Lord Malvern had gone out of town with Sir Frederick Marlowe the day after the Belfort ball. The bearer of this news was a young woman distinguished mainly by a crop of unattractive freckles, a dumpy figure, and a notorious penchant for taking feline pleasure in the occasional setbacks of more popular young ladies. It was an awareness of this last characteristic that enabled the twins to conceal their surprise and close ranks behind Didi in an automatic expression of family solidarity. By the time one or two of the other guests had uttered exclamations of dismay at losing two of the town's most attractive bachelors, Cassie was able to project a creditable air of rueful nonchalance as she admitted that though Sir Frederick had indeed mentioned his upcoming departure from town, her memory was so wretched that she could not recall how long he planned to stay away.

"My brother said Lord Malvern decided quite suddenly to accompany Sir Frederick," chimed in the sadly spotted miss with a penetrating stare in Cassie's direction. "He said Malvern sent him a note canceling a sporting engagement for early this week, and I know that he had the intention of attending Mrs. Alberton's rout tonight because she was crowing to my mama only last week about having secured him as a guest."

"Yes, I believe it was a sudden decision," Arie agreed, entering the lists in support of her twin. "Lord Malvern is so devoted to his true friends that he could not refuse Sir Frederick's importunities. We all miss their delightful company, do we not?"

"I am persuaded that Miss Aphrodite Farrish is the person to be pitied most at the loss of Lord Malvern's company," said the determined intelligencer with a spurious air of sympathy.

Cassie produced a merry laugh. "Didi? Oh, my, no. Her appointment book is so crammed she has to take great care to be impartial and not wound the feelings of any of the gentlemen who constantly seek her company."

"Still, she must miss Lord Malvern's attentions. He has long been her most favored admirer, has he not?"

"Would you say so?" Arie turned an innocently inquiring look on her sister, who paused and appeared to consider the question deeply while a circle of attentive faces focused on her with unnerving fixity.

"One of the most favored, certainly," Cassie said, coming at last to a decision, which she immediately qualified. "At least, that has been my impression. Others might not agree." She smiled a bit apologetically at the interested young ladies and took a dainty bite of her cream cake.

The upshot of an anxious conference between the twins on the way home that afternoon was a decision to keep the disturbing news they had learned to themselves for the present. Against Didi's problematic gratitude for the signal service her sisters had just rendered her must be weighed her certain outrage at learning of Lord Malvern's temporary—to put it no higher—defection from the ranks of her suitors. As bearers of the bad tidings they would be first in line to feel her anger. It wasn't until they were nearly home that another and even more disturbing thought occurred to them. What if Didi learned the news from a third party, as they had? She might be able to carry it off as well as they fancied they had done this afternoon, but her fury if she found out her sisters had been privy to this vital information would know no bounds. After a few minutes of uncomfortable contemplation they agreed that Didi would indeed discover their prior knowledge. From unhappy experience of her relentless pursuit of information they had wished to conceal in the past and their own inability to tell a convincing lie and stick to it in the face of her stronger will, they had to acknowledge that it was a foregone conclusion, as was the aftermath of prolonged misery they would undergo at her hands. Either option, to tell or not to tell, seemed fraught with danger, and it was not until they were ascending the staircase leading to the bedchambers that Arie came up with a solution. She spun around and stopped her twin's progress with an urgent hand on her arm.

"We'll tell Sandy," she whispered.

Hope came back into Cassie's eyes, but she said doubtfully, "It seems a rather craven thing to do."

"Well, of course it is, but it does solve the problem. If Sandy says we must tell Didi, then we must, but she is more apt to do it for us, do you not agree?"

Actually, Alexandra seemed to favor neither course of action when apprised of the news by the reluctant twins before dinner that night. Though her eyes narrowed and her lips firmed on reception of the intelligence, she displayed no sign of surprise or dismay.

"Thank you, girls, for what you did for your sister this afternoon. I think we shall not mention this to her just yet. You may leave it to me to decide when would be the right moment."

Greatly relieved to be free of their burden, the twins were quick to agree to any course their eldest sister favored.

It would have been idle for Alexandra to pretend that she was totally unmoved by the news that Lord Malvern had beat an immediate retreat out of town, but it only confirmed that he had spoken the truth when he declared that he was not going to marry Didi, though on the surface it had appeared to be a decision made on the whim of an instant that might just as easily be revoked on the next. Nearly a sennight had passed with no word from Lord Malvern, something unprecedented in the short history of their acquaintance with him.

Didi would have to be told of her suitor's unannounced departure within twenty-four hours of the episode at the ball. Actually, it was marvelous that one of her jealous court had not dropped a word in her ear before now. As she considered this stroke of good fortune, Alexandra could only hope that most of Lord Malvern's friends were unaware of his absence from town. Though the girls' admirers covered the spectrum of available gentlemen, the majority were younger than Malvern and therefore not well-known to him. The twins' intelligencer had not included the probable length of his absence from town in her bulletin, but his nonappearance in Harley Street was already of sufficient duration to give Didi cause to reevaluate her chance of becoming Lady Malvern. When Alexandra had communicated this latest piece of information to her, she thought she could trust her shrewd sister to take steps to protect herself from the worst of the gossip.

Alexandra's view of the situation seemed reasonable at the time, but matters fell out differently. She had every intention of speaking with Didi that very evening, but they were forced to rush to be ready to leave for the theater in time, and once there, they were besieged with visitors to the box, as usual. She still had not managed the requisite privacy in which to divulge the unpleasant news to her sister the next morning, for Didi had been asleep when she had slipped into her room after everyone had retired for the night. Alexandra finished with her breakfast before anyone else was downstairs, and she spent the next two hours conferring with the cook and Edson and checking over invoices in the morning room.

She looked up in surprise when Edson knocked to tell her of the presence of callers in the main saloon. "So early?" She glanced at the clock, surprised to find morning callers actually arriving before the noon hour. "Who is it, Edson?"

"Lady Standish and Miss Standish, ma'am."

As Alexandra checked her appearance before going up to the saloon, she wondered what had brought these particular visitors to Harley Street. The Farrishes had been introduced to Lady Standish and her daughter at the Harrogate Assembly last fall by Lady Marielle Trent after Lee had presented her to his sisters. Apart from a naturally sweet nature, Lady Marielle had been prepared to like the Farrish girls because they were Lee's family, but Miss Julia Standish had no such compelling reason to look with favor on three young ladies who outshone her in looks and personality. In the month that the Standish family had been in town this spring, Lady Standish had done no more than bow formally in passing. The twins had occasionally been present at female gatherings that included Miss Standish, but there had been no advances toward real friendship, and it was well known that the blond Julia had the utmost difficulty in concealing her dislike of Didi. The cause of this ill feeling was not far to seek. One merely had to watch the chit's manner change from faintly bored to an almost feverish gaiety and animation whenever Lord Malvern came within earshot to know she had aspirations in that direction. Didi was certainly the most formidable obstacle to the realization of those aspirations at present.

Alexandra's footsteps speeded up as she approached the top of the stairs, seized with a sudden conviction that this morning call was somehow connected with Lord Malvern. An instinct for trouble lent wings to her heels and she drew up outside the saloon door nearly at a run.

She collected her breath and her wits before entering quietly.

A quick survey of the room located Lady Standish and her daughter sitting close together in the middle of a sofa in an offensive alliance, flanked by the twins occupying the cane-back chairs at right angles to the sofa. Didi, her head bent over the embroidery lying in her lap, was seated a bit apart in one of the gold-colored bergère chairs. Alexandra disciplined a smile at the twins' identical expressions of relief at sight of her, then turned it into one of welcome as she came forward, hand outstretched.

"Lady Standish, what a pleasant surprise, and, Miss Standish, how do you do? Has anyone ordered coffee?"

"How very kind, but no coffee for us, thank you, dear Miss Farrish," gushed the sharp-eyed matron, showing all her large teeth in a wide smile. "We can stay but a moment, but as I told Julia this morning, 'Here are the Farrishes, practically neighbors in Yorkshire, and we have not even found the time to call on them in London. They will think us perfect barbarians,' I told her, though I am persuaded you must find yourselves caught up in the same mad whirl of activities. I declare, I don't know where Julia gets her stamina from. For my part, I would welcome a quiet evening at home occasionally, but the invitations just keep pouring in, as they no doubt do for your sisters also."

"Yes, we go out a great deal," Alexandra confirmed as Lady Standish was forced to interrupt the flow of words to draw a replenishing breath.

"It is said your sisters are quite the most-sought-after young ladies in town, and who can wonder at it?" Lady Standish went on. "Why, the twins must draw every eye when they appear together, so uncannily alike as they are, and I am told Miss Didi is considered by many to be the Season's outstanding beauty."

Despite the flattering words, the impression was left that the twins' appeal was of the same order as the two-headed calf in a traveling freak show, and that Didi's claim to beauty was debatable among persons with more discriminating taste.

"There are many lovely girls to be seen in town this spring, ma'am, your daughter among them," Alexandra said, producing her best smile for the benefit of Miss Julia Standish, whose blue eyes dropped in confusion.

"You are too kind, dear Miss Farrish. You must forgive a fond mama if I agree that Julia's looks will wear well and be enhanced by maturity, unlike some that bloom early and fade almost as quickly."

"Are you enjoying this Season as much as last year, Miss Standish?" Alexandra asked, sending a warning look at the twins, whose strugglingly polite expressions showed signs of cracking. Didi continued to direct her attention to her embroidery.

"No," replied Miss Standish shortly. "My best friend last year was Lady Marielle Trent, and she is dead. I miss her company."

"Speaking of the Trents," Lady Standish interposed quickly, "we wondered if, being such a great family friend, Lord Malvern might have given you some indication of when he plans to return to town. I should like to reschedule the dinner that he had to miss when he was called away so suddenly. The poor boy was devastated at having to beg off at the last minute, but naturally we understand that emergencies do arise from time to time."

Didi's head had shot up at the mention of Lord Malvern, and she was staring fixedly at Lady Standish while she spoke, but Alexandra got in the instant the matron paused.

"I believe Lord Malvern's return will depend on Sir Frederick Marlowe's schedule, Lady Standish, since the unexpected trip was at his instigation. I am sorry we cannot be of more assistance to you."

Lady Standish gathered her gloves together and began to put them on. "It is of no real consequence, dear Miss Farrish. As I said before, Julia and I were in the area and decided it was past time to do our neighborly duty, but we must be going now. You must all come to drink tea with us one afternoon," she finished, displaying her teeth again while Miss Standish mustered up a pale smile at a look from her parent as both ladies rose to their feet.

"How very kind." Alexandra spoke for her sisters.

"Yes, thank you," echoed the twins.

Didi said nothing. After a brief valedictory nod, her attention was again directed at her sewing while they waited a few seconds for Edson to appear. The instant the door closed behind the visitors, however, she cast aside her handiwork and leapt out of her chair.

"That horrible, patronizing woman! She came here for the express purpose of finding out what we know about Malvern's absence, or if we knew about it—and you did!" she finished, confronting her eldest sister with an accusing glare.

"Yes, but only since yesterday," Alexandra admitted, directing a dismissing gesture of her hand at the wide-eyed twins, who were only too glad to scurry to safety.

"What do you mean, keeping such information from me?" the enraged beauty demanded, paying no heed to her sisters' hurried departure.

Alexandra waited until the door was closed once more before she spoke. "When you have composed yourself, Didi, I'll be happy to enlighten you about what has just transpired." She sat perfectly motionless until her sister, her lovely face quivering with impatience, perched on the edge of one of the cane chairs vacated by the twins.

"First of all, I must say that I heartily concur with your assessment of Lady Standish's motive in coming here today, and I admit that I found it a real chore to keep mindful of the hospitality owed a visitor in my house."

"That poisonous female does not deserve hospitality."

"You had better learn that you owe it to your own consequence and that of your husband to maintain a standard of behavior in situations you do not necessarily welcome, Didi, if you expect to become the wife of a man of stature, but I do not wish to digress. The simple truth is that yesterday the twins learned that Malvern went out of town with Sir Frederick the day after the Belfort ball. From what they reported to me on their return from Lady Georgiana's tea party, they managed to conceal their surprise and even parried one or two ill-natured speculations about your probable disappointment at his absence. I asked them to let me break the news to you, but as you may recall, we had not a single moment of privacy at the theater. You were asleep when I went to your room last night, and Lady Standish arrived before we met this morning. Believe me, I am very sorry for your chagrin, but it was just an unlucky happenstance, not a deliberate policy to keep you ignorant."

The anger faded from Didi's face under her sister's sympathetic scrutiny and she offered a quick apology. "I'm sorry I snapped at you just now, Sandy. I just wish I knew what he meant by this," she added half to herself in a dispirited tone, looking uncharacteristically young and defenseless.

Alexandra mentally echoed this sentiment. She would give a lot to have just five minutes alone with Lord Malvern in which to deliver herself of her opinion of his outrageous actions, starting with his refusal to commit himself to making Didi an offer after involving her in what might well have been a compromising situation, and then crowning his iniquity by forcing an embrace upon herself and immediately disappearing from the scene to avoid accountability.

"Men are strange creatures, Didi," she began, feeling her way with caution, "given to sudden passions which can be quite ephemeral. Your beauty is not necessarily an unmixed blessing. Men tend to be so fascinated by your face that they don't really take the time to get to know you as a person. Initially they might believe they've fallen in love with you, but I do not believe one can really love a person without knowing him or her. Perhaps when he kissed you he realized this and felt he must get away for a time to examine his feelings."

Didi listened to her sister's halting explanation with intense concentration; then her expression hardened as she forcefully rejected the weak hypothesis. "What about my feelings? How dare he treat me with increasing particularity in front of the whole world and then pull back so abruptly that everyone must remark his action?" Her magnificent brown eyes fairly sparked with anger as she said through gritted teeth, "Those horrid girls at that tea party are all jealous of me. How they must relish the hope that Malvern has dropped me. I could kill him for that!''

Alexandra eyed her sister doubtfully and ventured, ''If Malvern has caused you some embarrassment—though, mind you, I do not believe many people are aware of his absence—surely the best tactic is to show the world that you care nothing for his apparent defection and are more than content with your other followers. Is there another whom you might favor as a husband? Sir Adrian Calvert is well connected and a personable young man. He seems to be sincerely devoted to you, and I am persuaded it would take just a very little encouragement to get him to offer for you.''

Didi tossed her dark curls disdainfully. ''Do not be so stupid, Sandy. I intend to make Malvern offer for me.''

''You just said you wanted to kill him,'' Alexandra reminded her more sharply than a joke would warrant.

''So I did, but as the law frowns on murder, it will be safer to marry him instead.'' Didi rose and shook out the creases in her pink polished-cotton dress. ''Or it might be more amusing to jilt him at the altar,'' she added with a glittering smile that sent a chill feathering down Alexandra's spine.

''Do be serious, Didi,'' she begged. ''He obviously does not wish to marry you.''

''We shall see about that,'' the beautiful brunette said pleasantly as she turned the doorknob and left her elder sister alone, a prey to the liveliest misgivings about the immediate future.

11

GENEROUS SPLOTCHES OF MUD begrimed the spokes of the wheels on the solid traveling carriage that drew up in front of a large red brick house in Hanover Square. One or two small globs even dotted the side windows in mute testimony to a messy trip. The two gentlemen who jumped down from the vehicle displayed no signs of travel weariness, however; their *point de vice* appearance, from the crowns of their brushed beaver hats to the soles of their shining Hessian boots, was everything that could be expected of members of the highest stratum of society.

"Your house is very grand, sir," the younger man said, gazing with appreciation from the beautiful fanlight over the door to the topmost range of windows three stories above the entrance.

"Too big for me," Lord Malvern agreed. "My grandfather must have had visions of founding a dynasty when he bought it. It hasn't quite stopped raining. Let's get inside. Stokes will see to our baggage, and here he is, prompt as usual.

"Stokes, this is Mr. Ballard, who will be staying with me."

"Very good, sir. Right this way, Mr. Ballard."

As the men removed their hats into the butler's keeping in the commodious entrance hall, Mr. Ballard said diffidently, "It is awfully kind of you to have me in your house, sir, but I feel a bit awkward about the imposition. I assure you I don't mean to be a bother to you, whatever promise my father may have exacted from you."

"If you think Sir Henry twisted my arm to invite you to London, Gervaise, let me disabuse you of that false notion right now," Malvern said in firm tones, taking his guest's elbow to guide him into a paneled study with one wall given over entirely to bookshelves. "Not that your father could not command me in any neighborly duty in the name of his long friendship with my parents, but it happens that it suits me to have company in this empty house just now, so when Sir Henry mentioned that you were thinking of coming to town for a spell, I offered a roof, and that is the whole of it. A little Madeira?" he asked, indicating the bottle he had taken from a tray on a side table.

"Thank you, sir, but you must not think I expect you to bear-lead me around town. You have your own circle of friends, and many engagements, I make no doubt. You need not be concerned with amusing me. I shall do fine on my own."

"I'm sure you would," his host replied mildly. "Your father wishes you to acquire what he refers to as 'town bronze,' and I was not so presumptuous as to tell him you stood in little need of it after managing his plantations in Jamaica for the past two years, but I trust you are not so stiff-rumped as to refuse an introduction here and there?"

"I . . . I beg your pardon, sir. I . . . I did not mean to sound stiff-rumped," Mr. Ballard denied swiftly, his color a little heightened. "It is just that I do not wish to become a nuisance to you."

"Take it from me, you won't. I have no difficulty at all in disposing of persons whose nuisance value becomes significant." Lord Malvern handed his embarrassed young friend a glass and lifted his own. "To your stay in town."

"Thank you." A gleam of amusement enlivened Mr. Ballard's habitually serious countenance for a moment. "If my nuisance quotient starts to rise, a hint will be sufficient to detach me, sir."

Malvern smiled. "I'll remember. Now, there is just one more detail we must settle before I show you your quarters. I am afraid, my dear boy, that you will have to renounce your stern parental training and drop the title.

I really cannot have you constantly 'sirring' me. It makes me feel positively ancient, decades more than the eight-year gap in our ages would warrant. You called me 'Robert' when you were a boy, as I recall. If that sticks in your throat, 'Malvern' will do.''

''Of course, s . . . Robert,'' the young man agreed with a shy smile that gave life to the sober planes of a well-sculptured head.

Lord Malvern's feelings as he left his guest to settle into his rooms were not quite the complacent ones arising from a good deed performed at some personal cost to the performer. He was guiltily aware that he did not deserve the quiet gratitude expressed by Gervaise or the more fervent thanks of his father. When he had said it suited him to have company in his house at present, he had certainly spoken the truth, but with little expectation of being believed. His penance therefore must be the discomfort of having to accept thanks he did not merit.

Malvern ran back downstairs to collect the post that had accumulated in the eight days of his absence from town. He thumbed quickly through the obvious bills and invitations and opened anything he could not immediately identify. When he reached his own rooms he tossed the whole disappointing lot onto the satinwood table desk under the window and dropped into a chair, frowning into space.

What had he expected? The likelihood of receiving a communication from the one person in the world he yearned to be in communion with was absolutely nil unless she wrote to tell him never to darken her door again. He ran massaging fingers along the spinal cord in his neck to ease the tension that beset him regularly these days. How had matters come to such a pass? Or, more accurately perhaps, how could he at two-and-thirty have been so stupid as to fail to recognize what was happening to him?

After a sennight of thinking of little else, he still had difficulty believing that it was not until an enchanting little termagant with forget-me-not blue eyes had scornfully demanded whether he intended to kiss every girl in

London that the knowledge that he had been courting the wrong Farrish sister all these weeks had hit him with bludgeoning force. While his eyes and competitive spirit had sought out the spectacular Didi, his heart had been wending a steady underground route toward her elder sister. In the instant before he had kissed Alexandra, he finally understood why he had not fallen in love with Didi despite her beauty and charm. Something in his nature had derived more satisfaction from quarreling with Alexandra than flirting with her beautiful sister.

At that point instinct had taken over. Quarreling was fine and stimulating, but he needed to know the feel of her in his arms. For a few blissful seconds heaven seemed within his blind grasp; then the stunned young woman had quivered in his embrace and begun battling strongly for release. He had been reluctant to abandon the quest so close to success, but sanity had come flooding back with the discomfort of the furious jabs she rained upon him. Not all the disadvantages of the situation had been instantly apparent, but Alexandra's blistering tongue-lashing had left him in no doubt as to her reaction to his ardent impulse. She had exploded with all the fury of one of Whinyates' unpredictable rockets.

Having come down to earth with a decided bump, the remnants of his recently dormant intelligence had prompted him to take himself out of Alexandra's firing range before her inflamed temper or his aroused passions should provoke an action from which there was no possible retreat. All the cogitation he had indulged in since that moment had merely confirmed that he had been all kinds of a fool. If he were at point-non-plus, it was his own prideful dash for the prize that was the beautiful Didi's favor that had brought him there.

His nature was neither passive nor pessimistic, however, and he never considered taking the path of least resistance and offering for Didi. Thank heaven he'd had the wit to make that clear to Alexandra before his inglorious retreat from the Belfort antechamber. He'd completed his strategic rout by sending a message to Freddy late that night to make arrangements to go into Kent with him the next day. Alexandra would be quick to see that he had meant it when he told her he would not offer for Didi, and she would begin to prepare her sister. God knew what she was thinking of him at this point! The only thing that enabled him to look himself in the eye in the mirror when tying his cravat this past sennight was the knowledge that Didi's feelings for him had not been strong. He'd have sensed it during that week of intensified courting; indeed, he'd been looking in vain for signs that she really cared for him apart from the ladylike encouragement she had always given his suit.

If Freddy and Lord Cathcart had found his company more unnerving than stimulating as his mood swung from gloom to high spirits to mental abstraction, they were too kind to comment on it. Nor had Freddy displayed the curiosity he must have felt over the *volte-face* that had his comrade accepting an invitation he had turned down not five hours before. Grateful though he was for their forbearance, he became too restless after four days to continue to inflict his wearing company on his friends.

He had left Kent for a quick visit to his home in Sussex rather than return to London to the fray with no clear idea of what he could do about his dilemma. There was always plenty to occupy his time on the estate, but the restlessness increased as his thoughts winged back to Alexandra's multiple attractions. Although he'd spent much more time with Didi, his encounters with her elder sister, some decidedly acrimonious, but enjoyable for all that, had remained fixed in his mind. He could recall in detail their first meeting, when he'd have been delighted to take her over his knee and spank her, so shocked had he been to hear profanity from someone who looked too delicate to blow her nose. The illusion of delicacy had been chased away by the overwhelming evidence of the varied capabilities and responsibilities demonstrated by the dynamic young woman who held a large family intact singlehandedly. Despite her obvious intention of remaining quietly in the background, he had become aware of her selfless devotion to her siblings and had admired her increasingly as the full extent of her loving custody was gradually revealed.

Until the scene at the Belfort ball, the most vivid image he had of Alexandra was the haunting recollection of the quiet acceptance in her face as she had told him of her father's disaffection and her stepmother's resentment of her existence. At this removed point he could see his violent rejection of this story as an indication that he was already beginning to fall in love with her. Life owed Alexandra some return for the years she had spent nurturing her young brother and sisters, and he passionately desired to be the instrument of this long-overdue return. As matters stood at present, however, the unlikelihood of this outcome was a continual source of frustration as he prowled around the empty apartments at Fairlawns after dining alone. Even had there not been Didi's disappointed ambitions to cloud the picture, Alexandra must hold him in such low esteem as to challenge any man to change her opinion. And he could not even attempt to initiate this seemingly star-crossed campaign while Didi remained hopeful of his eventual capitulation to her manifest charms.

The first gleam of light in the muddy picture was shed unknowingly by his neighbor, Sir Henry Ballard, who paid a social call on him on the second day of his sojourn at Fairlawns. When in the course of the conversation he mentioned that he'd like to see his son become more at home in London society, Robert had glimpsed a way to introduce some new blood into Didi's court while providing himself with a valid excuse to diminish his pursuit of her without arousing wagging tongues. The boy was decidedly eligible—personable, well-educated, and heir to a healthy fortune. If he was more serious-minded than was common among the followers of the year's reigning belle, his comely face and lean athletic body were attractions not to be denied. Sir Henry and his father had cherished the hope of making a match between Gervaise and Marielle, but the two had grown up almost as brother and sister, and neither had looked upon the other with new eyes by the time Marielle reached the age to make her come-out. It did not aid their parents' cause that Gervaise had been in Jamaica for over a year by then. So far as he knew, the lad was heart-whole still.

Robert had gratified his old neighbor immensely by issuing a warm invitation to Gervaise to stay with him in Hanover Square for the remainder of the Season. At the very least he could hide behind the lad while pulling back from Didi to allow her numerous suitors to fight it out among them. If she should take a fancy to Gervaise, so much the better.

It was always in the cards that he would have an uphill battle to reverse Alexandra's poor opinion of himself after what any woman would perceive as his caddish behavior at that wretched ball. Until Didi made her choice—and he heartily wished her success in achieving a brilliant connection—Robert Trent would figure as a contemptible philanderer in her sister's estimation. Even should Didi happily accept another offer in the immediate future, there was no guarantee that Alexandra would listen to his pleas or respond to his ardor, but he had no choice but to try to storm her defenses. Nothing had ever mattered so much in his life, and so far he had made a complete hash of it.

Lord Malvern took his houseguest along to a private ball the very evening they arrived in London, having sent along a polite note begging his hostess's indulgence. Mrs. Compton was all complaisance upon meeting the attractive Mr. Ballard. New faces were always welcome at this stage of the annual circus, and anyone sponsored by Malvern was bound to be eligible. Miss Maria Compton, a dashing redhead, was only too willing to add the names of the late arrivals to her dance card.

Behind his customary air of debonair civility, Malvern's mind was distinctly unquiet as he quartered the ballroom with a sentry's thoroughness, looking for the Farrish party. He had determined on pleasant nonchalance with regard to his unannounced absence from town. It would be much trickier to strike a balance between sufficient attendance on Didi to appease the gossips and a significant diminution in intensity for her private appraisal to convey his change of heart to her. One could never predict how a young lady would react when she perceived an injury to her pride. Aware that he did not deserve to be let off scot-free, he could only hope to achieve his purpose with a minimum of discomfort and public speculation.

Alexandra was the first to spot Lord Malvern when he entered the ballroom in company with a young man who was unknown to her. Her heart executed an uncomfortable leap in her breast and she swallowed dryly as apprehension gripped her and blocked all response. It was a second or two before she could tear her eyes away from that Nordic fair head to nudge Didi at her side.

"Malvern has just come in."

Didi stiffened at her sister's whisper but did not turn her head or remove her attention from the two young men who were entertaining her with the story of a comical curricle race. Alexandra's breathing grew difficult as she watched the approach of the man who had said he was not going to marry her sister. Didi had been acting strangely ever since learning of Malvern's absence from London. She had promptly accepted an invitation to view the exhibition at Somerset House with Lord Hexton that same afternoon, as well as two offers to go driving with other admirers in the upcoming days. On the surface it would seem she had decided to make the best of the situation, but the brittle gaiety of her manner and her refusal to talk about anything except the merest trivialities warned Alexandra that the girl was far from reconciled to losing Lord Malvern. Her behavior in the next few minutes could be crucial to the ultimate success or failure of their social venture.

Lord Malvern's imminent arrival derailed Alexandra's anxious thoughts as he very correctly greeted her first with one of his best smiles before presenting young Mr. Ballard. Though she managed the correct responses, she was unable to summon any warmth into her voice, aware as she was of her own chaotic thoughts and of Didi's continued pretense of total absorption in her companions.

As her name was spoken by Malvern, the brunette girl

gave a start of simulated surprise and affected a pretty confusion that even her critical sister could not fault. One lovely hand fluttered briefly near her heart as she begged, "Pray forgive my lack of manners, sir. I did not expect to see you tonight. I thought someone said you were out of town, but I must have misunderstood."

"I was called away rather unexpectedly, but it is most humbling to learn that I have returned before I was missed," he said mournfully as he bent over her hand.

"I protest, sir. You are putting unkind words in my mouth," Didi declared gaily. "Of course we missed you." Her brilliant smile skimmed over Malvern and lighted questioningly on the man by his side.

As Lord Malvern made the introduction, Alexandra relaxed her clenched jaw and released the little fold of skirt she had been fingering nervously. She sensed they were the cynosure of all eyes at the moment, but Didi was carrying it off in a magnificent fashion, aided without doubt by the look of stunned admiration in the fine hazel eyes of Lord Malvern's friend. She even produced a look of shy confusion on hearing herself described as "the most beautiful girl in London," and Mr. Ballard received the full benefit of her sumptuous black lashes lowering to her cheek to shield her eyes for a moment.

"I trust we are not too late to secure a dance, Didi? It is all Gervaise's fault for ruining no fewer than four cravats before he was satisfied with his efforts."

Alexandra guessed by the startled flicker of Mr. Ballard's eyelids that his host was lying in his teeth as he continued in cajoling tones, "Won't you please take pity on a man denied the sight of your smile for better than a sennight?"

"Well, it happens that I do have one country dance left at the end of the evening." Didi had hesitated before this capitulation, and her beautiful eyes looked squarely at Malvern, whose disappointment was plain to see.

"Then as punishment for my absence, it is clearly incumbent upon me to forfeit this dance to my young friend, whose first night in London must be made memorable by securing a dance with the most popular girl in town.''

Alexandra's teeth clenched again as her sister, after a recognizable pause, handed her dance card to Mr. Ballard with the glittering smile that always struck trepidation in the hearts of those who knew her best. ''Naturally, Lord Malvern must defer to his guest,'' she said to give Didi time to reestablish her control. That the girl longed to give her former suitor a piece of her mind was beyond doubting, and that would be disastrous.

The orchestra struck up again as Mr. Ballard finished writing his name on the dance card, and one of the men with whom Didi had been in conversation swept her onto the floor. The other drifted away to seek his next partner. Alexandra's eyes met Lord Malvern's as she said woodenly, ''I am persuaded you must wish to make Mr. Ballard known to some of your friends, sir. I see that Lady Amberdale has finished her conversation, so I shall be joining her. It was a pleasure meeting you, Mr. Ballard.'' She gave the inoffensive young man a special smile to make up for her coldness as she turned away, but Lord Malvern's quiet voice arrested her motion.

''I hope I may give myself the honor of calling upon you soon, Miss Farrish.''

Her face devoid of expression, she glanced at him over her shoulder. ''Do you think that is wise at present?''

''Wisdom hasn't characterized my actions lately,'' he replied with a wry twist to his mouth, ''but I think it . . . advisable.''

''Very well.''

Lord Malvern bowed and walked away with his puzzled friend in tow. Alexandra automatically checked on the whereabouts of her sisters, locating all three dark heads among the dancers, before she headed for the small group of matrons Lady Amberdale had joined. She went with the greatest reluctance, having no desire to deal with the curiosity that would be rampant among them after the meeting that had just taken place. In fact, she thought it a great pity there was no titillating scandal brewing at the moment to divert attention from the interesting situation between Didi and Malvern. Lady Amberdale must have divined her mood, because she murmured to the woman beside her and unhurriedly rose to meet her goddaughter before she reached the group.

"Come over here where we can be private, and smile, for goodness' sake. You look rather like Antigone awaiting her sentence. I must say, from a distance at least, that Didi came off better than you in that little pageant just staged. Malvern, of course, was his usual suave self, drat him."

Was he? As Alexandra followed her godmother to a fortuitously vacated settee at the far end of the ballroom, it struck her that Lord Malvern's guard had dropped at the end. For a second she could have sworn she detected unhappiness in those unrevealing pewter eyes, but she was probably mistaken. Villains were notoriously invulnerable to human emotions.

"Sit down." Lady Amberdale patted the cushion beside her as she eased her well-corseted bulk onto the settee with a sigh. "It feels good to rest my knees, and you, my dear, look like you could do with a large brandy. Alas, that isn't possible here, but at least you may regather your strength while we are undisturbed. I shall raise my lorgnette and frown furiously at anyone bold enough to approach us."

Alexandra laughed weakly, cheered as always by the dear lady's support and bracing affection.

"That's better. Was it very bad? Is there no hope that the match will still come off? They were taking bets on it at White's a fortnight ago, I hear."

"How . . . how disgusting!" Alexandra exclaimed between gritted teeth. "I could kill him with my bare hands!"

"I apprehend that my question is answered?"

"Oh, yes, it is over. I knew that before he went away." She regretted the unwary admission the next instant, when her godmother pounced.

"You did? How?"

Alexandra bit her lip. "Malvern told me he did not intend to offer for her, but it would be unbecoming of me to relate the circumstances in which he . . . he made his sentiments known to me, even to you, dear ma'am.''

"Hmmmm." Lady Amberdale generously concealed her disappointment at being denied what must be the most fascinating aspect of the situation. "Show your teeth," she commanded. "People are watching us. Does Didi know?"

Alexandra obediently produced a meaningless smile. "She does now. He requested a dance for himself and his young houseguest, and when Didi said she had only one left, he promptly resigned his claim in favor of Mr. Ballard. He made it sound terribly self-sacrificing, but Didi knew. For a moment I was afraid she'd lash out at him, but she behaved beautifully. I had attempted to prepare her all week, but you will apprehend that she found it difficult to accept in the circumstances. She is the toast of the town," she added loyally, "and he has been so particular in his attention of late. Why did he do it, ma'am? I would never have believed him capable of such coldhearted villainy."

Lady Amberdale gave the cold fingers pleating and unpleating a fold of blue skirt a quick warm squeeze as she studied the lovely young face that looked more baffled and wounded than angry. "According to Augusta Marlowe, whose son is very close to Malvern, he took his sister's death very hard. Freddy believes that in consequence he made a deliberate decision to look for a wife. Naturally, Didi captured his fancy. What man in possession of his faculties could resist that face? They all fall in the beginning. I hope you will pardon my plain speaking, dear child, when I say that in time the more discriminating men will be cured of their blindness as they recognize that her looks are really all Didi has to offer. She is not . . . warmhearted," she added, choosing her words with care, "and some men demand more than that their wives should be decorative."

As Alexandra stirred in dawning protest, Lady Amberdale went on, "Do not misunderstand me. Malvern has done badly by Didi, and you have every right to be angry. He has assured the clacking tongues a field day by drawing back so suddenly when it seemed he was on the verge of making her an offer. The only point I wish to make in his defense is pure conjecture; do not ask me to furnish evidence, for I could not, but I believe I am correct.''

"And what point is that, ma'am?"

"Well, if it is any comfort to you, and it won't be unless you wish to think better of him," the matron added with a sideways glance at the tense young face turned slightly away from her, "I am persuaded Malvern did intend to offer for her until he suddenly awoke from the spell her beauty cast over him. How it happened, what she did or did not do, does not signify. All that matters is that he ran for his life, an understandable but injudicious decision that has set tongues wagging. If, as I believe, he intended no harm to your family, he will try to put the best face on the matter now. I am persuaded he will be happy to let it appear that Didi has thrown him over, if you play your cards right. The fact that he made a beeline for her tonight can be taken as an indication that he is cognizant of his fault and eager to make amends.''

"You may be right, ma'am. If Didi will only cooperate, we may brush through this affair with no more than a little harmless talk.''

Lady Amberdale stared at her goddaughter uncomprehendingly for a second. "Of course Didi will cooperate. It is in her best interest to do so.''

12

LADY AMBERDALE'S BRACING WORDS enabled Alexandra
to do her part by concealing her anxiety behind a cheerful
demeanor, which she maintained throughout the trying
evening. To anyone who inquired of her feelings at having Lord Malvern once more in their midst, she delivered
a smile and a pat rejoinder stressing the whole family's
delight at this happy event. To those crass persons whose
curiosity took them further, she agreed that it was indeed
a shame none of her sisters had had a spare dance to
bestow upon him, adding with a teasing inflection that
latecomers got their just deserts.

"Dreadful woman, always has been," Lady Amberdale snorted late in the evening when one such interro-
gator had departed with nothing to add to the mix.

Sir Frederick was sitting with Alexandra and Lady
Amberdale at the time. He had been back in town for
two days, ample time to have heard the rumors, Alexandra realized as he turned to her and said more seriously
than was his wont, "It was entirely my doing that Malvern left town so abruptly, Alexandra. He is very fond of
my grandfather, who has been feeling poorly of late. I
urged him to drop everything for a few days and come
with me into Kent. I'm afraid I gave him no time for
deliberation, but neither of us could have foreseen that
his departure would give rise to gossip. I am really most
awfully sorry."

A faint smile touched Alexandra's lips as she said, "I
hope Lord Malvern appreciates what a very good friend
he has in you, Freddy."

"No, it is the other way round more often than not.

Robert has pulled my mutton out of the fire a score of times, and I cannot help but feel I've played him a backhanded trick, and you too, though it certainly was not my intention.''

"I do not hold you to blame for anything, Freddy, I assure you.''

"Since when are you responsible for Malvern's distempered freaks?'' Lady Amberdale put in over Alexandra's quiet assurances.

"No, I say, ma'am, nothing of the sort, really,'' Sir Frederick protested, looking acutely uncomfortable. "Robert was merely trying to oblige me in something. It queers me how anyone could create so much talk out of nothing.''

"The answer is that they could not.''

Before he actually had to perjure his soul by calling Alexandra's statement into question, one of the twins came up, much to Sir Frederick's relief. He jumped to his feet and bowed to the elder ladies. "If you will excuse me, I am promised for the last dance to Cassie; that is, I thought I was. It is Arie, isn't it?'' he asked the smiling charmer in pale yellow net over a taffeta slip of a deeper hue.

"Yes, if you will accept me as a substitute, Sir Frederick? Didi was scheduled to partner Lord Malvern's friend Mr. Ballard, but she has developed a bad headache, and Cassie is standing in for her so Mr. Ballard won't be left in the lurch.'' Arie gave Sir Frederick her best smile, but he had not missed the warning look she sent her sister, and he tackled her about it when they were out on the dance floor.

"What is the real story on Miss Didi's headache?'' he asked boldly when she curtsied to him as they joined a set.

Now it was he who received the warning look as they began to execute the figures of the dance. Patiently he waited until they came down the line together, and tried again.

"It won't wash, Miss Arie. I do not believe in fairies or your sister's headaches. If you don't wish to satisfy my curiosity, I'll get it out of Cassie later. She is not proof against my blandishments.''

He spoke lightly, but Arie gave him a searching look before she said, ''Please, sir, do not badger Cassie.''

Again they were separated by the movements of the dance.

''I would not dream of badgering Cassie,'' he promised at the next opportunity. ''Has someone been doing that—Miss Didi perhaps?''

Arie's lovely brown eyes dilated with quick alarm, then dropped as she circled behind her partner, leaving him with a picture of curling lashes and a gentle mouth. His conscience smote him and he begged her pardon the next time they came together. ''I had no call to badger you just because I wondered what Didi has talked poor Cassie into this time.''

''Nothing, sir,'' Arie reassured him eagerly. ''Didi intended to simply excuse herself from dancing with Mr. Ballard. It was Cassie who felt sorry for him and offered herself in Didi's place. She barely had time to beg me to carry her apologies to you. Cassie would rather dance with you, but she can never bear to see anyone hurt, and this is Mr. Ballard's first night in town.''

It was Sir Frederick's turn to do the reassuring, and he murmured soothing platitudes to his earnest young partner. The twins were a loyal pair. Despite the provocation, Arie had not exposed Didi's action to criticism, but he would take his oath that the spoiled beauty had left the unfortunate Mr. Ballard in the lurch solely to spite Malvern. It would seem this particular chapter was not yet ended. Those observers with a nose for news who were still circling might yet have their hoped-for scandal to chew over.

Sir Frederick noted that Didi had not joined her sister and Lady Amberdale by the time he returned Arie to these ladies. People would be leaving soon, and one might expect that a young lady suffering from the headache would be among the first to get her wraps. Alexandra was determinedly smiling, but he could read the tension in her jaw. As he bowed his farewell he caught sight of Didi approaching out of the corner of his eye. She was demonstrating a miraculous recovery from her headache by laughing and flirting with a fellow he would unabashedly stigmatize as a rakehell, not a sight to gladden the heart of any chaperone.

Whether out of consideration or pure cowardice—he'd have been loath to state which—Freddy unobtrusively removed himself from the scene, though he had hoped for a word with Cassie, who was a dozen paces behind her sister. Unhappily, Mr. Ballard was still in faithful attendance upon his rescuer, proving that the darling dimwit had no flair for intrigue, or perhaps had simply overestimated her sister's generosity and sense of propriety. Not content with notching up a score against Malvern, Didi had elected to offer a gratuitous slight to his innocent friend into the bargain. Safely on the other side of the room, Freddy observed that Mr. Ballard had the presence of mind to take a smiling leave of Cassie before they reached the family circle, at the point where she had stopped abruptly, having apparently just noticed her ungrateful sister and her escort.

"Under other circumstances, I'd say it was more entertaining than the play," drawled a familiar voice behind him.

Freddy moved his shoulders to allow more room for Lord Malvern. "Will it concern you overmuch if the fair lady continues to make it clear that she wishes nothing more to do with you?"

"It will if her enthusiasm for the role makes her appear to be the proverbial woman scorned."

Freddy turned and looked straight at his friend. "I do not believe anything out of the ordinary was perceived by the company to have occurred here tonight, Robert."

"I hope you are correct. It is of surpassing importance that she should not be perceived by society to have been humiliated by me."

Mr. Ballard's arrival at that moment was only partly responsible for silencing Sir Frederick. He had just discovered that his assumptions about what was bothering his friend did not fully explain his present urgency. Noth-

ing had been said between himself and Robert on the
subject of Miss Didi Farrish since the day he'd helped
select a parasol for her. Despite personal qualms as he'd
seen his old friend narrow his sights to exclude all girls
but Didi, he had kept the promise he'd made to himself
that day to say nothing against the girl. What was more,
he'd been careful to conceal his elation when Robert had
abruptly decided to accompany him out of town. He'd
assumed, of course, that his friend had received some
kind of jolt that had illuminated the beauty's real character, but he'd refrained from any attempt to satisfy his
natural curiosity on the subject while in Kent. In due
course Robert would confide the episode to him—or perhaps he would not. That would be all right too. There
must be a certain reluctance to disclose, even into sympathetic ears, that one had been a colossal idiot, not to
mention a gentleman's disinclination to impugn a lady's
character. As he observed the urbanity with which Robert received Gervaise Ballard as they all prepared to leave
the ball together, Freddy's active intelligence was busy
trying to account for the brief revealing exchange just
concluded with his friend.

In Harley Street the next day, Alexandra was only pe-
ripherally concerned with her own exchange with Lord
Malvern on the previous evening. Didi's behavior had
become her main worry. Her natural store of sympathy
for her sister's predicament had been considerably de-
pleted by the girl's unwarranted breach of etiquette at the
innocent Mr. Ballard's expense. She'd been so incensed
that she'd taken her sister severely to task in the carriage
on the way home, a mistake she readily conceded in the
calm of a fresh day. She should have spoken to Didi privately to begin with, but it was the girl's defiant attitude
that caused her the most concern. She was frankly un-
repentant about the trick she had pulled and unpossessed
of any compunction for Mr. Ballard. Her anger at Malvern blinded her to the rights of anyone else and even to
propriety, a dangerous combination that filled Alexandra
with dread. In the mood Didi was in at present, she was
capable of ruining herself and sinking the family in the

process. The saving grace in this instance was that no one at the Compton ball could have known of Didi's action save Lady Amberdale and Freddy Marlowe and, of course, the victims. Alexandra could take small comfort from this circumstance, since past history had left her with little confidence that fear of public disclosure would prove enough of an inhibiting factor when Didi was intent on achieving something. Last night she had seen a way to avenge herself on Malvern for daring to pass her over to his guest for a dance, and she had acted on it. Alexandra could not convince herself that Didi would have behaved differently had the entire company been aware of the real situation, and this was at the root of her present malaise.

When Lord Malvern and Mr. Ballard were announced, Alexandra and the twins were doing their best to entertain an eager young man who had arrived fifteen minutes before the appointed hour to take Didi driving. Since the twins were well-versed in the art of soothing the irrational anxieties of gentlemen who feared something might intervene at the last minute to prevent their long-awaited tryst with their goddess, Alexandra was able to sit back, sewing in hand, to think her own thoughts at such times. She looked up with a start, having at last gotten around to a worried contemplation of Malvern's intentions for the interview he had urgently sought. It would not have surprised her to receive a polite note regretting that unexpected business would prevent his keeping the appointment, but perhaps the inclusion of his houseguest was meant to achieve the same end.

Alexandra rose and came to meet the visitors just as Didi appeared in the doorway, hatted and gloved and carrying the charming parasol that had been Lord Malvern's gift. "Ah, there you are, Didi. Mr. Cadbury has been waiting, and Lord Malvern and Mr. Ballard have just arrived."

"Oh, what a pity that I am just going out," her sister said with the convincing sweet mendacity that served her so well in her dealings with the opposite sex. She paused long enough to slide the beginning of a smile past Lord

Malvern to Mr. Ballard, where it rested and bloomed into that captivating entity that had been exhaustively praised by poetically inclined gentlemen and inarticulate youths alike.

Alexandra noted with interest that Mr. Ballard's response was nicely calculated to be a trifle warmer than polite without being effusive. It would seem he had already progressed beyond the helplessly adoring state of poor Mr. Cadbury, who had jumped out of his chair on Didi's appearance, fearful even now that a cruel fate would snatch the prize from his grasp. Lord Malvern wore the lazy look of slightly derisive enjoyment in the human comedy that was one of the traits about him Alexandra most disliked.

The next half-hour passed in the pleasant manner of countless others this spring. The Misses Debenham arrived on a wave of giggles and were well-rewarded by the presence of four entertaining gentlemen, for Lord Callum and a jolly friend of the twins had joined them by then. Malvern was at his debonair best, agreeable, willing to talk about any topic raised, but never standing in the young people's light. Alexandra thought that he took care to avoid meeting her glance as she remained in the background as usual, unless a guest was feeling left out momentarily. This confirmed her hunch that since last night the urgency had gone out of his request for an audience. It was just as well, since they could have little to say to each other after what had happened. The only novelty of the social interlude was supplied by Mr. Ballard, who found a moment of comparative privacy in which to invite Cassie to go driving with him the day after his phaeton arrived from Sussex.

Though not precisely of a retiring nature, Mr. Ballard had allowed others to do most of the talking. Alexandra considered that the few remarks that passed his lips had been distinguished more by their good sense and pertinence than their value as amusing tattle. She thought his smile particularly winning, since it had the happy effect of making the person at whom it was directed feel suddenly witty and well-liked, judging by her own reaction when it was turned on her. In her shy way, Arie too seemed to be entranced by Mr. Ballard's smile. For his part, he appeared wholly captured by Cassie's bubbling gaiety. From her vantage point Alexandra saw the dimming of the light behind Arie's own smile when Cassie referred Mr. Ballard's invitation to her elder for approval. There was no legitimate reason to deny the request; indeed, she was pleased that the Farrish family could make some amends for Didi's callous treatment of this pleasant young man, but she had a sudden premonition of more unhappiness in the future.

So far the twins had unconcernedly shared all their friends, both male and female. They were perhaps a bit young yet to be thinking of forming permanent attachments. Alexandra had been content to see them enjoy themselves and acquire some town polish. She would be well-satisfied to leave the question of their marriage to the future if she could only establish Didi in a position to be of use to them later. A fortnight ago that was exactly what seemed to be happening. Didi had appeared on the point of contracting a brilliant marriage, and the twins were gaining rich experience of a world outside of Yorkshire. She suspected that Cassie had formed a mild *tendre* for Freddy Marlowe, but he could be trusted not to toy with her feelings, and the girl's high spirits and short-lived enthusiasms indicated she was still relatively heart-whole. No need to fear the unhealthy sort of attachment Marielle Trent had formed for Lee.

Arie was another story. She had quite a different personality from that of her more forceful twin. Once she had given her affection, she did not withdraw it and move on unscathed if the recipient disappointed her. Her feelings went deep and her loyalty was complete.

Alexandra assured herself she was worrying needlessly as Lord Malvern and his attractive protégé prepared to depart. Arie had seen Mr. Ballard for the first time less than twenty-four hours ago. Love at first sight was a phenomenon more prevalent in poetry and fiction than in everyday life. There was no point in borrowing trouble. She shook off her temporary lowness of spirits and roused herself to speed the parting guests. All the gentlemen took their leave within minutes of each other, but the twins persuaded the Debenham girls to remain behind. Alexandra left them to their chatter and headed down to the morning room to tackle the household accounts.

She was on the top step when she met Edson coming back up.

"Lord Malvern desires a private word with you, Miss Alexandra. I have put him in the morning room."

"Thank you, Edson." She started down the stairs slowly, readjusting her thoughts in view of this unexpected development. "Where is Mr. Ballard?" she asked the butler with a puzzled frown.

"Mr. Ballard went on without Lord Malvern, Miss Alexandra. Shall I bring refreshments to the morning room?"

"No, thank you, Edson." A wryly amused smile crossed Alexandra's lips as she walked toward the back of the house. Edson had a sixth sense for anticipating family events, but this time he was way out in his reckoning if he thought this conference would end in celebration.

She paused in front of the pier glass in the hall and stared at her sober reflection for a moment, tucking a stray curl back among its brethren. Scarcely the coiffure for a mature woman, but she'd always found her riotously curling thick locks a time-consuming burden and had adopted this short crop many years ago rather than expend time and thought on dressing her hair as changing fashions dictated. She made a face in the glass, suddenly dissatisfied with every aspect of her appearance. She'd long ago accepted the disappointing reality that she would never be tall with dramatic coloring like the rest of the family, and she scarcely ever gave her looks a passing thought. She did so now in her disinclination for the meeting ahead of her.

Determined to take a positive view of the matter, she acknowledged that she could be grateful at least that she wasn't ugly, situated as she was in this beautiful family. She supposed her features were not displeasing, but neither were they arresting, and her stature was and would remain insignificant. Her eyes were probably her best feature—many people regarded their deep blue color as attractive, but she'd have preferred to have the thick dark lashes that went with brown eyes. Hers were thick enough, but one could not deny their straightness, and she considered that the uninteresting golden-brown color detracted from their length. Her cheekbones were high and pronounced—that was a definite asset. They redeemed her face from round insipidity, but her nose was nothing special and her mouth was too large for beauty, though her teeth were good. Her brows drew together again as she pondered whether the irregularity in Penny's teeth would become less evident as she grew. They were beautifully white, thank heaven, and her smile, in Alexandra's opinion, was one of her little sister's most attractive features.

A door closed somewhere in the house, effectively recalling Alexandra's wandering thoughts to the present. She rubbed her cheeks briskly to stimulate some healthy color and walked with purposeful steps to the morning-room door, gathering her dignity about her as she did so, but still refusing to think of the man awaiting her on the other side of the door.

"Come in, Miss Farrish," Lord Malvern said from near the fireplace, where he'd evidently been studying Penny's portrait of her brother. "Thank you for agreeing to talk with me."

Alexandra came a few steps closer, then stopped, still a half-dozen paces from the tall compelling man who looked at her without the social mask for once. "I do not really see that there is much to be said between us, my lord, to any positive purpose," she replied, producing each word with an effort under that steady, unknowable regard.

"Do you not?" His narrow gray eyes seemed intent on peering into her mind, and Alexandra folded her lips one in back of the other as she nervously moistened them behind the barrier they formed before relaxing her mouth and giving a slight negative shake of her head.

"Well, perhaps you cannot," Lord Malvern admitted with seeming reluctance, removing his eyes from her face briefly. "Won't you please sit down? There is a proposal I wish to put before you for your consideration."

She stiffened instantly and her eyes unloosed blue fire. His pupils contracted in surprise for an instant; then he must have heard his own words, for a muscle twitched in his cheek and his lips firmed. "I beg your pardon, Miss Farrish. A poor choice of words, I agree. Alas, my maladroit tongue. Perhaps I had best begin with an apology."

Again he indicated one of the armless chairs with the chintz cushions, and when she was seated, took possession of the one on the other side of the tea table from hers.

"I realize that my decision not to offer for Didi has placed you in an unenviable position *vis-à-vis* the town gossips, and I apologize most sincerely. Please believe it was never my intention to hurt Didi or cause you distress."

"Then why . . . ?" she blurted when he came to a full stop. She stopped in her turn and stared at him, one hand opening briefly in an unconsciously supplicating gesture.

"I wish I could make you understand. I *thought* I meant to offer for her—that it was just a matter of waiting until I was sure I was in love with her. I *expected* to fall in love with her. Does the word 'love' seem out of place coming from me?" he asked abruptly.

Her lips parted but she said nothing. Their eyes met, but her face was full of incomprehension. He took an audible breath.

"I cannot blame you. No one, least of all myself, thought I was capable of falling in love, as that is understood by the poets, and I fully expected to select a wife on a more rational basis, until Didi crossed my path. I do not have to tell you that her beauty is extraordinary. When she is in a room, one's eyes return to her face no matter who is speaking, for the sheer pleasure of looking at her. As I said, I expected to fall in love with her, and when I suddenly realized that it was not going to happen, I found I could not go through with it after all.''

Alexandra digested this for a moment. All her anger had drained away in the face of his obvious contrition. She struggled against pity for his suspected unhappiness and forced her mind to consider the sense of his explanation.

"Why?" she asked at last. "Why, if you did not expect to marry for love in the first place, did you change your mind about offering for Didi just because you decided you weren't in love with her after all this time? Why wasn't whatever drew you to her in the beginning sufficient later?"

This time the silence stretched out and became a palpable entity. She knew he did not wish to answer, and she refused to withdraw the question that hung in the silence as if roasting over a spit and getting blacker by the second.

A veil of blankness settled over his countenance and was reinforced by the uninflected tone in which he replied, "It was no longer sufficient once I discovered I was in love with someone else."

Alexandra slumped a little in her chair without realizing it. Whatever she had expected, it had not been this bald confession. She felt hollow inside, and defeated and stupid with it, as she blinked at him. "I . . . see," she managed in a voice as deadened as his had been. She tried again, and this time produced a brisk tone. "Well, then, there really is no more to be said."

"Have you forgotten that I came here with a proposition for you to consider?"

"What kind of proposition?" She still felt dull-witted and uncaring.

"I would like to ensure that Didi will suffer no embarrassment because of this, and it seems to me the most effective step in this regard would be to make it appear that she has turned me down. I thought I might give a small dinner party for your family as soon as it may be arranged. People would be bound to learn of it, and if afterward Didi is seen to prefer other suitors, the implication will be plain that she has refused me." He summoned a faint self-mocking smile and elaborated on his scheme. "I shall look suitably crushed for a time, and any gossip will soon die a natural death."

Alexandra concentrated fiercely on his words while he outlined his plan. Two objections occurred to her at once. She could not very well tell him that there was no guarantee that her sister would cooperate in the scheme, so she brought forth the second. "Is it quite fair to the girl you are in love with to allow the polite world to think Didi has thrown you over? Won't it later appear that she is merely your second choice?"

"The person I love would wish me to do this for Didi."

She eyed him doubtfully. "You seem very sure of that. I do not believe any female would care to be put in the position you propose. She'd never be certain that she was the one you really wanted."

Something flared in his eyes for a second, and he appeared to be keeping himself motionless in his chair by an enormous effort of will. "After this situation with Didi is cleared up, I shall hope to spend the rest of my life convincing her that she is the woman I love."

"Have you not explained the situation to her already?"

He stirred then. "I cannot. It would . . . compromise her."

"I don't think I understand."

"Miss Farrish, you will have to accept my word on this point."

"Of course," she said stiffly, hearing the impatience behind his words. "It is none of my affair. I beg your pardon."

"No, it is I who should beg your pardon. I'd beg Didi's if I thought it possible, but in these delicate—"

"Lord Malvern, do not, I beg of you, say anything at all to Didi," Alexandra cried on a rush of words, interrupting him ruthlessly.

"Calm yourself, O Prudent Miss Farrish. I shall not add awkward explanations that must only mortify us both to the growing list of my follies." He smiled then, a smile that warmed and comforted her at the same time that it brought home to her that Didi was not the only loser in this affair. She was losing a friend she had come to value.

She rose from her chair and held out her hand, desperate to get the interview concluded. "Once more, I am sorry, sir, and I thank you on behalf of my sister for the suggestion of the dinner party. I hope it will serve to end all this." She gestured vaguely and did not meet his eyes.

"I shall let you know the details when I have spoken again with Lady Marlowe, who has agreed to act as my hostess."

"Thank you," said Alexandra, edging him toward the door.

13

"PSST, ARIE, I NEED TO TALK TO YOU. Come in here."

As her sister walked into the morning room, Cassie went over to check that the door to the dining room was closed. "Shut the hall door," she commanded.

Mystified, Arie went back and closed the door. "Why all the secrecy?" she asked, watching her sister cast off her straw hat and throw her gloves into the crown as she settled onto the sofa, running her fingers through her flattened curls.

"I want you to do something for me, and Sandy mustn't find out."

Arie paused in the act of drawing off her gloves. She had taken the other end of the sofa, and now she stared at her twin. "What are you up to that Sandy would disapprove of?"

Cassie ignored that for the moment. "Do you recall earlier this afternoon that I took our books back to the library while you and Penny were in the confectioner's and Didi and Sandy were looking for gloves for her orange gown?" Arie nodded, and Cassie went on, "As good fortune would have it, Sir Frederick was in Hookham's when I arrived, and—"

"Good fortune or good planning?" Arie asked with a grin.

"I swear." Cassie held up her right hand, then sternly enjoined her sister to let her tell her story before someone came into the room. Arie folded her hands and assumed the exaggerated expression of a saintly child, which provoked an appreciative giggle from her twin, though she insisted, "This is serious, Arie. To come directly to the point: Sir Frederick invited me to go driving with him, and I must go!''

"I'm not stopping you," Arie pointed out, "and I shouldn't think Sandy would either. She dotes on Freddy.''

This familiar use of the gentleman's name brought a quick frown and a stern rebuke. "Stop interrupting. The problem is that he invited me for Wednesday afternoon, and that is the time I am promised to Mr. Ballard.''

Now Arie's expression was as serious as her sister could wish. "Did he not name another time when you told him you had a previous engagement?'' She read the answer in her twin's evasive eyes. "You did not tell him," she said slowly.

"How could I? He has never asked me out before, just that time when Didi could not go, and that doesn't count. I was afraid he might not ask me again if I refused, and I want to go—badly.''

"What are you going to do?''

They both knew the question was unnecessary. Cassie looked pleadingly at her twin, who waited in numb silence for the blow to fall. "Won't you do it for me, Arie, please?''

"You wish me to take your place with Mr. Ballard, even though Sandy has expressly forbidden us to lie for each other?''

"You won't have to tell a lie. Just be me for that one little hour. No one will ever know. Mama never found out when we switched places as children; neither did the governesses.''

"Sandy always knew. She did not tell on us when we were children, but we are not children now, and she would think it monstrously unfair to Mr. Ballard. I think so too. It is you he wishes to take driving, not me.''

"But he doesn't know me. He only invited me out of gratitude for rescuing him that night. He has seen us only twice, and we are so alike, he would not know the difference—or care, for that matter. Most of them don't know us apart or care which twin it is, but I am hoping so much that Freddy does. Oh, Arie, please do this for me. It is so important.''

Arie was weakening visibly under Cassie's persuasions, but she came back to her first objection. ''Sandy would forbid it if she knew, and I do not see how we can keep her from finding out. In fact,'' she went on slowly, ''the rest of us are due at Lady Amberdale's that afternoon for a nuncheon. It is impossible, Cass. If you wrote a note to Mr. Ballard explaining the situation and asking him to excuse you, I am sure he would understand.''

''So am I, but he would be hurt, and I don't wish to hurt him further after what Didi has done. He is so very nice. It is all so ridiculous, really,'' she said in exasperation. ''He is a rather serious-minded person and probably won't even like me above half when he finds out how frivolous I am. And it can be done, Arie,'' she added, reverting to the main issue. ''If you were to beg off from going to Lady Amberdale's on account of a bad head or a sore throat or something, we could easily be back here before Sandy, Penny, and Didi return from the nuncheon.''

''Perhaps, but . . . Oh, you've forgotten Edson. He'll give the whole show away when two men arrive separately, each expecting to take Miss Cassandra driving.''

For a moment Cassie was stymied. She jumped up and started to prowl around the room under her sister's troubled eyes, throwing out disjointed phrases and suggestions, only to dismiss them immediately as unworkable. In the end it was Arie who said slowly, ''Did not Lee say he expects to be here early Wednesday afternoon waiting for an old friend to arrive? If we tell him the story, I am persuaded he'd help us. At least he'll keep Edson at bay and answer the door during that period.''

''Oh, Arie darling, thank you. I'll tackle Lee this evening. See, I knew it could be done if we put our heads together.'' Cassie was her old optimistic self once more, so excited she did not notice that her twin, though committed to aiding and abetting, was not at all happy about the scheme.

''Suppose he guesses I'm not you? I should just wish

to die on the spot if he found out we were deceiving him."

Cassie glanced at her apprehensive twin in amazement. Once the physical details of the situation had been accounted for, her natural ebullience had reasserted itself. "He won't guess. Why should he? I told you, he doesn't know me."

"I might inadvertently say something that would betray you. What did you talk about during that dance the other evening?"

"Calm yourself, Arie. We talked the same nothings one does with new partners, exchanging opinions on the decor and the music and so forth. I remember he commented that people had seemed more friendly toward a stranger than he had expected, and I said everyone would naturally be well-disposed toward a friend of Lord Malvern's. Then he waxed rather eloquent on Malvern's kindness, I agree with all of it, and that was about it, except that like everyone else we've ever met, he declared us uncannily alike. Now, do you feel better? He told me nothing about himself; there is nothing I know about him that you do not, so pray cease worrying, Arie. Everything will go smoothly, and I am so grateful to you for helping me to have Freddy to myself for once."

The twins exchanged smiles of perfect understanding, not needing to put their feelings into words.

For once, the way of the transgressors was not made hard, though Sandy did indeed note and comment on the twins' rather extreme behavior. Cassie's characteristic optimism and blithe spirits seemed to contain a touch of the manic on Wednesday morning. She appeared to have difficulty containing herself, a reaction more allied to a child's impatience for a promised birthday treat than a young lady of fashion's anticipation of a quite ordinary outing with a gentleman with whom she was barely acquainted. At the other extreme, the habitually quiet Arie seemed in imminent danger of sinking into a fit of the dismals for no appreciable cause. When she asked to be excused from attending Lady Amberdale's luncheon party because her throat hurt, Sandy took a closer look at her flushed cheeks and dull eyes and concluded that this was the explanation of the girl's low spirits.

Lee was amenable to smoothing his sisters' paths by playing porter when first the real Cassie and then her nervous twin were called for by the unsuspecting gentlemen involved. He already knew Sir Frederick and was pleasantly surprised to find Mr. Ballard a more responsible individual than the commonality of his sisters' friends. In due course Mr. Ballard bade Lee good-bye and left, perfectly content with his companion.

The conspirators had agreed that widely separated destinations were vital to the plot's success, so when Mr. Ballard asked his passenger's preference, Arie was able to speak composedly in favor of seeing the flowers in the gardens at Kensington. Except to confirm his directions, those were the last words she spoke for an appreciable time as conscience and unwonted shyness kept her dumb. In point of fact, all kinds of symptoms beset her suddenly, with the possible exception of the sore throat she had claimed earlier. Certainly there were palpitations of her heart to contend with, and she was grateful for her gloves to conceal the fact that her palms were clammy as she wished desperately in those first moments that they had not embarked on such a perfidious deception. Mr. Ballard was too good; he did not deserve to be so shabbily treated.

Mr. Ballard turned and smiled at his silent passenger. "You are unusually quiet today, Miss Cassie."

This would never do! He must suspect! Arie gathered her courage together and produced a charming little moue of dismay. "Oh, dear, I can see that you have been told that Arie is the quiet one and I am a veritable chatterbox. In essence it is true, but I do not prattle quite all the time, I promise you."

"I would not mind if you did. No one has ever characterized me as an adept at social conversation, so I shall be glad of any assistance," he said lightly, but with an element of underlying truth to which Arie responded.

"I would not have said you were in need of any conversational assistance, judging by your contributions the other morning in our drawing room. When you said something, it was pertinent and made a real contribution.''

Mr. Ballard shot his passenger a look of mingled appreciation and curiosity. ''You are as kind as I remember from the Compton ball. Is your sister very like you—in character, I mean? It is obvious that you are nearly indistinguishable physically. Is it like being halves of one whole? No, that sounds as if each of you were incomplete without the other and is an insult to both, but it is almost eerie to see you together. I beg your pardon; I am talking nonsense.''

''No need,'' he was assured. ''We are quite accustomed to being regarded as an intriguing oddity, and perhaps we do feel a bit incomplete without the other. We have always been treated as one entity, you see, though not at home, of course.''

''Do you mind that? Do you feel cheated of your own identity?''

''Not really, because those who get to know us well soon learn that we are indeed two separate persons who are not more similar in disposition than other members of one family.''

''Then it would behoove those who wish to become your friends to get to know each of you better, would it not?''

''Yes,'' agreed Arie, dimpling at him.

''But I shall remember which twin I met first,'' he said softly, giving her a look that softened her bones.

Arie turned her head away, struck silent by the dawning complexity of the situation Cassie had created. A compliment intended solely for Cassie would have disturbed her less, but at this point she had spent as much time in company with Mr. Ballard as her sister had, and might be entitled, all things being equal, to a share in his approbation. She was miserably conscious that things were not equal in this case, and danger lay in allowing her thoughts to wander in that direction. The last thing Cassie had said to her before happily running down to join Freddy was a laughing warning not to be too nice to

Mr. Ballard because it would not do to encourage him to dangle after her. Firmly suppressing her own desire to be herself and let Mr. Ballard take whatever encouragement he might from her response to him, Arie squared her shoulders in her twin's rose-pink muslin dress under a lacy white knitted shawl and flashed a bright "Cassie smile" at her escort.

"This process of getting to know people works both ways, Mr. Ballard. All we know of you so far is that you are a neighbor of Lord Malvern's in Sussex and, by inference, that you do not possess a twin brother," she said, laughing up at him. "Go on from there."

No more than most young men was Mr. Ballard proof against a lovely lady's professed interest in his life story, and he willingly regaled her with a short history of his family. They whiled away another hour in growing harmony, and Mr. Ballard declared himself enchanted with the gardens through which they strolled most companionably. At the end of their outing Arie thought she could say with truth that she had kept the conversation on an impersonal level. Mr. Ballard had been quick to sense her slight withdrawal earlier and had subsequently shown himself willing to let her set the tone thereafter.

They were safely back before anyone else, and Arie managed to conceal her surprise when Edson greeted her at the door as Miss Cassie. Her relief was great when she attained the privacy of the room she shared with her twin, however. This was one of the rare moments when even Cassie's company would be an intrusion. She needed solitude in which to subdue the glow of happiness left in the wake of her time with Mr. Ballard and to try to compose herself to give a factual account of it when her twin returned. For the moment, at least, she hugged to herself these strange new feelings, unwilling to examine them in the light of reality or share them even with the person whose support and sympathy were unconditionally at her disposal.

When Cassie arrived home twenty minutes later, Arie was sitting in the rocking chair, quite composed. She watched her sister float into the room with a dreamy little smile on her lips and her hat dangling from her wrist by its yellow ribbons. "No need to inquire if you enjoyed your outing," she said teasingly as Cassie cast herself, straw hat and all, across the big bed and spread her arms wide.

"How could one not? Freddy is such fun to be with."

"Where did you go?"

Cassie turned her head and stared owlishly at her twin. "Promise you won't laugh?"

"I promise."

"He took me to see the exhibition at Somerset House. Stop that—you said you would not laugh." Cassie stuck out her lower lip in the mode of a spoiled child.

"I'm sorry, dearest. It was unpardonable of me," Arie apologized, "but the thought of you parading past all those allegorical pictures, trying to sound as if you knew what you were about, was too much for me. Did you admire all the most praiseworthy canvases and offer sound and knowledgeable criti—*Ouch!*"

The exclamation was occasioned by the smart of Cassie's straw hat hitting her on the shoulder as that young lady sat up with a rueful grin. "Wretch! You know very well I sounded as dim-witted as I am when it comes to painting. At first I did try to pretend to be halfway knowledgeable, but I gave up after I saw Freddy nearly convulsed with silent laughter at my performance."

"How horrid of him!"

Arie was indignant on her sister's behalf, but Cassie said, "No, no, of course it wasn't. Freddy couldn't be horrid if he tried. He apologized handsomely and promised to educate me on the subject of great painting some other time. We left the exhibit then and he took me to Gunter's for ice cream. We had a marvelous time."

"Didn't you mind that he was laughing at you?"

"I would rather have Freddy laughing at me, yet still liking me very much and wanting to protect me from all real and imaginary dangers, than listen to a string of meaningless compliments from men who merely wish to be seen with the prettiest girls in town."

"Is that the way you feel about some of our escorts?"

"Yes, do not you? We must be very pretty," Cassie went on matter-of-factly, "because we look so much like Didi, and she is ravishing, but it seems an inadequate reason for liking people and wanting to be in their company frequently. For that matter, Freddy is not nearly so handsome as Lord Malvern or even Mr. Ballard, but he is so kind and such fun to be with; in short, the nicest man I know."

Arie smiled mistily at the somewhat defiant expression on her twin's face. "I do hope he will ask you, Cass. And now, we had best speak of Mr. Ballard."

"I'd rather continue talking about Freddy," Cassie said, the dreamy expression returning to her face as she settled back down on the bed.

"No doubt, but in view of the fact that Lord Malvern has secured a voucher for Almack's for Mr. Ballard and will be taking him there tonight, it would behoove you to learn a few things that happened today, like which flowers you most admired at Kensington."

"The lilacs, of course, you always do," Cassie said absently, but she was sitting up alertly, and Arie had all her attention now as she frowned. "Now, why must the wretched man decide to go to Almack's tonight?"

"He is not a wretched man, and you might have expected it," her sister replied unsympathetically. "He is staying with Malvern, who generally comes to the balls."

"Well, he might have decided to stay away now that he has thrown Didi over."

"Cass! We don't know that he has."

"Why else has Didi lost that cat-at-the-creampot look of hers, and why else did Malvern leave town so suddenly, and if that isn't enough evidence for you, why does Sandy go about with a worried look all the time lately?"

"I don't know," Arie admitted reluctantly, "and I think perhaps I would rather not learn."

"Oh, certainly," her twin agreed. "Ignorance must be considered a highly desirable state in this case for our own sakes. It is difficult enough around here right now, just dodging Didi whenever possible. Well, back to your outing with Mr. Ballard. Quick, I think I hear people downstairs.''

"First of all, his father is Sir Henry Ballard, Gervaise is the only son and has two sisters, Alice and Evelyn. Both are younger, though Alice is married. Evelyn is only sixteen.''

"Freddy has two sisters also.''

"Cass, pay attention! You won't be quizzed about Freddy's sisters.''

Cassie looked uneasy. "Why did you have to talk about his family at all?'' she grumbled.

"What would you have had us talk about?''

"The gardens, that's what. We decided on that destination because we were there last week and could describe it.''

"We had to have some conversation on the drive to Kensington,'' Arie pointed out. "We could scarcely discuss the gardens until we had seen them.''

"You could have described them to him.''

"Cassandra!'' For the first time Arie's patience wore a little thin, and hearing the exasperation in her voice, Cassie hastened to beg her pardon and thank her for her sacrifice.

"I am truly grateful, dearest. It's just that it has suddenly struck me what a dangerous undertaking it was and how awful it would be to be found out.''

"Yes,'' Arie agreed soberly, "and, Cass, have a care with Mr. Ballard tonight. He likes you a lot.''

"Pooh, that's the least of our worries. Tonight Mr. Ballard is going to be treated to a revealing glimpse of Miss Cassandra Farrish at her most frivolous and fickle.''

Cassie was as good as her word. She smiled brightly at Mr. Ballard when he sought her out that evening, but refused to see the warm look in his hazel eyes. Nor could she be prevailed upon to grant him a second dance, assuring him with gay nonchalance that most of her dances were already promised, though she had saved him a waltz. Mr. Ballard's manners were irreproachable, but he could not quite conceal his surprise at this cavalier treatment at the hands of the same young lady with whom he had spent a delightful afternoon.

Arie, standing quietly at her sister's side, experienced an unprecedented urge to shake her for wounding him, though she perfectly agreed with the necessity of cooling his interest. She was unaware that her own smiling warmth in accepting his invitation to dance formed a stark contrast to Cassie's careless good humor. It was necessary to exercise the strictest self-discipline during the evening to keep her mind from leaping ahead to the moment when she would move into Mr. Ballard's arms, for their dance was to be a waltz. Even so, her responses to her other partners were a bit mechanical and her smile lacked something of its natural sweetness. From time to time she was conscious of a racing pulse, and it became imperative to take a calming breath and refocus her attention on the partner of the moment.

In contrast, her twin was apparently in high gig, whirling about the room in a state of laughing good humor that was contagious. Cassie's partners had every reason to congratulate themselves for being irresistibly entertaining that evening.

By the time Mr. Ballard came to claim Arie for the scheduled waltz, her throat was dry and her heart was exhibiting an alarming tendency to leap about in her breast in an irregular rhythm of its own. She moistened her lips and produced a tentative smile, for he looked quite serious as he held out his arms to her. Within a few seconds of feeling her partner's right hand at her waist and allowing her movements to blend with his, she had relaxed, however. Arie loved to dance and knew herself to be the best performer of the waltz among her sisters. In less than a minute she realized she had found the perfect partner in Mr. Ballard. Her body seemed to know instinctively where he was leading and when he wished to change direction. There was a comfortable difference in their heights that would make conversation easy, though for the first half of the number, not a single word passed between them. Arie was wholly given over to the exquisite pleasure of the experience, her mind empty of thought, her senses filled with the beautiful sounds of the music and a lovely kaleidoscope of changing colors as the women's dresses spun by them. She blinked up at him dazedly when his rich voice finally sounded in her ear.

"I . . . I beg your pardon?"

Mr. Ballard smiled down into eyes like velvet pansies. "No need; I merely muttered that that was a close call as an eager young man charged across our path."

"Oh." Arie looked a little uncertainly at him, and Mr. Ballard smiled with great charm.

"If that clumsy lout has spoiled the mood, I promise I'll call him out. I cannot remember when I have enjoyed a waltz more or had a finer partner," he said with a gallantry that deepened the roses in her cheeks.

Arie's slow smile started with the glow in her eyes and spread over her face. "May I return the compliment, sir?"

Mr. Ballard's gaze sharpened for a second; then he said lightly, "I told Miss Cassie this afternoon that it was my intention to become better acquainted with you in the hope that I'll soon be able to tell you apart."

"It's not difficult, really. I'm the quiet one." The glow that had given her a unique beauty subsided under his eyes and she was again just a very pretty girl with shining dark hair and large dark eyes, which were no longer meeting his.

They danced in silence for another minute or two before Mr. Ballard said, "Your sister is certainly a vibrant personality. Is she always the life and soul of the party?"

There was a trace of mischief in Arie's soft brown eyes as she said, "Sandy is always preaching decorum to us, but the problem is that Cassie simply likes almost everyone she meets and wants people to enjoy themselves, and her nature is impulsive to boot. If on occasion she goes beyond the line of what is considered by high sticklers to be ladylike behavior, at least it is never done to call attention to herself or put herself forward. She doesn't like to see anyone languishing in a corner when he might be having a good time with a little push in the right direction."

"You are her staunch champion," Mr. Ballard commented.

"Why, of course." Arie looked at him in surprise, but he made no reply except to accelerate their turns until they were circling the room in a fashion that would have been dangerous except for his exceptional skill.

Heads were turning to follow the attractive couple, whose performance made the other dancers look enervated by contrast. Watching them from her vantage point among the chaperones, Alexandra thought she had never seen Arie look so radiant. She had no hesitation at all in attributing this to Mr. Ballard's influence and not much in deciding it was more than his terpsichorean prowess that had brought the transforming glow to the girl's lovely quiet features. They looked so right together in a more elemental way than a mere physical compatibility. It would be premature and presumptuous to claim she discerned a mental attunement between them, but a little seed of hope germinated nonetheless.

14

THE IRONY OF THE SITUATION was not lost upon Miss Alexandra Farrish on Friday evening as she dawdled over dressing for Lord Malvern's intimate little dinner party. On the most practical level it was exquisitely ironic that ten people should be taking pains with their preparations for an event whose sole purpose was to throw sand in the eyes of the rest of society. Hopefully, the oddity of having a number of the most notable faces among the younger set missing from Almack's on the same evening would give rise to speculation as to the cause and help in spreading news of Lord Malvern's dinner quickly enough to create the desired climate for the hoax.

Of more permanent importance to the Farrish family perhaps was the unexpected swing in the marital expectations of the three girls. Didi had lost the premier catch of the Season at a time when two highly eligible young men seemed to be increasingly particular in their attentions to the twins.

No counting chickens before they hatched, Alexandra reminded herself sternly. That had gotten them nowhere in Malvern's case, and it was certainly too early in the game to expect an offer from Mr. Ballard, though he had been parked in her drawing room both days since that spectacular waltz he and Arie had performed at Almack's on Wednesday evening. His demeanor was most correct always, but his eyes had a tendency to follow Arie's every movement. Dear Cassie had somehow seen to it that his early interest in her had shifted to her twin. Hopefully, Arie's charm and sweetness would complete the transfer and make it permanent. There was less actual evidence that Freddy Marlowe's choice might be settling on Cassie. He was not one to wear his heart on his sleeve, and he had been too successful at avoiding the lures cast out to him Season after Season to be stampeded into a rash action by a transitory attraction. It was this very factor plus her faith that he would never allow Cassie to become an object of unkind gossip that gave Alexandra hope for this union. If she were correct and Freddy continued to distinguish Cassie by his attentions, it was because he had decided she was the girl for him.

Alexandra resolved to keep her own counsel and take what comfort she could from these developing attachments as a compensation to Didi's situation, which was a source of continued worry and distress. Didi never referred to Malvern by name these days as she flirted madly with any number of obliging gentlemen, some of whom were the type of inveterate pleasure seekers whose advances no sensible chaperone would wish to encourage. So far Alexandra had suppressed a strong desire to shake the girl out of this defiant mood; she was prevented by a deep understanding of what must be the chagrin of someone whose confidence in her ability to enslave any man she favored had been absolute. There was nothing to be gained by pointing out the unrealistic nature of such an attitude. Alexandra confined her advice to strict admonitions to Didi not to dare deliver any public snubs to Lord Malvern.

After an initial flash of undisguised anger in deep brown eyes there had been nothing to read in her sister's face when Alexandra had tactfully explained the reasoning behind the dinner party. Certainly, gratitude for Malvern's generous gesture was entirely absent. Didi had merely nodded her understanding and gone into a brown study for a moment or two, the results of which she obviously did not propose to share with her uneasy sister. Alexandra had thought it advisable to hold back the news that Malvern was in love with someone else. This information could have no other effect than to exacerbate Didi's resentment of her former suitor's defection.

No explanation of the invitation had been offered to the

twins, who displayed no curiosity about the upcoming event, which in itself was worthy of note. Alexandra was unsure whether their own affairs were consuming all their attention these days or they had simply adopted a policy of diplomatic blindness where their sister's blighted hopes were concerned.

All things considered, Alexandra was dreading the evening ahead of her, though it should put any unfavorable gossip to rest permanently. The Season was dwindling to a close, and Didi had shown no signs of singling out any of a number of perfectly acceptable young men who continued to vie for her favors. It did no good whatever to dwell on the matter, but her uneasy thoughts kept returning to Didi and her lack of reaction to this new development. It was more typical of the girl to reiterate her complaints about any aspect of life *ad nauseam* to anyone who would listen. This present tight-lipped avoidance, coupled with an emanation of deep anger that Alexandra sensed every time she was in her sister's presence, put her forcibly in mind of a slow-simmering volcano. If she were only certain it presaged an eruption, she would sit the girl down in an empty room and not let her out until they had talked the matter over from every angle, no matter how much resistance she had to overcome to accomplish it. There was, however, a slim possibility that Didi had received the kind of jolt that produces self-examination and reform. If this were so, it was vital to permit her to think it all out for herself, and it would be insulting to treat her like a child having a temper tantrum. Alexandra felt she must give her sister the benefit of the doubt, but she would be relieved when the farcical dinner party was behind them.

Still, she took unusual pains with her appearance, choosing the most flattering gown in her limited wardrobe, a sapphire-blue silk that enhanced her eyes and whose long simple lines, she fondly believed, made her look taller. She brushed her unruly curls until they shone, and even went to far as to darken her eyebrows a trifle to give more definition to her features. In a way, she felt she owed it to herself to give Lord Malvern a good look

at the family he had declined to join. When he had un-
willingly confessed to being in love with someone else
the other day, she had experienced a sense of rejection
almost as acute as if she had actually been the one rejected instead of her sister.

Didi must also have been thinking along the lines of
letting Malvern see what he was giving up, because she
had chosen to give the burnt-orange gown its debut. In
Alexandra's opinion, the girl had never looked more
beautiful. Lee stopped in the middle of a sentence when
she walked into the drawing room, where the rest of the
family had already congregated.

"By Jove, Didi, that's a dashed attractive dress. It re-
minds me of the deepest part of a sunset sky before the
purple takes over."

"Didi, it's magnificent," Cassie squealed, "and the
gloves you had dyed are an exact match. What a stroke
of luck!"

"You look really lovely, Didi," Arie said. "Mama's
topaz set has never had such a dramatic background before."

Always responsive to admiration, Didi pirouetted
slowly to show off the streamers of gold ribbon in all
different lengths that drifted down from the sash at the
center back for an unusual touch. She glanced questioningly at her elder sister, who said quietly, "It is beautiful,
Didi, and the gold net fan you found in the Royal Opera
Arcade is the perfect finishing touch."

"I am persuaded no one could tell the gown did not
come from the finest French modiste in London," Didi
said, which was her way of thanking her sister for her
labors.

The twins bore the major share of the conversation in
the carriage on the way to Hanover Square, speculating
happily on the degree of luxury to be expected in the
large house they had seen only from the outside. Didi
remained almost totally silent, answering in monosylla-
bles when directly addressed. Alexandra, observing her
closely under cover of the good-natured badinage between a teasing Lee and the twins, discerned an unusual

degree of tension in the girl's bearing that increased the amorphous sense of pending trouble that had tormented her ever since she had told Didi of the dinner party. Sullen resignation was Didi's typical style when forced to do something against her own inclination. Of course, she did stand to gain from tonight's carefully staged event, but leaving society with the impression that it was she who had refused Lord Malvern was at best a hollow victory after being so sure she had secured the match.

Evidently Alexandra was not entirely successful in her attempt to portray a carefree spirit, because, upon welcoming the Farrish party, their host held her hand a fraction longer than was customary and urged softly, "Do not look so worried. There is no reason why we all should not spend a pleasant evening together. Leave everything to me."

The reception of Didi's gown was everything she could have hoped. Lord Malvern said gallantly that he had never seen her look lovelier, Sir Frederick and Mr. Ballard were most complimentary, and Admiral Dunbar, who generally eschewed society parties but had obliged tonight at Lady Marlowe's request, actually dropped his monocle in stunned admiration at his first sight of the Farrish family en masse. He was later heard to utter to Lady Marlowe in what he fondly thought was an undertone:

"Demmed fine-looking group, that, Augusta, especially the gel in that orange dress. Can't remember when I've laid eyes on a prettier-rigged little bark."

Didi succeeded in looking demurely unconscious, but Cassie was betrayed by a giggle that was choked off by a nip on her elbow from Sir Frederick. Alexandra's eyes met Lord Malvern's, alight with laughter, and suddenly her spirits soared out of the dumps as she mentally resolved to banish this newly acquired tendency to magnify their troubles. There was no reason why they should not enjoy a cozy evening among friends. It should be especially welcome after the surfeit of large crowded parties they had all experienced lately.

Perhaps everyone else shared her feelings. At least the small party proved marvelously congenial. Didi's strange mood had lightened somewhat under the benign influence of her host's deferential treatment, though this must be the only time since the girls had made their come-outs that she had not been surrounded by men trying to gain her attention. With such a small group it was possible to keep the conversation general, and Lord Malvern, ably assisted by Sir Frederick and his mother, saw to it that this pattern prevailed until dinner was announced.

Alexandra was seated to Lord Malvern's right at table that evening, with Didi on his left, as befitted their position as the eldest of the female guests. Freddy, on Didi's other side, claimed her attention frequently enough that she was unable to monopolize her host, which would have left Alexandra to converse solely with her brother. A discreet lowering of one eyelid at one such moment conveyed to Alexandra both his knowledge that he was not among the beautiful Didi's favorites and his determination to make her do her duty by him as he turned on his considerable charm full force for her benefit. A lurking smile in Lord Malvern's eyes as he began a gentle conversation with Alexandra showed that he too was aware of the byplay.

At the other end of the table, Lady Marlowe held forth, ignoring the claims of Admiral Dunbar and Mr. Ballard for a time in order to describe the scene at the recent evening party at Carlton House for the benefit of the eagerly listening twins, who had never been privileged to gaze upon the fabulous interior of the Regent's home. Their eyes sparkled at a description of the Gothic conservatory filled with flowers for the occasion and containing the prince's own band, which played for the guests on and off throughout the evening.

The food served at Lord Malvern's table was of a quality to complement the conversation. Though not an elaborate meal by London standards, each course, from the first, a cold poached salmon in a heavenly sauce flavored with dill, was carefully selected, beautifully prepared, and elegantly presented in a dining room that featured a magnificent Chinese garden wallpaper that was an unending delight to the roving eye. At the end, Alexandra was able to tell her host with absolute truth that she had not eaten a more satisfying meal since their arrival in town.

The men did not linger long in the dining room after the ladies were conducted to the main drawing room that contained an exquisite satinwood pianoforte among its furnishings. While they were absent, Lady Marlowe carried out a kindly but thorough interrogation of the Farrish family. Having spent the better part of the Season among the dowagers, Alexandra had no difficulty in handling the lady's curiosity. She showed her a smiling face and an apparent air of openness while divulging only what she chose to have circulated about the town. The twins came in for their share of the garrulous matron's attention, but Didi enveloped herself in a cloak of bored abstraction that discouraged any attempts to include her in the questioning. Alexandra noted with some disquiet that the strange tension had returned to her bearing.

It was with mingled relief and pleasure that the younger ladies welcomed the gentlemen back to the group. A request for some music from the twins was made by Freddy and acceded to after a slight nervous hesitation.

At that moment Didi put her fingers up to her ear and said suddenly, "Oh, dear, I seem to have lost one of my earrings. Will you excuse me, sir, if I just run down to the dining room and look for it?"

"I'll ring for a servant to do that, Didi," Lord Malvern said equably.

"Oh, but I do not wish to disturb anyone unnecessarily. It won't take a moment to locate it," she insisted, rising from her chair.

"Very well. I'll go with you. Perhaps you might like to look over the music in that cabinet while we are gone," he suggested to the twins with a smile. "Gervaise will show you."

As Didi and Lord Malvern left the room together, those remaining disposed themselves about the softly lighted room with its elaborate plaster ceiling and green marble fireplace whose color was repeated in the brocaded upholstery of chairs and sofas. The twins selected some sheets of music after a short discussion, and Arie took her seat at the piano. Mr. Ballard helped Cassie to her feet where she had been kneeling before the rosewood music cabinet.

"I almost forgot this for the third time in a row," he exclaimed, reaching into his breast pocket. "Here is the glove you dropped in my carriage when we drove to Kensington on Wednesday, Miss Cassie. I hope you have not been inconvenienced by its loss," he added politely as the scarlet-cheeked girl stood dumbly staring at him, making no move to accept the glove he was holding out to her.

Alexandra glanced in puzzlement from the petrified Cassie to an ashen Arie, who seemed to be holding herself upright at the pianoforte by a white-knuckled grip on the keyboard. Her gaze swung to Sir Frederick, seated beyond her near the music cabinet, when he murmured, *"Déjà vu,* as I live and breathe."

Cassie's stricken eyes flew to Sir Frederick's face, then dropped to her feet.

The pregnant silence that had fallen upon the large room was ended a second later by the arrival of Didi and their host.

The smiling brunette flashed a swift glance around the room. "Goodness, it is so quiet in here. It seems the perfect moment to announce that Malvern and I have just become betrothed."

It would be unfair to state that Lord Malvern's sangfroid deserted him completely as this gay announcement rang in his ears. A look of consternation did indeed cross his face briefly as he met the shocked blue eyes of Miss Alexandra Farrish, but his voice was only a shade more crisp than usual as he said, "Loath though a gentleman must always be to correct a lady in public, Didi, and much as I sympathize with your desire to jilt me at the altar in due course, I must insist that you correct your misstatement."

"What did the lad say, Augusta? Are they or ain't they betrothed?" hissed Admiral Dunbar in the loud whisper of the hard-of-hearing.

"We are not, Admiral," Lord Malvern stated unequivocally when Didi, white and furious, did not immediately reply.

"Didi," Miss Farrish croaked in a husky little voice, "what have you done?"

"He deserved it for making me a laughingstock," the girl said through tight lips. "I want to go home."

"I am sorry, sir. Please. . . ." Miss Farrish implored, her face now as pale as all her sisters', for Cassie's embarrassed color had faded in this last moment of high drama.

"Of course, ma'am." Lord Malvern pulled the bell. "Won't you sit down again? It will take a few moments for a message to be delivered to your coachman."

Miss Farrish sat, more because her legs refused to support her than from any desire to prolong the agony.

Lady Marlowe in an attempt to lighten the atmosphere, offered a suggestion that they might still enjoy a little music while they waited for the coach to arrive. The admiral harrumped and declared it a capital idea, but Arie blanched even more as their eyes turned to her, and she rose precipitately from the bench in front of the instrument.

"I . . . I could not, ma'am. I . . ." She swayed and would have fallen to the floor had not an alert Mr. Ballard sprung to her side and caught her before she hit the ground.

"It wanted only this to round out the evening," Sir Frederick murmured to no one in particular.

"Your levity is ill-timed, sir. Please let me pass."

Miss Farrish pushed past him and directed Mr. Ballard to deposit Arie in a chair. Her practical action in forcing the girl's head down toward her knees brought her to her senses within a few seconds. By then Lord Malvern had given orders to his butler. He approached the little group consisting of Miss Farrish in attendance on her sister, anxiously watched by Mr. Ballard, with a glass in his hand, which he proffered to Miss Farrish.

"Give her a few sips of this."

Alexandra took the glass from his hand, uttering a per-

functory thanks without looking at him. She was vaguely
aware that Lady Marlowe had engaged the admiral in soft
conversation. Though she appreciated the intent to be
kind, there was nothing anyone could do to retrieve the
evening from total disaster. As she bent over Arie, urging
her to take a couple of sips of the brandy Lord Malvern
had provided, she was as aware of every movement in
the room as if it were being played out in that peculiar
slowed-movement effect of a dream sequence. If only it
were just a dream instead of this extraordinary, unreal
reality that had transformed a pleasant evening into a
nightmare in the wink of an eye. Even before Didi had
dropped her bombshell and covered the family with
shame, there had been an explosion of tension in the room
following Mr. Ballard's return of Cassie's glove. The
twins and Freddy had reacted most strangely, but Didi's
appearance had prevented any light from being shed on
the earlier incident.

She glanced around the room from under her lashes.
With the exception of Lady Marlowe and Admiral Dunbar, everyone seemed to be frozen in the postures they
had assumed when Arie had fainted. Didi stood stony-
faced and alone on the spot where she had made her lying
pronouncement. Lee sat stunned in his chair. Freddy
seemed to be trying to speak to Cassie, whose attention
never left her twin, and Lord Malvern, like Mr. Ballard,
stood silently watching her own ministrations to Arie.

The door opened and the butler appeared carrying the
Farrish family's wraps. "The carriage will be here directly, my lord."

The words addressed to his master had the effect of
releasing the players in this strange scene from the pa-
ralysis that had held them in suspended motion. Lord
Malvern separated out Didi's gold velvet cloak from the
rest and handed it to Lee, along with his hat and gloves.
Freddy stepped forward and claimed Cassie's wrap while
Mr. Ballard did the same for Arie, leaving their host
holding Alexandra's cashmere shawl.

As he assisted a stiff Cassie into her cape, Sir Frederick said in an undertone that was audible to Miss Farrish, "I would like to call on you tomorrow if I may?"

"No," said Cassie flatly.

"May I call tomorrow to see how you are feeling?" Mr. Ballard asked as he provided the same service for a still-shaky Arie.

"Please, no!" she whispered, clinging to her brother's arm as Lee went to her side at the direction of Miss Farrish after assisting Didi into her cloak. She did not look at Mr. Ballard.

Didi, who had not said a word since expressing her desire to leave, turned on her heel and headed for the door. Lee muttered a general good-night and followed with a hand under the elbow of each twin, leaving to Alexandra the delicate task of conveying the family's sentiments on the occasion.

Things were still happening in the slowed motion of a dream, she thought in some confusion as Lord Malvern's hands seemed to linger on her shoulders as he arranged her shawl. She blinked at the banked-down fire in his narrow gray eyes and swallowed.

"I . . . what can I say, my lord, except that I am dreadfully sorry for everything that has happened here tonight."

"You are not to worry about anything, do you hear me?"

A faint smile touched her pale lips briefly at the fierce, low-voiced command, but she made no reply except to extend a collective farewell to the company. As he escorted her to the door, he said, "I'll see you tomorrow."

"Please, no," she said on a shudder, unconsciously echoing Arie's response to Mr. Ballard.

They were on the stairway now, a few steps above the others, and Lord Malvern did not argue. Within a minute they had all gone out to their waiting carriage.

A steady parade of persons plied the brass knocker on the front door of forty-nine Harley Street the morning after Lord Malvern's memorable dinner party, but none succeeded in gaining entrance. Edson's response to each

application was to declare that the ladies were not receiving that day.. To the more persistent he amplified this
statement as applicable—thus to Mr. Ballard, who sought
an interview with Arie, he announced that Miss Ariadne
was indisposed. Sir Frederick Marlowe, inquiring for Miss
Cassandra, received a similar excuse. It was necessary
to exercise even greater firmness with Lord Malvern, who
seemed to be laboring under the misapprehension that
Miss Farrish would wish to make an exception for him,
but Edson was equal to the task, and all callers were
denied admittance.

Inside the house, all was in turmoil.

Not a word had been spoken in the carriage on the
drive home from Hanover Square. When they entered the
house, Alexandra dismissed the twins to their room.
When Cassie said timidly that they had something to tell
her, she said with weary patience, "I know, but it can
wait until morning. Good night, girls." To Didi she said,
"Come into the morning room, please."

"No, I am going up to bed," the still-defiant beauty
had replied, setting her foot on the first stair.

Lee spoke up unexpectedly then. "If I have to carry
you kicking and screaming into that room, you are going.
Which is it to be?"

Didi hesitated, staring in fury at her brother until she
had assured herself that he did not mean to back down
from this threat, whereupon she turned and headed down
the hall, her face set grimly.

"Do you wish me to stay, Sandy?" he asked.

"No, my dear. She is resentful enough to say a lot of
things she doesn't really mean, and your presence will
only prolong this reaction."

"Very well, but call me if you feel she should hear
some home truths from a masculine point of view."

Lee trailed the twins up the stairs and Alexandra
walked to the morning room with fixed purpose but little
relish for the necessary interview.

It had been every bit as difficult as she'd anticipated.
To her initial query as to how her sister could ever justify
such a dishonorable act, Didi had replied sullenly that a

gentleman would never have exposed a lady to the criticism of others.

"Yours was not the action of a lady, but let us for the sake of argument suppose that Lord Malvern had been weak enough to let you get away with that lying announcement tonight to save your face. How would it have served you in the end? You would have had to break the engagement sometime in the future in any case."

Didi had stared at her as if she had two heads. "Of course I should not have broken the engagement."

It was Alexandra's turn to stare in disbelief. "But he doesn't wish to wed you! He could not have made that more plain during these last weeks. You *cannot* have seriously contemplated forcing an unwilling man to marry you! Your life would be a living hell!"

"I'd be a marchioness and I'd have a great deal of money to spend."

The simple stunning reply had finally brought home to Alexandra the utter futility of trying to get Didi to acknowledge the immorality of her action. In the most fundamental sense, this beautiful girl was essentially amoral; she recognized no moral guidelines. An expedient fear of public censure was the only staying force that operated on her when in pursuit of her goals.

A crushing conviction of failure weighed on Alexandra's spirit. She was tempted to end the discussion right then so she might try to get some much-needed rest, but they still had the practical repercussions to deal with. She squared her shoulders and announced, "Tomorrow you will write an apology to Lord Malvern for the embarrassment you caused him tonight."

"I shan't. I hate him. He deserved to be embarrassed after what he did to me."

Unmoved by the passion in her sister's reply, Alexandra had spelled it out for her in no uncertain terms. "Until you have penned an acceptable apology to Malvern, you will not leave this house except to return to Yorkshire, and you will receive no visitors. Now you may go to bed."

Alexandra had left the room then to the accompanying

sound of breaking china as Didi had taken out her rage on every breakable item within reach.

In contrast to the intensely disturbing interview with Didi, Alexandra's session with the twins the next morning offered something akin to comic relief. Tearful, ashamed, and penitent, they sought her out before breakfast and confessed the trick they had played on Mr. Ballard.

"It was all my fault, Sandy," Cassie had insisted. "Arie did not wish to do it, but I had waited so long for Freddy to notice me that I was afraid to put him off when he finally asked me to go driving. We knew it was wrong and that you would not approve, but we really did not think Mr. Ballard would be hurt by the switch because he didn't know us at all well then."

"And we thought he'd never find out," Arie put in.

"But Freddy knows," Cassie added, a tear spilling from her long lashes. "I heard him last night. I believe he has always known about Didi's going off with Lord Malvern that day she excused herself from driving with him, because he has never really courted her since. She seems to amuse him, which is why I particularly noticed him in the first place. Most of her suitors are blinded by her beauty. And now he must think I am just like her!" she wailed, bursting into tears.

"And I shall have to confess everything to Gervaise if he has not already guessed, and he will lose all respect for me," Arie added on a pitiful sob.

Another of life's little ironies, Alexandra reflected as she did her best to convince her shattered sisters that their one peccadillo did not make them sinners beyond redemption. Here were the twins clearly suffering from overactive consciences, while nothing she or anyone could say would every persuade Didi that an action of hers was wrong from an ethical standpoint.

Though she did not share the twins' pessimism that their moral lapse had permanently blighted their love lives, Alexandra decided for the sake of rest and restoration of their spirits to keep the world at a distance for that day at least, especially since she could not guarantee that other factors might not in the end prove more critical. If word of Didi's attempt to entrap Malvern ever leaked out, the girl would be sunk quite beneath reproach. She would continue to be surrounded by men, but few would have marriage on their minds. The invitations from respectable hostesses would cease abruptly and they would all very likely be cut by many of their acquaintances, which would certainly give Freddy and Mr. Ballard pause if they had been seriously considering the twins as potential brides. A man would have to be wholly lost in love to risk his family's disapproval of his choice of bride. Freddy's mother already knew the worst, and if word got around about the happenings at that dinner party, Mr. Ballard's family would learn of it in time. He, unlike Freddy, was not financially independent of his family.

Didi spent the day sulking in her room and the twins passed the time alternately crying and consoling each other in theirs. Lee, with the consideration he could exhibit on those rare occasions when his family's affairs broke through the barriers of his preoccupation with his scholarly pursuits, went off after breakfast, taking an ecstatic Penny with him. Though grateful for the child's sake, Alexandra was left with time and solitude, qualities usually in short supply in a large family, and which she squandered that day in an unprofitable and unhappy mental recapitulation of their experiences thus far in London society.

Perhaps she had been too ambitious for her family. Except for Didi, they had been happy in the limited society of their Yorkshire community, but having had a taste of the world beyond Yorkshire, would they ever know that simple contentment again? Here they were, several months into their great adventure, and all four were more miserable than they could have dreamed back at home with the prospect of an exciting time before them. The three girls had personal reasons for their depression, but what was her excuse for glooming around like the day before the end of the world? It was up to her to get a grip on herself and find a way out of this coil for all of them.

Lord Malvern had told her not to worry, and she would concentrate on that advice. If word of Didi's reprehensible behavior last night could be kept from spreading, then the situation was far from hopeless. At least the girls would not be ostracized even if their specific hopes did not materialize. Strictly speaking, Didi did not deserve the consideration, but everyone shared equally in the fortunes of the family.

By the end of a day given over to introspection, Alexandra, though far from happy, was not entirely sunk in the gloom that had oppressed her twenty-four hours previously.

15

~~~~~

IT WAS SCARCELY PRACTICABLE that the Farrish ladies should remain in seclusion indefinitely. On Sunday morning Alexandra decided they had wallowed in misery long enough and she issued instructions that all the girls except Didi, who still refused to pen the required apology to Lord Malvern, ready themselves for church service. At the twins' protest that they could not bear to face any of their friends, not knowing what stories of Lord Malvern's dinner party might be circulating about the town, she relented to the extent that they took the carriage that day and went to St. Margaret's Westminster, where they were unlikely to meet any of their particular friends.

The high-ceilinged Gothic church had been extensively renovated in the eighteenth century and now contained the magnificent painted-glass window that had been made by order of the magistrates of Dort in Holland and intended as a gift for Henry VII's chapel in Westminster. It dominated the east end of the lovely church with its many-figured depiction of the Crucifixion, which included, near the bottom, the king and his queen kneeling on either side of the cross.

As they followed Alexandra and Penny into the pew, the twins were somewhat subdued in spirit, nervously glancing around to assure themselves of anonymity, as if those two peas could ever share a pod without attracting considerable attention. By the time the service ended, however, they had relaxed enough to smile naturally at the familiar stares of strangers.

Feeling calmed and uplifted after the last notes of the final hymn had faded away, Alexandra stepped out into

211

the sweet spring air and lifted her face toward the sun.
"Ah, that warmth is delightful. Aren't you glad to be
outdoors on a glorious day like this, girls, instead of hid-
ing out in your room? Let's drive through the park on the
way home, shall we?"

Alexandra had glanced over her shoulder as she spoke,
so she could not fail to see the dismay that crossed the
twins' faces, and the contrasting delight that irradiated
Penny's. She did not have far to seek for enlightenment
as a rich drawl sounded above her ear.

"Good morning, ladies, and my favorite elf. What a
fortunate decision of mine to show Gervaise one of our
finer churches this morning. May I offer an arm, Miss
Farrish? I fear we are holding up traffic standing in the
path this way."

Alexandra had turned long before Lord Malvern concluded his smug little speech. She did not miss the significant glance that passed between the two men as Mr.
Ballard promptly offered an arm apiece to the hesitant
twins, and she felt herself being drawn away from her
sisters. She was not required to contribute anything beyond a tentative smile as Penny and Lord Malvern chatted comfortably over her head for a while until the
marquess said to the child, "We'll plan an outing to
Richmond Park one day soon, Penny, but for the moment
I need to speak privately with your sister."

Always quick to comprehend, Penny returned his special smile with interest and obligingly veered off to have
a look at the Abbey.

There was no expression save polite inquiry on his face
as he asked, "Where is Miss Didi on this beautiful morning?"

"She is indisposed," Alexandra said briefly, incapable
of manufacturing an illness that would account for missing church.

"Is this indisposition voluntary or imposed?" he asked
conversationally.

She bit her lip to keep back the smile that would have
confirmed his shrewd guess. The man was too quick by
half! On second thought, she decided that she owed him

the unvarnished truth. Meeting that enigmatic gaze, she said with brutal candor, "She is confined to the house until she composes the apology that she owes you."

After a searching glance into honest blue eyes, he stared ahead of him, a slight frown lending a stern aspect to the handsome profile. "Lord, what a coil," he said at last on a sigh. "There are so many men buzzing around her always. I had no idea how determined she was to . . . I'm sorry, I must sound like a complete coxcomb. I do not wish to insult you—" he tried again, and stopped abruptly.

Alexandra took pity on his masculine embarrassment. "Pray do not cavil at some necessary plain speaking, sir. Rest assured, my sister's heart is not broken. She was bent on becoming a marchioness, and yes, hers is a very determined nature. None of which excuses her action on Friday evening."

"There is no need for any letter of apology," he said awkwardly.

"I beg to differ with you. There is every need, and Didi will write it or we shall return to Yorkshire."

He turned, more than startled. "Whose nature do you call determined? Surely you would not go so far as that?"

Alexandra was strangely comforted by the concern in his voice, but she could not give him the assurance he sought. "It might be the best thing for all concerned. If word of her behavior leaks out—"

"It won't, Alexandra. I told you you could trust me on that. Admiral Dunbar and Lady Marlowe were each at pains to promise me quite voluntarily that no one would hear of it from them. Lady Marlowe liked the rest of the family," he added wryly, "but I'll spare you her opinion of Didi."

Alexandra bit her lip again and burst out, "I am persuaded beauty such as Didi's is more a curse than a blessing!"

Lord Malvern elected to keep to himself any opinions he might hold on that interesting philosophical question, preferring to offer some innocuous comments on upcoming events in the spring social calendar.

Behind them, the twins and Mr. Ballard had quickly reached a mutual understanding that cleared the air. Arie had gingerly placed her fingers on his proffered arm, but Cassie hung back until she had confessed the deception they had practiced on him on Wednesday afternoon, making it clear that the fault was entirely hers. Mr. Ballard had listened politely but with a gleam in his fine eyes that eventually penetrated her zeal to get the worst over with.

"You knew it all along!" she declared, stopping in her tracks until their smiling escort gently pulled her along with them.

"No, I promise you, I did not," he said. "I admit to being a bit confused at the rapid changes in personality of Miss Cassandra, who seemed different from my original impression on our outing, and appeared to change yet again at Almack's, but after that evening I no longer experienced any difficulty in telling you apart. Until I gave you back your glove, it did not occur to me that you might have switched places that day. At that point, though, it became instantly obvious. I fear neither of you is equipped by nature for a life of duplicity."

Now his smile was directed at Arie, who blushed rosily and added her own apologies to her sister's. It was a major relief to the girls to know themselves forgiven.

The visit to St. Margaret's resulted in a substantial lifting of the cloud that had descended over the Farrish family following Lord Malvern's party. If Cassie still feared a negative reaction from Sir Frederick, she generously put aside her own concerns to rejoice with her twin that any misunderstanding with Mr. Ballard had been erased. Alexandra told them in the carriage that Lord Malvern had assured her there would be no wider repercussions from Didi's action at his party, so they could look forward to resuming their London lives.

Didi finally put in an appearance at the dinner table, but her presence could not be said to add anything to the family's happiness. Far from expressing relief or gratitude when informed by the twins that no one would learn of the episode at the dinner party, a euphemism that brought a smile to Alexandra's eyes and a scowl to Didi's brow, the black-haired beauty turned on her elder sister and said snappishly:

"There, you see? You are forever making mountains out of molehills. Now, may we forget the matter?"

"Certainly, after you have made restitution to Lord Malvern," Alexandra replied in patient tones. "The fact that you have had the undeserved good fortune to escape any public notoriety does not lessen the original offense. Have you written your apology to Malvern yet?"

"No. It would be hypocritical in the extreme to say I'm sorry, when the only thing I regret is that it didn't work and he humiliated me in front of everyone. I think he owes me an apology!"

"If you care to know what I think," Lee said, entering the lists at that moment, "it is that you'll be lucky to find any man who's enough of a sapskull to offer for you. You cannot fool everybody forever. They might not find out what you tried with Malvern, but they're not all blinded by your beauty. Some must have noticed that you don't have a single female friend, and they'll begin to wonder why. Hexton isn't dangling after you quite so much these days, and the rest will follow suit as soon as they've twigged that sweet-as-sugar act of yours for the phony it is."

"That's enough, Lee," Alexandra said sharply, but she was too late to prevent an explosion once Didi recovered from her initial shock at her brother's attack. She abused him with the passion, if not the language of a fishwife, eventually bursting into tears of fury.

"And I'll have you know that Hexton is in love with me!" she cried, angrily brushing away tears. "Anytime I wish, I can get him to propose. If you haven't seen him lately, it's because his father sent for him for a few days. And I think you are the greatest beast in nature to talk to me that way, and I refuse to stay and listen to you!"

That was the last her family saw of Didi on Sunday, but on Monday morning when the twins and Alexandra were entertaining visitors in the saloon, she suddenly appeared in the doorway, greeting the callers with her famous smile. "Mrs. Ethelstone and Miss Ethelstone, how do you do? And, Sir Adrian, how sweet of you to call."

Didi glided into the room on her words, but Alexandra had been prepared for something of this nature. She rose unhurriedly and clucked in sweet reproof as she went to meet her sister. "Didi, my dear, you must not overtax your strength too soon. I have just been telling our guests of the wretched few days you've had with that putrid sore throat. I'm sure they are delighted to see you somewhat restored, but I know they will agree with me that it is dangerous to try to cheat nature's recuperative period. If you'll excuse me, everyone, I'll just see the poor child safely back to her room. She is still rather weak."

Alexandra had already clamped her sister's arm in a viselike grip while she spoke, and now she slipped her arm around Didi's waist and bundled her out of the room, a picture of sisterly solicitude.

The solicitude ended on the other side of the door. Alexandra marched the protesting girl up the stairs and along the corridor to her bedchamber, sheer determination making up for the difference in size between the two. Once inside Didi's room, she released her hold and stood with her back against the door, watching the enraged girl massaging her twisted wrist.

"Hear me well, Didi, and, for your own sake, believe me. You are going nowhere and seeing no one until you have made amends to Lord Malvern. No matter how hypocritical you might deem this apology, convention and decency demand it. And if you try anything like this again, I shall have Lee escort you back to Yorkshire within twenty-four hours."

Each word was enunciated with a clear snap, and Alexandra had the tainted satisfaction of seeing fear oust defiance in her sister's eyes before she returned to her guests without another word.

Didi was not one to cave in while there was the slightest chance that determination would prevail. She held out for another day, but at breakfast on Wednesday, when the twins reported that Lord Hexton had been at Lady Sitwell's musical evening and had spent most of the evening in close attendance on Lady Martha Sitwell, one of the Season's heiresses, she reevaluated her resistance in the light of self-interest. The apology was written and approved by Alexandra, and the *beau monde* was no longer denied the ravishing sight of Miss Aphrodite Farrish, London's greatest ornament.

Over the next few days life seemed blissfully normal after the alarms of the recent past. Alexandra could discern no difference in the way Didi was received, which lifted a great burden from her shoulders. In actual fact, Lord Malvern's dinner party appeared to have had the desired result, as far as shifting the stigma of rejection from Didi to Malvern was concerned. He gave this theory credence by continuing to beg the beauty's favors in public. Didi, who could not stand the sight of him by now, was quick to deny all his petitions, whereupon he invariably took himself off, tail between his legs, to seek out her elder sister's company. If society perceived him as still languishing after the beauteous star, it was because he took care to follow Didi's progress around the room with his eyes for the benefit of the curious whenever he remembered to do so. He also took care to disguise his high spirits behind a mask of dejection.

"Do not overdo it, Lord Malvern," Alexandra advised him on one occasion when he heaved a visible sigh as he watched Didi circle the dance floor in the arms of an overdressed young smart. "You would never make a successful actor."

He looked hurt. "Do not forget, O Critical Miss Farrish, that pantomine must be played broadly to make up for the lack of deathless prose at the actor's disposal. I thought I was quite convincing."

"What you are doubtless convincing the world of is that my company is excruciatingly tedious," she retorted.

"Never. Anyone privileged to know you will place the blame squarely on me."

"I was only funning," she protested, annoyed that the fervor of his denial should have set up a rapid tattoo in her chest.

"While I meant every word I said."

For a moment, confusion was evident in the flower eyes that met demanding pewter ones; then she rallied. "This girl you are in love with, Lord Malvern—I hope you have set her mind at rest about all this playacting?"

"I am trying, Miss Farrish," he said on another sigh. "And she is a woman, not a girl."

Alexandra was not required to reply to this *non sequitur* since Cassie came up to her sister just then, displaying a torn flounce. "Do you have any pins, Sandy? Someone stepped on my dress during the reel."

"Of course, my dear. I'll come with you to pin it up, since the tear is in the back. Will you excuse me, please, sir?"

Lord Malvern caught Lady Amberdale's eye as she was ending a conversation with a crony and he moved closer to her chair in response to her beckoning finger.

"Where is Alexandra off to?"

"She has gone to pin a tear in Miss Cassie's gown, ma'am."

Lady Amberdale's eyes trailed the departing figures, then came to rest on the blond Adonis at her side, whose gaze was still fixed on the same sight. "I don't believe that girl has had a thought in her head for anything but that family for the last ten years. Such a waste."

"I take your meaning, of course, ma'am, but I am persuaded that Alexandra would strongly disagree with that sentiment."

"Naturally. She has taken the place of mother and father in their lives. I'd give my diamond necklace for ten minutes alone with Thomas Farrish. His ears would be ringing when I finished telling him what I thought of a monster of selfishness who could abandon his children to the sole care of another child."

"But what a wonderful and formidable child it must have been," he said softly, "to have accepted the challenge and the duty. And she has done a magnificent job of raising them."

"With one notable exception," Lady Amberdale observed tartly, her eyes on the rose-clad figure of Didi

Farrish as she whirled by them with Lord Hexton, "and that was inevitable, given the fixation Isabella Farrish had with her own beauty. She was a very stupid woman."

Lord Malvern remained tactfully silent while his companion delivered herself of a long-repressed tirade against the second Mrs. Farrish for her shallow, narcissistic nature, invalidish ways, and neglect of her stepdaughter. She even scored the woman for the untimely death that had saddled that same stepdaughter with the care of her half-siblings.

"Yet I would not say that Alexandra is embittered or resentful at her lot, would you, ma'am?" he asked when the indignant matron had paused for breath.

"No, not yet, but what's to become of her when she succeeds in getting these three married off? As she informed me earlier this year, there is still Penny down the road. By the time she settles her, life will have passed Alexandra by. She'll dwindle into an old-maid aunt, still at the beck and call of that family but without the authority she has now. It does not bear thinking of."

"Somehow I cannot envision that terrible fate in store for the indomitable Miss Farrish. You must not let yourself become blue-deviled by future specters, ma'am," Lord Malvern kindly advised the agitated dowager.

"What's to prevent it?" she demanded crossly. "I was so hopeful when Tony Hazelton first arrived in town. Anyone could see he was still in love with her, and she was happy to renew their friendship, but he was complaining to me just the other day that he cannot keep her attention fixed on him for more than a minute at a time without one of her family needing her for something."

"Well, I can certainly sympathize with his complaint, but you never know what is around the next corner. Lord Callum may not be the only string to her bow," Lord Malvern said with a little smile. "Will you excuse me, ma'am? I see Lady Denison wigwagging her eyebrows at me in a summons. She will want to commiserate with me upon losing the most beautiful girl in London, and I should hate to deprive her of the pleasure." He favored Lady Amberdale with a serene smile that had that shrewd lady staring after his retreating back with awakened interest.

Alexandra, happily ignorant of the fate predicted for her by her concerned godmother, was skillfully mending the tear in Cassie's gown in the ladies' retiring room while that young lady chatted away nonstop. "There, that should hold for the rest of the evening, Cass. Now, if you'll help me up, these old bones are protesting this awkward position."

"What old bones?" Cassie laughed as she hauled her elder to her feet. "You could beat all of us in a footrace any day of the week. Do not try to cozen me into agreeing you are ready for a rocking chair." She gave her sister an exuberant hug that set her lace cap atilt.

The elder girl studied her glowing sister in the mirror as she straightened her incongruous headgear once more. "Your high spirits lead me to believe that Sir Frederick has forgiven you for your deception last week," she said. "I saw you dancing together earlier, but I have not chanced to speak with him myself this evening."

"Oh, yes," Cassie said sunnily. "He gave me a tremendous scold, though, and he said I was never to do such a thing again. Then he smiled that devilish smile of his and allowed as how the crime looked entirely different from the point of view of the beneficiary, and that he definitely preferred that role to the one Didi had cast him for. I told you he always knew about that, Sandy."

"I rather suspected as much," her sister agreed as they left the room together. "There isn't much that escapes that mild blue gaze."

Alexandra was not entirely unprepared to receive a private visit from Sir Frederick a few days later. Edson had put him in the morning room. She had her underlip gripped between her teeth and her expression was serious as she descended the stairs slowly and approached the small back room.

Sir Frederick rose when she entered, and came to greet her with a smile. As usual, he was neat as wax and dressed with quiet elegance in the finest fabrics, from his crisp spotless linen to the beautifully molded coat of burgundy superfine, which could have come from no other tailor than the great Weston.

"I have come to request your father's present direction, Alexandra," he began with another smile after the initial amenities were concluded. "I imagine you will not be slow to guess the reason."

This time his smile was not returned. "I apprehend that you mean to offer for Cassie," she said, her enormous eyes searching his countenance.

"The idea of acquiring me for a brother-in-law does not seem to have sent you into raptures." His smile had been replaced by a questioning lift of one dark eyebrow.

Alexandra's hands were clasped loosely in front of her as she gave him a direct look. "I think you know that I like you very much indeed, Freddy, and in the ordinary way there is no one I would rather have for a brother-in-law."

"But?" he prompted.

"Please sit down," she said, playing for time as she seated herself in one of the chairs in front of the sofa.

Sir Frederick took the other and said quietly, "You were about to qualify your joy at having me in the family."

She leaned a little forward in her earnestness. "Cassie has a special gift for spreading gladness in her wake. It comes from a loving heart."

"I have long been aware of this quality in her."

"Yes, well"—she glanced fleetingly at him and then away, and finished on a rush—"but her nature is very open and she is therefore vulnerable. She deserves to be loved." Her eyes pleaded with him for reassurance.

Two spots of red darkened Sir Frederick's cheekbones. "And you are not convinced that I am the man to provide this love?"

Her hands fluttered briefly. "Oh, dear, I am making a hash of this. I know you are fond of Cassie and that you would never be unkind to her intentionally, Freddy, but if you don't really care deeply for her, it might be kinder not to offer, because in time she will discover the truth." As Sir Frederick sat very still, staring into the fireplace,

Alexandra added hastily, "I beg your pardon for becoming so personal. Please believe that it isn't my intention to insult you, but Cassie's happiness means a great deal to me."

"It does to me also," he said, meeting her troubled gaze squarely. "I loved a girl once with that embarrassing singleminded passion and devotion only the very young are capable of, and my inamorata delighted in spurning it and me in a forthright fashion that could not fail to provide a permanent cure for romantic tendencies. It may be that a man—or a woman—can love that way only once, but I beg you to believe that Cassie matters very deeply to me. I have just discovered how deeply. I came here today secure in my own conceit of my eligibility and received the facer I didn't know I deserved. When you expressed your doubts to me, I suddenly glimpsed a future that might not contain Cass, and I can tell you it was a hellish vision, black and bleak."

"I should hate to be responsible for the bleakness of your future, Freddy," Alexandra said through a mist of tears. "Please forgive my presumption, but I had to be sure."

"There's nothing to forgive," he said gruffly. "I owe you a debt of gratitude for the love and care that have made her what she is, and I pledge my word that I'll cherish her the way she deserves to be cherished."

"If she'll have you," Alexandra put in mischievously.

Freddy laughed. "It would be vastly more becoming in me to express trepidation on that head, but as you said, Cassie is by nature open and honest. I've been basking in the warmth of her affection for some time now, and it has become as necessary to me as the air I breathe."

Alexandra got to her feet. "I'll send her to you."

As he scrambled out of his chair, she put her hands on his shoulders and kissed him on the cheek. "Welcome to the family, brother. I'll write down that address and give it to Edson. I think I can assure you that my father will not ask embarrassing questions before giving his consent," she added in dry tones as she opened the hall door before he could perform this service for her.

As she watched a radiant Cassie speed down the stairs a moment later, Alexandra breathed a silent prayer of thankfulness that she had not blundered irretrievably in questioning the quality of Freddy's feeling for her sister. A niggling fear that he regarded Cassie somewhat in the light of a pretty pet to be indulged had been thoroughly laid to rest, and she could now rejoice in her sister's good fortune.

No one in the Farrish family was totally surprised at Cassie's betrothal except Didi, whose self-centeredness had prevented her from seeing the growing attachment between her sister and Sir Frederick. To her credit, she managed to offer felicitations in a passably pleasant manner, but to Alexandra, at least, it was abundantly clear that the beauty had received another jolt to her self-esteem. Everyone, not least of all Didi herself, had assumed all along that she would be the first of the sisters to make a match. There would be no official announcement until Sir Thomas' consent had been received, but people would not be long in guessing the situation, what with the pair of them smelling of April and May. There was no point in Alexandra's attempting to soothe Didi's ruffled feelings, however, because her sister was still bitterly angry about being coerced into apologizing to Lord Malvern. Her resentment of her half-sister's authority had never been greater, and she could barely bring herself to be civil to her in public.

16

IT BECAME APPARENT TO ALEXANDRA over the next sennight or so that Didi meant to have Lord Hexton. She had curtailed her unrestrained flirtations and was giving the young viscount a deal of subtle encouragement to declare himself.

Alexandra was uneasy over the ripening affair on more than one count. It was common knowledge that the Earl of Caswell was in financial difficulties, which argued against an alignment with his family on practical grounds. Nor would Caswell be pleased to welcome an impecunious bride into his family; in fact, Alexandra would wager her back teeth that the lad had been called home precisely because rumors had reached his father that Hexton was dangling after the daughter of a provincial nobody. It did not require exceptional perspicacity to divine the context of the earl's instructions to his son on that occasion. Hexton had been seen squiring Lady Martha Sitwell on and off throughout the Season, but Alexandra entertained no doubts at all that his attendance on the pleasant-natured but plain-faced heiress was strictly in the line of familial duty. Anyone but a looby could see that the viscount was tail over top in love with Didi.

This last fact failed to reconcile Alexandra to the developing situation, even should the young man's inclination prevail against his father's wishes in the end. She liked and pitied Hexton in equal measure and could not deny a dash of contempt for his inability to gain, not the upper hand, but merely parity in any contest of wills with Didi. His blind adoration of the beautiful girl put him at a permanent disadvantage in all his dealings with her.

That Didi favored Hexton above all her other suitors in a personal sense, Alexandra had long suspected. He was young and dramatically handsome, with coloring as dark as Didi's own. He possessed a good understanding and was blessed with a sweet nature. Many a young lady's eyes had wandered wistfully in his direction this spring. If Didi really loved him, all Alexandra's doubts except the financial would have been swept away, but such could not be considered the case in view of her recent unprincipled efforts to land Malvern. Mutual liking and respect might be enough to promise a successful marriage, but in this instance the unfortunate truth was that Hexton's infatuation put him at Didi's mercy. She would dominate him, she could not resist this, but her complex nature was such that she had no respect for those persons she could control. Malvern was the only man among her serious suitors who could have stood on equal terms with the headstrong girl right from the start. What might happen eventually when her chosen husband, whoever he might be, had love's veils torn from his eyes was another matter and one too horrifying to contemplate.

Alexandra could not be sanguine about her sister's ultimate happiness in any case, but since her doubts were based on intimate knowledge of Didi's character, she had reached the decision to refrain from trying to influence the girl's choice. At Lady Amberdale's prompting she had passed along the warning about Caswell's monetary problems early in the acquaintance. Didi would not have forgotten this. It had most likely weighed in her earlier decision to set her cap for Malvern. Obviously, if she could not be a marchioness, she planned to settle for the coronet of a countess. Didi was in no mood at present to listen to any advice from her sister, so after much unsatisfactory reflection Alexandra reluctantly abandoned Lord Hexton to his fate.

At least she could rejoice in the twins' good fortune. Cassie was bubbling over with happiness these days, though Freddy knew how to keep her accompanying impulsiveness in check. Mr. Ballard had as yet made no formal application for Arie's hand, but anyone with eyes in his head could see that the attachment between them was deepening daily. They had known each other such a short time that Alexandra was content to let nature take its course slowly in their case. There could be no objection to the match from the Farrish point of view. The girls were not entirely dowerless, but their portions were meager compared with the majority of their contemporaries at Almack's. They must hope that Sir Henry Ballard, unlike the Earl of Caswell, would be satisfied with something less than an heiress for his son. If he needed any persuading as to Arie's background and character, Alexandra felt confident that they could rely on Lord Malvern to stand their friend with his neighbor. He would not otherwise have encouraged his young protégé to make their acquaintance in the first place.

As matters stood, Alexandra had no reservations about the twins' future. Barring personal reservations based on her understanding of Didi's character, if Hexton came up to scratch, she must consider that her purpose in coming to London had been accomplished in a more-than-adequate fashion. All of which made it the more trying that she could not seem to banish a vague but persistent case of the dismals.

In all probability those wispy clouds on her emotional horizon had to do with anticipating the changes that would take place in her life with her sisters' marriages. The permanent loss of three lively girls, none of whom would be within easy reach after her marriage, would be a blow to those remaining. Reminding herself that this was the natural order of things and the whole reason for this London sojourn did not erase the sense of loss. And if she were to be completely honest with herself, she would have to admit that it would take some adjustment to fit back into their quiet rural existence after experiencing the delights of the capital this spring. She had been contented with her life before, and she had greatly missed her country garden while dwelling in the city, but there would be aspects of their London life she would miss equally when they returned home.

As Alexandra shepherded her pretty flock from one

social engagement to another in the first weeks of June, she acknowledged that it was the wider social contacts she would miss most when they left London. There was no one like dear Lady Amberdale to confide in among their limited circle in Yorkshire, and gentlemen with the worldly knowledge and entertaining conversation of Lord Malvern and Tony Hazelton were thin on the ground—in fact, nonexistent—among her acquaintance at home.

Now she was coming to the heart of the matter. Alexandra faced her selfishness squarely and admitted that what she would miss most when they were back home were the flattering attentions of two extremely attractive men, for Lord Malvern had not ceased his attendance on her even after the news-hungry dowagers had turned their scrutiny upon Didi and Lord Hexton. Alexandra had been puzzled by this, but had concluded that the woman Malvern loved must be from his vicinity in Sussex. She could not be in London or he would have ceased his attentions to the Farrish family once the gossip about himself and Didi had died down. Alexandra was the prime beneficiary of this situation at present, but the other side of the coin would soon manifest itself when the pleasure of stimulating conversation with attractive men was permanently withdrawn. She had already noticed a lessening of Tony Hazelton's attentiveness since she had, with all the delicacy at her command, tried to impress upon him her unwavering intention of eschewing a personal life while she still had Penny in her charge. Her intuition had warned her that he was within ames ace of making her an offer, and she was grateful to have avoided the sad chore of refusing him. He still sought her out at social functions but the frequency of his visits to Harley Street had sharply diminished. She missed his cheerful repartee but was satisfied that, in fairness to Tony, she could have done nothing less. It would be another five years before she brought Penny to town, and she could not muster the courage to speculate upon her own personal life at this distance, the prospect was so unappealing.

With no power to influence the future, she attempted to enjoy the present, though it more than once occurred

to her that her situation bore a striking similarity to that
of the French aristocracy in the last century, who lived
for the pleasures of the moment while the Revolution
boiled up around them.

When Lord Malvern sought her permission to take Penny
to Richmond Park for a day in the country air, high-
lighted by an *al fresco* meal, she hesitated briefly, but it
seemed he'd anticipated her objection.

"Naturally my invitation extends to the whole family,
Miss Farrish, since it will require the better part of two
hours to reach our objective, not to mention an equal
span for the return trip."

The twins' enthusiasm for the projected treat increased
amazingly when Lord Malvern proposed to include Sir
Frederick and Mr. Ballard, but even the possibility of
Lord Hexton's attendance was insufficient to win Didi
over to the scheme. This young lady told her sister flatly
that, hating him as she did, a day in the marquess's company had all the appeal of a day spent in a contagion
ward in the hospital. Though deploring the violence of
her language, Alexandra quite understood her sentiments
and she passed along Didi's refusal to Lord Malvern, edited somewhat freely and rephrased for social accepta-
bility.

The day broke fair, with a promise of strong sunshine.
Alexandra experienced a few qualms at abandoning her
sister to a day of solitude, but was assured by Didi that
there were a number of personal tasks she planned to accomplish. Indeed, the girl seemed relieved to see all her
family pile into two carriages and depart after a flurry of
last-minute preparations and forgotten belongings. The
twins and their respective swains occupied one hired landau, and Alexandra and Penny joined Lord Malvern and
Lee, who had decided to accompany them in order to
spend some time with an astronomer friend who resided
in Richmond.

The day seemed designed for just such a purpose as
theirs. Though the ladies had need of their parasols, the
air was pleasantly warm rather than hot, and they all enjoyed the drive to the lovely hamlet that had formerly

boasted royal residences of the Tudor and Stuart monarchs. Only Lee had been there before, and his interest has not been in the scenic or historical aspects of the location. His sisters were enchanted with the large unspoiled green where jousting in the royal past had given way to cricket in the present. They appreciated the charm of the Greenside section adjacent to the green, where they dropped Lee at the home of Mr. Steven Rigaud, his astronomer friend.

There was not a great deal left of the Old Palace that had been built of dark red brick with indigo diapering, but they enjoyed wandering around the site. Fortunately, time had done nothing to diminish the serene beauty of the view from Richmond Hill. Here the serpentine river, much diminished in width, wound its way quietly through peaceful green meadows, almost totally devoid of the bustling river traffic that never abated in the metropolis.

They decided to drive through Richmond Park before coming back to eat where they could look down on the river. Penny was enraptured by several glimpses of the red deer that still roamed freely in the two-thousand-acre park. In comparison, magnificent oak trees of several hundred years' antiquity were as nothing, though she certainly joined the others in admiring the vista through Sidmouth Wood that gave a clear view all the way to St. Paul's Cathedral. Too hungry by then to be interested in visiting the Earl of Pembroke's White Lodge, the party went on to find a suitable spot above the river, where they happily consumed the bountiful provisions Lord Malvern's cook had prepared.

After lunch the twins wandered off on foot with their young men to explore their surroundings, and Penny settled herself under a tree to sketch the scene below her. Alexandra repacked the hampers with the remains of their feast and stored them in the shade. She smilingly shook her head when Lord Malvern asked if she would like to walk down to the river.

"I'm much too lazy and replete to climb back up the hill again. Do go yourself if you wish, sir. I intend to make myself comfortable under this tree and luxuriate in this beautiful scene.''

''If 'luxuriate' is a euphemism for 'nap,' I'll join you,'' he declared, stretching his long length beside her with his chin in his hand, propped up by one elbow. The other hand toyed idly with the strings of the netted reticule she had cast down on the quilt spread under the tree.

Alexandra sat with her back against the rough bark of an accommodating oak, her legs bent at the knees and tucked to one side, her hands relaxed in her white muslin lap, one cradling the other as she gazed out over the river. At her side Lord Malvern's appreciative gaze rested on his silent companion's delicate profile. She was hatless in the shade, and the honey-hued curls stirred invitingly in the slight breeze. Her soft, sensuously curved mouth disturbed him. He knew what he'd like to do right now, but Penny was busy with her sketchpad not twenty feet away.

''What are you thinking?'' he asked to sidetrack his own wayward thoughts.

Two lamps of intense blue were turned his way. ''Nothing earth-shaking,'' she replied, giving him the smile Freddy had once described as ''lighting up her whole face,'' ''just that this has been the loveliest day I have spent since coming to London. Thank you so very much for suggesting the excursion, and while I am at it, for being so consistently kind to Penny. Your attentions to her have made all the difference this spring, when she has been deprived of the freedom of movement she enjoys at home.''

''Today has been my pleasure, and I enjoy your little sister's company, so I cannot allow you to endow my actions with a virtue they do not possess.''

It was odd looking up at her like this. She was so small that his usual view was downward, but this angle gave him the full benefit of a veritable thicket of golden-brown lashes and a delicately rounded chin. He marveled, not for the first time, that such a fragile-appearing shell could house such an indomitable spirit. The truth was that appearances were ludicrously—to borrow Penny's favorite description—deceptive in the case of Miss Alexandra Farrish. She was tough in mind, body, and spirit. She was also tender with the young and weak, loving and generous-spirited, intelligent and perceptive, quick-tempered at times, and always captivating. And desirable—he mustn't forget that quality in cataloging her attributes, not that the omission was likely. He'd always found her mentally stimulating, but at this moment it was not his mind that was responding so insistently to her presence. He dropped his eyes to the quilt, afraid of what they might reveal when he had not the privacy to pursue the matter.

"Have you gone to sleep, Lord Malvern, after assuring me less than a fortnight ago that my company was not tedious?"

"No, Miss Mischief, I assure you sleep was the last thing on my mind." This time he did not lower his eyes until confusion clouded hers. "Tell me," he asked, switching topics swiftly, "does Didi mean to have Hexton?"

"I . . . I am not in her confidence, I fear."

"But your best guess, based on your knowledge of her is . . . what?"

"I would say yes, if he asks her."

"Oh, he'll ask her—the lad's besotted."

He was frowning thoughtfully, and Alexandra ventured, "Is it true that Lord Hexton's family is unlikely to approve a match?"

"I'm afraid so. Caswell is very ambitious for his family's advancement, principally because he needs to repair the depredations his own actions have made in their financial position. That is one male who will not be conquered by Didi's beauty. On the other hand, I would not put too much credit in the rumors of the earl's imminent bankruptcy. Matters are nowhere near that desperate. I'll back Hexton to get his own way eventually."

"I see." The expression of utter peace of a few moments ago had fled Alexandra's face, and Malvern regretted his intervention.

"Well, Miss Farrish," he said with an attempt at jocularity, "may I be the first to congratulate you on your singular achievement?"

"What do you mean?" she asked, not following his quick change of subject.

"You have given all the matchmaking mamas in the kingdom a new mark to shoot at. I do not believe anyone has ever succeeded in finding husbands for three girls in one short Season. The Gunning sisters spring to mind, but there were only two of them."

"I find this conversation in poor taste, my lord," she said repressively, "and premature to boot."

He grinned unrepentantly. "You are dissembling, O Hypocritical Miss Farrish." His eyes challenged her to deny the charge. Alexandra resisted stiffly, but eventually the smile dawned in her own eyes and her lips quivered.

"Ah, that's better. I always count on you for the truth, whether or not I wish to hear it." He smiled up at her warmly.

Alexandra looked down past his uncovered head of slightly waving blond hair, so fair as to appear nearly silver in the sunshine, to narrow gray eyes redeemed from insignificance by the intriguing black-rimmed pupils and brown brows and lashes. Though fair-complexioned, he did not possess the pale skin that generally accompanied very light hair. Her eyes roamed over stark cheekbones already tanned, past a chiseled mouth that could look straight and uncompromising but now was relaxed and beautiful, to linger on the deep cleft in his square chin. What a face of contrasts it was, appearing hard one moment and tender the next. She had thought him carved out of ice on their first meeting; now she was marveling at the endearingly boyish aspect that furrowed chin gave to his amused expression. She had always found her gaze lighting on that incongruous feature. It was silly and lovable at the same time, and—

"Why the look of sudden horror, as if you'd just come across a specter in your dreams? Or is it reality you have just discovered?" he added, a note of urgency in his voice as she wrenched her eyes from his and turned to stare out over the river once more. Only this time her hands were clenched in her lap and her lips were pressed firmly together. "Alexandra, look at me!"

Alexandra had no intention of obeying that tender command until she had herself under rational control once more, but she was spared any further distress by the opportune appearance of her little sister at the edge of the quilt.

"Would you like to see my sketch, Sandy?"

"Yes, of course, dearest." Alexandra accepted the proffered sketchbook with the same thankfulness with which a drowning man must grasp the extended hand of his rescuer.

She had repeated only two or three of her original phrases of commendation for Penny's efforts when the twins and their escorts appeared on the scene. During the recounting of their experiences and the ensuing decision to prepare to return to London, Alexandra was able to retire to the background to try to sort out her chaotic thoughts.

By the time they had picked up Lee at Mr. Rigaud's house, she had already passed beyond the stage of denial. There was no point in telling herself that she had not committed the ultimate stupidity of falling in love at her advanced age, and with a man who loved another woman, because she had obviously done just that. Shaken and appalled at the discovery she had just made, Alexandra still retained enough sense of self-preservation to maneuver herself into the seat next to Lord Malvern in the carriage. This way she would be able to avoid meeting his eyes on the drive home. She had no intention of allowing him to discover her secret before she had learned to disguise it.

Alexandra sat quietly in her corner of the landau, calling upon all the self-discipline at her command to preserve a normal appearance. Fortunately, Lee was in one of his rare chatty moods and he ably abetted Penny in keeping a light conversation alive on the homeward drive. At her side, Lord Malvern was much less forthcoming than was his wont, contributing only when his opinion was sought by the others. Alexandra shied away from speculating on the content of his thoughts, but if they concerned herself, she was determined to remove any impression that she was becoming too interested in him. Pride demanded that much. She would have to avoid him in the future. Now that it was too late, she could see that she had gradually come to depend upon his companionship over the course of the Season. Well, she had best get used to doing without it, she told herself uncompromisingly.

By the time the carriages pulled up in front of the Farrish house, a depression had settled like a heavy mantle over her shoulders, but she was calm and resigned. The tenuousness of her control was instantly challenged, however, when she tried to thank Lord Malvern for their lovely day.

"I'm coming in, Alexandra. We need to talk," he said brusquely, brushing aside her thanks.

"It . . . it is growing late, sir," she objected, making a production of closing her white parasol to avoid looking at him. "I fear a surfeit of sunshine and fresh air has rendered me too sleepy to speak sensibly on any topic."

"Good. I'll talk and you can listen. Come."

He held out an imperative hand to help her down from the carriage and kept hers imprisoned as they went up the shallow steps together.

The door was flung open by Edson before they reached the top. "Oh, Miss Alexandra, I am so relieved that you are returned at last. I regret to inform you that Miss Didi left the house within an hour after you did this morning and she has not yet returned."

All the others had crowded around in time to hear the end of Edson's announcement, including Sir Frederick and Mr. Ballard, who had been escorting the twins to their door.

"There's no sense in standing on the doorstep as if this were a public meeting," Lord Malvern said when Alexandra did not immediately react to the news. "Come inside, everyone."

He took Alexandra's arm and led her inside. The rest followed in silence, and Sir Frederick, the last person to enter, closed the door, shutting out most of the bright sunshine.

"Did Didi mention any appointments for today?" Lord Malvern asked Alexandra, who stood blinking in the sudden gloom.

She shook her head wordlessly, and Edson cleared his throat.

"Miss Alexandra, I took the liberty of sending a maid to Miss Didi's room when she had not returned by midafternoon. She found this on the mantel."

The hand Alexandra held out to take the envelope was not quite steady, but she ripped it open and mastered its contents in one swift glance. Wordlessly she held it out to Lord Malvern, who was no less quick to read the message.

"She and Hexton have eloped," he said curtly.

There was a concerted gasp from the twins, and two masculine arms slid around two slim waists in support.

"I . . . I don't know what to do," Alexandra whispered, still dazed.

"Well, I do. I am going after them," Lee snapped.

"May I suggest that you not go tearing off without giving the matter some thought," Malvern said, addressing the scowling young man. "They have at least a six-hour start, so a few more minutes won't matter one way or the other."

The silence that instantly settled over the gathering was proof that everyone saw the force of this argument. Lee shoved an impatient hand through his curly locks, looking more appalled by the moment. "I cannot just do nothing!"

"Why do we not repair to the saloon, where we can be comfortable while we talk this out," Lord Malvern suggested. "Edson, I think some tea for the ladies, don't you?"

"And wine for the gentlemen, Edson." Alexandra had herself well in hand now. She set her foot on the stairs and the others trooped up after her.

As the subdued party arranged itself about the room, with Sir Frederick and Mr. Ballard each in close attendance on his beloved and Penny huddled next to Alexandra in a corner of a sofa, Lord Malvern watched Lee prowl about the room. There was sympathy in his tones as he commiserated. "I appreciate that you feel you must be doing something, Lee, but it never pays to go off half-cocked in these affairs. Tell me, do you disapprove of Hexton for your sister?"

Lee shrugged. "He's a sapskull, but I do not have any moral objection, if that is what you are getting at."

"It is precisely what I am getting at. Then I take it your objection is not to the match but to the elopement?"

"Of course," Alexandra cried. "An elopement will ruin her socially!"

The twins echoed this sentiment in unison, but subsided when Lord Malvern held up a staying hand.

"Believe me, an unsuccessful elopement would be infinitely more damaging to her reputation." He let this sink in for a second before continuing. "There is no possibility of catching up with them today. They have too much of a start, and we cannot begin to guess where they'll rack up for the night."

"Robert is in the right of it, I'm afraid, Alexandra," Sir Frederick spoke for the first time. "Even if you do succeed in catching up with them tomorrow, the damage will already be done to her reputation."

Alexandra and her brother exchanged glances, after which Lee slumped into the nearest chair. "Then what is to be done?"

Again it was Sir Frederick who articulated the unwelcome advice. "I do not see that you have any choice except to put the best face on it you can when the news leaks out."

"Sally Jersey eloped," Cassie put in suddenly. "And she is one of the patronesses of Almack's."

Alexandra smiled faintly at the earnest girl; then her expression became more anxious once more. "Why must she do this thing?" She posed the question at random. "There was no need to create all this scandal."

"If you wish to know what I think," Penny piped up suddenly, "I think Didi *likes* to be the talk of the town."

Sir Frederick laughed, Mr. Ballard was seized by a fit of coughing, and Lee scowled at his little sister as she edged even closer to Alexandra, taking her sister's hand for comfort, though who was offering and who receiving was perhaps a moot point by then. Alexandra continued to look bewildered and hurt, but she smiled at Penny, who snuggled closer as the door opened and Edson entered carrying the silver tea service, followed by one of the maids with another tray containing bottles and glasses.

The gentlemen jumped up to assist in the distribution, except for Lord Malvern, whose brooding gaze rested on Alexandra for another few seconds before he reached a decision. He got to his feet and strode over to the sofa, looking down at Penny with a smile in his eyes.

"Thank you, most delightful elf, but I'll take over now," he said as he removed Penny's hand from her sister's and pulled Alexandra to her feet.

She was too surprised to protest at first, but as it became clear that his intention was to remove her from the room, she dug in her heels. "Stop! Where do you think you are taking me?"

"What about your tea?" Cassie called after them.

"We're going to have our little talk now," he replied to Alexandra, and, "Keep it for us," he tossed over his shoulder to Cassie.

Alexandra found herself flying down the stairs in his lordship's wake. "What will everyone think? Unhand me this instant!" she demanded and ordered in the same breath.

"I have every confidence that they will come to the correct conclusion," he replied to her question, but a tightening grip on her hand was all the answer she received to her imperious command.

"Lord Malvern, where are you taking me?" Alexandra asked for the second time as they reached the entrance hall.

"Back where it all began."

Lord Malvern hauled his protesting captive into the morning room and released her. While she was still trying to catch her breath, he smiled whimsically. "It has been said before that a man cannot keep your attention fixed on him for more than sixty seconds without some member of your family putting in a call to distract you. I find myself in sympathy with that sentiment and trust our dramatic exit may preclude interruptions this time."

He approached the young woman staring at him in disbelief and said softly, "I am selfish enough to want all your attention all the time, but I can be persuaded to spare some for Penny for the next few years." He reached for her hands.

She snatched them away and took a step backward. "What are you raving on about? You are in love with some woman! You told me so!" she cried while her eyes begged to be contradicted.

"Yes, I did, and if you'd asked her name I might have told you then and there, but it was too soon. I barely understood what had happened to me that night at the Compton ball, and afterward there was Didi to consider. I knew well you'd never give me a thought while you were so worried about her."

This time when he took her hands she did not resist and came willingly into his arms, though there were questions forming on her lips. "But why did you not tell me later?"

"I tried, my darling, but until this afternoon you never looked at me as though you saw me as anything but a friend of the family. A man requires a little encouragement to bare his heart."

"Coward," she taunted.

Those were the last coherent syllables Alexandra uttered for an appreciable length of time. Lord Malvern accepted the challenge to his manhood with alacrity, sweeping her into a crushing embrace that might have daunted a lesser woman. Alexandra emerged shaken but smiling, though her lashes sank in response to the ardor in his eyes, and she buried her face in his neckcloth while she fought for breath.

"Did I hurt you, darling?" he asked in quick contrition. "You pack such a wallop, I forget how tiny you are."

In answer she lifted her face for another kiss.

When at length he released her lips, Lord Malvern stared down in bemusement at the face of his beloved, her chin gently cupped in his hand. "Those amazing eyes of yours," he murmured. "The first time I saw them, I thought of forget-me-nots, never dreaming how prophetic that was. Even though my only wish that day was to take you over my knee, I couldn't forget them."

She grinned and said with relish, "Liar! Like every other man in London, all you saw was Didi's big brown eyes."

He pinched her chin in retaliation but answered seriously, "Like every other man in London, I acted the fool over Didi for a while. She filled my eyes but never my heart. I did not understand for a time that a very different image had already crept into my heart and taken up residence. All I knew was that I found quarreling with you more stimulating than flirting with your sister."

"Not, perhaps, a very good omen for future domestic bliss," commented his love, wrinkling her nose.

"Are you concerned that we won't discover any activity more stimulating than quarreling?" he asked meaningfully.

She blushed and the lashes descended again. His laugh rang out, carefree and young, as he hugged her. "Will you marry me soon, Alexandra?"

"What is your idea of soon?"

"Tomorrow, by special license."

"Robert!"

He laughed and relented. "All right, if you insist, we'll put up the banns, but how about stealing a march on Didi by putting an announcement in tomorrow's paper?"

"Didi!" Her face clouded instantly. "Oh, dear, for a moment I completely forgot about Didi and this awful elopement. Do you think people will refuse to receive her?"

"A few of the highest sticklers perhaps, but when all's said and done, there is really nothing about the match to give food for scandal broth except the style of the nuptials.''

"I do hope you are correct in your assumptions," she said fervently.

"Besides, if we spring all the betrothals on society at once, the talk will have to be split up among all the Farrish ladies. Didi will not get the lion's share of the town's attention.''

"*All* the betrothals?" One brown brow arched upward.

"Did I not tell you Gervaise has written to his father? He'll be requesting an interview any day now.''

Alexandra smiled. "I like him very much and I believe he and Arie will suit admirably.''

"And what is your prediction for Robert and Alexandra?''

"Oh, my very dear, I will try my best to be the kind of wife you wish.''

Lord Malvern caught his betrothed in his arms again and rested his chin against her soft curls. "There is only one way to answer a promise like that," he said with a husky note in his voice. The gentle touch of his lips lingering on hers brought a mist to Alexandra's eyes as she clung to him with all her strength.

When at last they drew apart, having exchanged a silent promise of devotion, Alexandra said a trifle shakily, "Everyone will be wondering what has happened to us, Robert.''

"Perhaps it is time we put them out of their misery. Come, darling.''

As they approached the door to the main saloon a few moments later, there was a tiny pucker between Alexandra's brows.

"What is it, dearest?''

"How will we ever explain what has happened, Robert? It has all been so sudden. They'll never believe us.''

Lord Malvern's little chuckle sounded above her ear as he pushed open the door.

Sir Frederick's jovial voice greeted them as they entered. "Ah, Robert and Alexandra, here you are at last. Edson has already uncorked the champagne.''